TEMPTING FATE

A COLORADO HIGH COUNTRY NOVEL

USA Today BESTSELLING AUTHOR

PAMELA CLARE

TEMPTING FATE

A Colorado High Country Novel

Published by Pamela Clare, 2017

Cover Design by © Carrie Divine/Seductive Designs

Image: 4x6/iStockphoto

This is a work of fiction. Names, characters, places, and incidents are products of the author's imagination or are used fictitiously, and any resemblance to actual persons, living or dead, business establishments, events, or locales is entirely coincidental.

ISBN-10: 0-9987491-2-5

ISBN-13: 978-0-9987491-2-9

Chapter One

Monday, July 10

Roosevelt National Forest

Above Scarlet Springs, Colo.

Naomi Archer put another log on the fire, the blaze offering warmth against the evening chill. The sun had set behind the mountains a few minutes ago, its last rays stretching pink across the sky. Although it was July, there were still patches of snow on the high peaks, their summits bright in the waning light.

It was breathtaking.

She sat back in her camp chair and inhaled, the soft crackling of the fire and the mingled scents of smoke, pine, and fresh mountain air bringing a sense of peace. How long had she dreamed of this vacation?

Forever, it seemed.

She'd first come to Denver for a silversmithing workshop, had seen the mountains through the dirty window of her cheap hotel room, and had promised herself she'd come back to visit those mountains one day when she could afford it. It had taken her five long years of waiting tables and making jewelry on the side to keep that promise, but here she was—not in a cheap hotel room, but camping on National Forest land with her own gear.

A big raven landed on a pine branch across from her and gave a throaty caw.

Naomi wished she had her camera within reach. "Hey, there."

Corvus corax.

She used ravens in her jewelry more than any other creature, and when a client had asked her why, she hadn't had an answer. She'd mumbled something about ravens being intelligent and playful. Only later, after she'd had time to think about it, had the answer come to her. For her, ravens were a symbol of freedom.

She had watched them fly over the fields of the farm where she'd grown up, watched them tumble in the wind, watched them defy Peter's attempts to keep them out of his corn, and she had envied them.

The bird cocked its head at her, its feathers gleaming blue-black in the twilight. It hopped down the branch and cawed again, moving a bit closer.

Oh, this would have been the perfect shot. *Damn!*

She supposed the little guy was hoping for a handout, but she knew better than to feed wildlife. Even if it weren't bad for the raven, National Forest rules prohibited it. "Sorry, buddy. I don't have anything for you."

The bird cawed once more, then flew off, as if it had understood her.

She watched it until it had disappeared into the forest canopy. She'd seen a small herd of mule deer and a tiny kit fox while hiking today. They hadn't seemed afraid of her but had gone about their business with barely a glance in her direction while she photographed them. She was hoping to use her photos and sketches to inspire jewelry when she got home again—if she went home.

She'd been here for only two days, and already she was in love with Colorado. She could imagine herself living in a little mountain cabin, stands of aspen for a front yard, maybe a little creek gurgling somewhere nearby. True, she would have to start from scratch, meeting with merchants, getting her jewelry into their shops, building her clientele. But most of her income came from her website and catalog sales. If she wanted to relocate to Colorado, she could make it work.

The idea excited her. If she relocated, she'd be able to spend every day up in the mountains, not just rare vacations. She might even be able to open her own boutique in one of these small mountain towns. Best of all, she'd be able to make a new start far from everything that reminded her of her past.

She got to her feet and washed her supper dishes, then packed them and the rest of her food in the back of her battered old Honda CR-V, her mind lost in thoughts of her imaginary boutique. She would sell her jewelry but also that of other artisans, along with paintings and photography and maybe even textiles if—

"Well, hello, there."

She spun around, a startled cry trapped in her throat.

Two men stood just beyond the firelight. She took in their appearance at a glance—unkempt hair, scraggly beards, baggy jeans, and jackets—and took a step backward, instinct telling her to jump into her vehicle, lock the doors, and drive.

One of the two men raised his hand in greeting, his unshaven face breaking into a smile. "Sorry to spook you, miss. We're just camping yonder and thought we'd say hello. I'm Arlie, and my buddy here is Clem. We're from Texas."

"Hey." Clem gave her a nod.

"Hey." She slipped a hand into the pocket of her jacket, searching for her cell phone, then remembered she'd left it in her backpack, which was in the tent a good ten feet to her right.

Damn it.

She couldn't be sure the two men meant her harm, but she knew better than to ignore her instincts. These men were predators.

Arlie pointed toward her license plate and turned to Clem. "Don't you have a cousin in South Dakota?"

Clem nodded. "Small world, I guess."

"Mind if we share your fire for a while, keep you company?" Arlie took a step forward. "If you'd rather keep to yourself, we can go. We don't mean to intrude."

There was something silky in his voice, as if he desperately wanted her to trust him. Too bad for him.

She took a step to her left, ready to pivot and run. "I came up here to get some space, so I'd really like my privacy. Please go."

Her pulse ticked off the seconds as she waited to see whether they would respect her wishes—or whether they were as bad as her gut told her they were.

"That's not very friendly, is it, Clem?"

Shit.

Naomi tensed to run—then froze, heart seeming to stop in her chest.

A gun.

Clem held it in his right hand, the barrel pointed straight at her. "We haven't had a decent bite in a few days. You've got plenty of food. Get to cookin', woman."

Naomi sat near the fire while Clem and Arlie ate the chili they'd forced her to make for them, a needle file she'd snuck from her toolbox hidden in her coat pocket. She knew where this was headed. Arlie's wandering hands and the slimy grin on Clem's face left no doubt in her mind what they planned to do once their stomachs were full.

She wouldn't give them the satisfaction.

There are two of them and one of you, and Clem has a gun.

She squeezed that thought from her mind. She couldn't let fear get the best of her, not if she wanted to get out of this untouched and alive.

Naomi had gleaned from the men's conversation that they had escaped from a Texas prison and had been hiding out in Roosevelt National Forest for at least a week, eating food stolen from campsites and sheltering in some old abandoned ranger cabin. She and her SUV were their ticket to getting out of here and moving down the highway.

Arlie belched. "Bring some firewood, squaw. The fire's burning low."

Naomi glared at him, got slowly to her feet.

"That's what you are, ain't you?" Arlie reached for her, but she dodged him. "You're part Indian. Your daddy must've been white on account of them blue eyes."

She didn't answer. She couldn't have answered even if she'd wanted to because she didn't know. Not even the people who'd raised her had known who her parents were or where she'd come from.

"She's part Indian?" Clem sniggered. "Which part? Seems like we ought to spread her legs and find out."

His vile words sent frissons of fear through Naomi. She picked up an armload of firewood from the stack near her truck and carried it back to the fire, the needle file burning a hole in her pocket. She would do whatever it took to defend herself, though the idea of killing someone made her stomach ache.

Don't think about it.

She dropped the wood beside the fire pit, took one of the smaller pieces and poked at the fire, embers glowing orange. And then it came to her—a way out.

She adjusted her hold on the wood, jabbed at the fire again, her body tensing, her pulse beating faster. All at once, she scooped up flaming wood and embers and flung them into Clem's lap, then swung the wood like a bat into Arlie's face, knocking him onto his back.

"Son of a bitch!" Clem howled. "I'm burned!"

Arlie grunted. "Fuck! Get her!"

Naomi bolted toward the forest. She didn't wait to see how badly the bastards were hurt or to find out whether Clem was pointing his gun at her. If she could just get far out of the firelight where they couldn't see her…

BAM!

A gunshot split the night. The blast made Naomi shriek, turned her blood to ice, but she kept running. It was only after the darkness of the forest had swallowed her that she realized she'd been hit.

Chaska Belcourt hiked up the trail with his sister, Winona, the sun just up, the air fresh and cool after a night rain. Ahead of them, Shota loped down the trail, stopping every so often to sniff something before taking off again. The wolf had a large enclosure—almost a square mile—but he got restless if he didn't get out to run at least once a week. In his heart, Shota would always be wild.

The only place they could let him run free was on National Forest land. No, it wasn't strictly legal to run a wolf off leash here, but there were significantly fewer people. Folks had a tendency to freak out when they saw a big, gray wolf running toward them down the trail. Fewer people meant a lower probability of confrontations.

"Are you going to do it?" Winona asked.

"Do what?"

"Ask Nicole out."

Not that again.

"I like Nicole. She's a good climber. She's smart. She's—"

"She's pretty—and she really likes you." Winona said that last part as if it were impossible to believe.

"She's on the Team, Win. You know how I feel about that."

"Don't dip your pen in the company inkwell, I know. Okay, but you don't work together. You *volunteer* together. Lots of people meet that way."

Chaska had been a primary member of the Rocky Mountain Search & Rescue Team for a little more than four years now. Though the Team was an all-volunteer organization, he and everyone else took the work seriously. Lives were at stake. "I won't risk getting distracted or bringing personal baggage with me on rescues."

"Oh, come on. I don't believe for a moment that you or Nicole are so unprofessional as to let your relationship get in the way during a rescue."

"We don't have a relationship." He aimed to keep it that way. "Besides, she's not my type."

"A gorgeous climber who wants to tear your clothes off isn't your type?" Win looked up at him. "Is this because she's *wasicu*?"

"You know me better than that." It's true that Chaska had always imagined himself settling down with a woman who shared his heritage and way of life, but that didn't mean he'd turn away from loving a woman because she was white. "Why are you still going on about this?"

"You're thirty-three. When our parents were your age, they—"

"Were already divorced, and Mom was drinking."

Their mother had killed herself with alcohol as surely as if she'd put a gun to her head and pulled the trigger.

Winona was quiet—for a moment. "I just don't want you to be alone."

He reached over, tousled her dark hair. "I *wish* I were alone, but I have a pesky little sister who thinks she's my granny and acts like a matchmaker."

Win laughed. "Someone has to watch out for you."

He supposed that was true. They were far from family, far from *Oglala Lakota Oyate*, far from Pine Ridge. Then again, he and Win had looked out for each other ever since they were small children. When he'd left the reservation to study mechanical engineering at the University of Colorado in Boulder, he'd known she would follow. Now he worked on propulsion and launch systems for satellites for an aerospace engineering firm, and she was a wildlife vet with her own clinic.

Life was good.

As for having a woman, yeah, that would be nice, especially at night. There were times when he was lonely, and there many nights when his sex drive left him feeling like he might explode. But sex was a bad reason to rush into a relationship. As far as he knew, no Lakota man had ever found his half-side—his perfect, matching female half—by going wherever his dick led him.

"Don't you want to be with someone?"

Of course, he did, but he didn't want to end up divorced like their parents.

"I'll wait till the right woman comes along. Creator can feel free to put her in my path anytime."

Ahead of them on the trail, Shota stopped. He raised his head, seemed to sniff the wind, then gave a strange howl. His ears went back, and he took off, running off the trail and disappearing among the trees.

Damn.

Chaska ran, following the animal through the forest, Winona's voice following him as she ran, calling for him, asking him to stop.

"Shota! *Ayustaŋye*!"

But Shota didn't stop, didn't so much as glance back, running until he had vanished.

Chaska stopped when he came to the place he'd last seen the animal, Win close behind him and breathing hard.

"Do you think you can track him?"

The ground was wet from last night's rain. "Maybe."

From nearby came Shota's howl. He was calling to them, calling his pack.

"Maybe I won't have to."

"That way." Winona set off again.

Chaska ran beside her, the terrain rocky and dropping steeply to a ravine below.

"There!" Winona stopped, pointed with a jerk of her head.

Shota lay on his belly partly concealed in what looked like a small cave or an old mine shaft, his gray fur like camouflage in the shadows. He craned his head to look over at them and whined.

Chaska moved toward him. "What's gotten into him?"

"You're asking me?"

"Aren't you the wolf whisperer?"

They approached Shota slowly, not wanting to spook him into running. Chaska let Win take the lead. She was the expert, after all, and Shota's official guardian.

She switched to Lakota, spoke in a soothing voice. "*Waste, Shota. Lila waste.*"

The wolf stayed where he was, tail thumping on damp pine needles.

Winona reached him first. "Oh, God. Chaska!"

But Chaska had already seen.

There beside Shota lay a woman, eyes closed, blood on her jacket, her dark hair damp, tangled, and full of pine needles. She was partially hidden inside the collapsed mine shaft. She had probably taken shelter there. The wolf had scented her—and come to help.

Chaska dropped to his knees beside her, felt her throat for a pulse, relief rushing through him to find her alive.

"What happened to her? There are blood and bruises. Did she fall?"

"I don't know." Chaska had seen a lot since he'd joined the Team, and this didn't look like a simple accident to him. A half dozen ideas chased each other through his mind, none of them pretty—kidnapping, sexual assault, partner violence.

He shrugged off his backpack, pulled out his first aid kit, radio, and hand mic. He turned the radio on, waited for traffic to clear. "Sixteen-seventy-two."

"Sixteen-seventy-two, go ahead."

"I'm at about the four-mile mark of the Lupine Trail with an unconscious adult female, break."

"Sixteen-seventy-two, copy. Go ahead with your traffic."

"She appears to have multiple injuries, possibly from falling or a physical altercation. Tone out the Team and medical, emergent. Better send a deputy as well. I'll be on FTAC Two going as Lupine Command."

"Sixteen-seventy-two, copy." Then dispatch came back with the time, part of the official record. "Six-twenty."

It would take most of an hour for the rest of the Team to mobilize, reach the trailhead, and hike here. Until then, it was Chaska's job to do what he could for her—which wasn't much. She felt cold, her skin damp from the rain. But she had a steady pulse, and her breathing was regular and unlabored. He pressed a hand to her shoulder and gave her a little nudge, taking in the bruises on her cheeks, her long lashes, her pale brown skin, the blood on her jacket. "Ma'am, are you okay? Can you hear me?"

She moaned but didn't wake up.

Shota whined, inched closer to the victim, licked her cheek.

Chaska tried again. "Are you okay, ma'am?"

Her brow furrowed, but her eyes didn't open.

He grabbed his hand mic again, switched his radio to FTAC 2, the county's tactical and rescue channel. "Lupine Command."

"Lupine Command, go ahead."

"I've tried to rouse the victim without success. Her clothes are damp. I suspect she's hypothermic. There's also blood loss from unknown injuries."

"Lupine Command, copy. Six-twenty-two."

He set the radio aside and reached into his pack for hand warmers. "We need to get her core temp up."

Hypothermia killed people every summer in Colorado's mountains.

He bent the metal discs at the bottom of the gel packs to start the exothermic reaction and handed them to Win. "Massage those to distribute the crystals evenly, and then tuck them inside her jacket. Don't put them against her bare skin."

While Winona did that, he reached into his pack again and drew out an emergency blanket.

"Look." Win held up a leather cord that hung around the woman's throat, a small beaded medicine wheel dangling from it like a pendant. She tucked it back inside the woman's jacket. "Do you think she's Lakota?"

Win might have time to wonder about such things, but Chaska didn't.

"I think she needs to get to the hospital." He knelt over her, about to tuck the emergency blanket around her, when he noticed something in her clenched fist. He pried her fingers open and took a small, needle-sharp *something* from her hand.

"Is that a knife?"

He handed it to Win. "It looks like a file."

"Maybe she was trying to defend herself."

"Maybe." Chaska studied his sister for a moment. "Are you okay?"

Two years ago, she'd been assaulted by an injured fugitive who'd forced her to give him medical aid at her clinic. The bastard had paid her back by drugging her with an overdose of animal tranquilizer that might have killed her had help not arrived. Chaska wouldn't be surprised if seeing a woman in this state dredged up those memories.

"I'm fine."

Chaska covered the woman with the blanket, tucked it around her. It would help hold in her body heat and the heat from the hand warmers. "Ma'am, can you hear me?"

This time, the woman's body went stiff, and she cried out. "No!"

Chaska found himself staring into a pair of terrified blue eyes.

Chapter Two

Awareness crashed over Naomi in a wave of pain and fear, nothing around her making sense. "Stop!"

She tried to strike out, tried to get away from the man who seemed to be on top of her, but pain lanced through her arm and leg, bringing her up short.

"Easy, ma'am. It's okay. No one's trying to hurt you. We're here to help."

"They have a gun. I have to go!"

"*Who* has a gun?"

"Arlie and Clem." She struggled against the fog in her head to explain, memories returning piece by piece, along with an awareness of every part of her body that hurt—her head, her left shoulder, her right ankle. "Escaped cons. They came to my campsite. They shot me. What if they find us?"

Fear slithered up her spine, made her pulse spike.

The man took her right hand in his, brown eyes looking intently into hers, the strength in his gaze settling the rapid thrum of her heart. "You're safe now. We're *not* going to let anyone hurt you. What's your name?"

Relief washed through her as his words hit home. "Naomi Archer."

"How old are you, Naomi?"

"Twenty-seven."

"Can you tell me where they shot you?"

"My shoulder." She tried to raise her left arm, but it hurt too much. Besides, it was all but pinned to her side by a space blanket.

"Lupine Command." He had a hand-held radio.

There was a burst of static, and a woman's voice answered him. "Lupine Command, go ahead."

"All incoming units be advised the victim says she was attacked by two armed assailants who might still be in the area, break."

"Go ahead."

"The victim is conscious and oriented. She says two men named Arlie and Clem came to her campsite with a firearm. She says they're escaped convicts. She has a gunshot wound to her left upper arm."

Naomi's eyes drifted shut, the man's voice sliding over her.

From beside her came a dog's whimper, and a cold nose nudged her cheek.

She opened her eyes and turned her head to the left to see a big gray dog sitting beside her, paws tucked under its chin. "Hey."

"Shota found you." A woman Naomi hadn't noticed until now ruffled the dog's fur. "I'm Winona. That's my brother, Chaska."

Naomi wanted to pet the dog, but she was just too tired.

"Naomi, do you know what day it is?" The man—Chaska—had put his radio down for now.

She tried to think. It was now morning. Yesterday had been Monday. "Tuesday?"

"Do you remember where you are?"

"Colorado." She'd come here for a vacation. She'd come to keep a promise to herself. She'd come to relax, to photograph wildlife. And now…

"Is there anyone I can call for you—your family, a significant other, an employer?"

"No." The last thing she wanted was for someone to call Ruth and Peter. She'd done everything she could to get away from them. She wouldn't turn to them to save her own life. "No one."

"Can you tell me what happened, Naomi?"

She did her best to remember, to tell him everything, but it wasn't easy. Her head ached, and she was so sleepy. "I didn't know they'd shot me at first. I ran, but it was dark. I fell and hurt my ankle. I couldn't stand or walk. When it started to rain, I crawled in here. I tried to stay awake but …"

She was trembling now, memories of the long, dark night chilling her to the bone. "I was afraid they'd find me. I was afraid they'd kill me."

"They can't touch you now." There was sympathy in the man's eyes, but steel in his voice. "If they were nearby, Shota would warn us. I doubt even escaped convicts would want to tangle with him."

He spoke into the radio again, relayed what she'd told him to others.

Naomi looked up at Winona. "Is he a police officer?"

Winona smiled. "Chaska? He's an engineering geek, but he's also part of the Rocky Mountain Search and Rescue Team and an EMT. We were just out walking when Shota took off running. We followed him and found him sitting next to you."

"Shota?" The dog licked Naomi's face.

"It means 'smoke' in Lakota," Winona told her. "We came to Colorado from the Pine Ridge Reservation in South Dakota."

Lakota. Pine Ridge.

Naomi was about to say she came from South Dakota, too, but the thought was lost when Shota licked her face again. "Thank you, Shota. He's a beautiful dog."

"He's not a dog. He's a wolf."

A wolf. Right.

And Naomi wondered if she was still unconscious and dreaming.

Chaska looked up at Winona. "Be careful."

He didn't like sending his sister off by herself, but the wolf couldn't stay. Shota, though more socialized to accept humans than most captive wolves, wouldn't take well to the sudden arrival of law enforcement and Team members, and there was no reason to risk a confrontation. If Shota believed that any one of them were a threat to his pack, especially Winona, he might attack.

She clipped the leash Chaska had made of climbing rope onto the wolf's collar. "Shota will watch over me. You worry about Naomi."

Chaska gave his sister a nod, watching as she scrambled up the steep slope to the top of the ravine and then disappeared, Shota beside her.

Naomi had slipped into unconsciousness again, and Chaska was pretty sure she had a concussion. She'd let him take a look at her arm, and he'd been relieved to find only a deep graze. It had bled a fair amount and probably hurt like hell, but the bone wasn't broken, and there was no bullet for surgeons to remove.

Her ankle was another story. It was badly swollen, and there were streaks of blood beneath her skin. He'd bet she had a fracture.

Radio traffic told him that he had at least fifteen minutes before anyone reached them. He got to his feet and looked up and down the ravine for a good evacuation point. He saw a spot about twenty yards to the south. There weren't any big obstacles—no fallen trees, no boulders, no large shrubs—and there were two sturdy ponderosa pines at the top to use as anchors.

He walked back to Naomi and knelt down beside her, not wanting her to come to and think she was alone. He ran through the evac in his mind. This was the part of rescues that he loved—besides saving lives, of course. A rescue was a high-risk engineering challenge in motion.

He worked on the anchor problem, doing the math in his head. Six rescuers with gear and the litter with Naomi meant the anchor would have to hold at least fifteen hundred pounds. He rounded up for safety's sake. They would run ropes from the two ponderosa pines. Once they had her out of the ravine, it would be a simple trail evac back to the parking lot.

He checked Naomi's breathing and her pulse, his gaze shifting to her face, concern for her stirring in his chest. Even bruised and smeared with dirt and blood, she was beautiful—big eyes, high cheekbones, a little nose, full lips. She couldn't be much taller than five-four or weigh more than one-twenty. The two bastards who'd walked into her camp had probably watched her for a while and thought she would make easy prey. It was just their bad luck that their intended victim was courageous—and smart. How many women in her situation would have thought to use live embers as a weapon?

Chaska wanted the bastards to pay.

As if Naomi could feel him watching her, her eyes fluttered open, pain making her brow furrow. "When will they get here?"

He glanced at his watch. "It won't be long now."

If he'd been a paramedic and had a full medical kit, he could have given her morphine, but that wasn't an option.

She turned her head to the left. "Where is Shota?"

"Winona took him home."

Fear filled Naomi's eyes. "How will we know if they're here?"

He didn't have to ask who "they" were. "I doubt they're still in the area. If they were smart, they would have gotten the hell out of here the moment you escaped."

"They didn't strike me as smart."

"In that case…" He rose to his knees and lifted his T-shirt so that she could see the Sig Sauer P250 compact pistol concealed in a holster inside the waistband of his jeans. He always carried when he went hiking. It wasn't the four-leggeds that worried him, but those that walked on two legs. "I won't let them hurt you, Naomi."

She seemed to relax—a little. "What's your name? I'm sorry … I forgot."

"Chaska." He spelled it for her. "It's Lakota. It means first-born son. Not very original, since I *am* the first-born son."

A burst of static from his radio cut him off. "Lupine Command, this is fourteen-oh-eight."

Fourteen-oh-eight was Deputy Marcs.

He picked up the radio and answered. "Lupine Command, go ahead."

"I'm nearing your position. Can you give me some indication how far off the trail you are?"

Chaska guided her through it, telling her to leave the trail and head east fifty or so yards until she came to the ravine. "Just follow it north."

"Fourteen-oh-eight, copy."

A few minutes later, Deputy Marcs came into view, another deputy a few steps behind her, both of them heavily armed.

"I told you they'd be here, soon." He glanced down to find that Naomi had lapsed into unconsciousness again.

Pain and the sound of voices crashed in on Naomi again. Someone was saying her name. Someone was talking to her.

"Naomi, can you hear me?"

"Chaska?" She opened her eyes.

It wasn't Chaska who knelt beside her now, but a man in some kind of uniform. "I'm Austin. I'm a park ranger, and I'm also a paramedic. I'm going to give you an injection for pain, okay?"

Thank God.

"Okay."

She tried to turn her head to glance around at what was happening, but they'd put something around her neck to keep her still. "What…?"

"We've got you in a cervical collar to immobilize your spine until we can rule out a head or spinal injury. Does your head hurt?"

"Yes. My arm, too, and my ankle." Not to mention a half dozen other places where she was bruised and scratched up.

"Belcourt said you faced down a couple of serious bad guys."

"I didn't do a very good job of it, did I?"

"I don't know about that. You got away from them, and you're alive. Seems to me you handled it just right."

He was just being nice to her.

"Do you have any drug allergies, Naomi?"

Did she? "No."

"Morphine is going to decrease your pain, but it will also make you sleepy. It can depress your blood pressure, too, so I'm going start an IV and then put you on oxygen when we get you to the ambulance. You're going to feel a sharp prick in your thigh."

"Okay."

It was more like a jab, but a moment later she was floating, her pain melting.

"I'm going to start that IV now."

A strange sense of euphoria made her smile.

"You're feeling better, aren't you?" Austin asked.

Hell, yes, she was.

She heard a snipping sound and saw that he was cutting through her jacket and shirt with sharp scissors, and some distant part of her mind remembered how much she'd spent on this jacket. But then she was drifting.

She knew when they put a splint on her leg because it hurt, even with the morphine. She knew when they strapped her to a body board and lifted her into the litter. Then she felt herself falling.

Her eyes flew open on a jolt of adrenaline. "Chaska!"

"It's okay, Naomi. We're just headed up a steep slope." A man looked down at her—not Chaska, but someone else. "I'm Jesse Moretti. We won't let you fall. We've got you strapped in tight. Chaska is up at the top on belay."

Naomi had no idea what "on belay" meant, but she figured it had something to do with getting her out of here.

Six people—three men and three women—were carrying her litter, all of them wearing bright yellow T-shirts that had the words "Rocky Mountain Search & Rescue Team" printed on the back.

Because she was immobilized, she couldn't see what was going on, but step by step, they moved up the steep slope.

She must have drifted off because the litter abruptly leveled off, bringing her eyes open again.

"See?" Jesse grinned down at her. "We didn't let you fall."

"I guess Belcourt didn't tell you that we're pros," said one of the women. "I'll have to dock his pay."

Laughter from the others told Naomi that the woman was joking.

And then Chaska was there. "You okay?"

"Yeah."

They attached ATV wheels to the litter—she couldn't see this, but they told her that's what they were doing—and then they rolled the litter down the trail, the rocking, bouncing motion quickly lulling her to unconsciousness again.

The next time she opened her eyes, she was being lifted into an ambulance, voices surrounding her, one of them Austin's.

"She's A and O times four. She's had ten mgs of morphine IM. In addition to the bullet graze on her left arm, I think she's got a concussion and a broken tibia."

"She's probably dehydrated and hypothermic, too." That was Chaska.

He was still there, still nearby.

A man's face swam into view. "Can you tell me your name?"

"Naomi … Archer."

"I'm Eric Hawke, and I'll be your paramedic today."

"Hey, I was her paramedic first," Austin said.

Erik got a look of feigned annoyance on his face that told her the two men were friends. "Okay, so I'll be your other paramedic. Let's get you to the hospital."

Chaska stayed at the scene, answering Deputy Marcs' questions.

"Did she give you a description of the men?"

Chaska shook his head. "She was in and out of consciousness and in a fair amount of pain. I was more focused on first aid than asking questions."

Marcs nodded, then pressed a finger to her earpiece, listening to something coming over her radio. She had taken over as IC—Incident Command—after she'd arrived, and all traffic was going through her. After a moment, she spoke into her hand mic. "Lupine Command, copy."

Chaska had put his radio away. "News?"

"They found her campsite. There were several spent casings—forty-five ACP. Her vehicle was there, but its windows were broken, and the tires had been slashed. The steering column was messed up, too. It looks like they tried to hotwire it but didn't know what they were doing. They rifled through her tent, too, and slashed her sleeping bag."

They'd been angry at her and had taken their rage out on her belongings. There was no doubt in Chaska's mind that they would have done the same to her if they'd caught her. "They couldn't have gotten too far on foot."

"No, but these mountains are full of mine shafts and abandoned cabins. There are lots of places for them to hide. Don't look now, but the feds are here."

A shiny black Ford Expedition with government plates pulled up and parked, and three men in suits stepped out, all wearing aviator sunglasses. Chaska recognized one of the men as the chief deputy US marshal who had helped catch the bastard who'd drugged his sister. McBride was his name.

Taller than the others, he walked over to Deputy Marcs, shook her hand, and introduced himself. "Chief Deputy US Marshal Zach McBride."

Marcs shook his hand. "Deputy Julia Marcs, incident commander."

The other two were from the FBI. Chaska respected McBride because of his past contact with him, but it was in his DNA not to trust the feds, especially the FBI. "You need anything else from me?"

Marcs glanced down at her notes. "I'll call if anything comes up. Good work today, Belcourt."

"Thanks." Chaska was about to walk away when McBride held out his hand.

"You're the member of the Rocky Mountain Search and Rescue Team that cuts sign. You helped with the capture of a fugitive a couple of summers back."

Chaska was surprised McBride remembered. "Yes, sir. Chaska Belcourt."

Marcs cut to the chase, clearly not happy to have feds at her crime scene. "Is the Marshals Service or FBI claiming jurisdiction on this one?"

McBride shook his head. "We're hoping to partner with local law enforcement. You all know the area. We know who you're looking for."

He drew two photos out of his jacket pocket and held them out for Deputy Marcs and Chaska to see.

Chaska leaned in and found himself looking at the mug shots of two hard-faced middle-aged men. One of them grinned at the camera, a cruel glint in his soulless eyes.

"Arlie Harding and Clem McConnell." McBride handed the photos to Marcs. "They murdered two correctional officers two weeks ago while en route to the hospital with faked injuries and escaped from a private prison outside Fort Worth. I'll have my team send over their records. They've both got a long list of priors that include assault, sexual assault, armed robbery—you name it. The victim is damned lucky she got away. I doubt they would have left her alive when they'd finished with her."

A jolt of rage shot through Chaska to think of these two bastards intimidating Naomi, planning to violate her, hurt her, kill her. "It wasn't just luck. She was smart."

"Belcourt is the one who found the victim and called it in," Marcs explained.

"I've been hoping to run into you again, Mr. Belcourt. Every once in a while, the Marshals Service here in Colorado encounters a situation where someone with your skills could come in handy, our current case included. Would you be willing to consult with us, help us out?"

Consult with the U.S. Marshals Service?

Little in life surprised Chaska these days, but this did. "Don't you have your own people for that, or a canine unit?"

"Yeah, we've got dogs, but they can be misled. We've gotten so dependent on technology that basic skills like tracking have largely been lost. I spent some time working with the Shadow Wolves along the U.S.-Mexico border, learned from members of the Tohono O'odham nation, but I don't have your skills. I've seen you work. While the dog followed a false scent trail, you found the real one."

Chaska's respect for McBride rose a notch. He'd used the word *nation* instead of *tribe,* and he'd pronounced *Tohono O'odham* correctly. On top of that, he'd spent time with the Shadow Wolves. They were legends in the Native community.

Still, could Chaska see himself working for the feds? He glanced at the FBI agents, who watched him from behind mirrored lenses. "I'll help you track these bastards, but I answer to you and not the Marshals Service or the FBI. After that, we'll see."

"That works for me." McBride seemed to study him. "Are you acquainted with the victim?"

It was a fair question. The last time he and McBride had spoken, Chaska had failed to disclose the fact that the man they were tracking had attacked and drugged his sister. McBride had not been amused when he'd found out.

Chaska couldn't help but smile. "Not this time."

Chapter Three

Naomi drifted in and out of consciousness on the way to the hospital, oxygen mask on her face, Erik's reassuring voice an anchor. Once she arrived at the ER, she found herself at the center of a whirlwind. She was examined, X-rayed, and given a CT scan. After that, the bullet wound on her shoulder was injected with anesthetic and cleaned by a kind RN whose name was Lolly.

"Dr. O'Brien will be in to stitch you up soon."

"Thanks."

"You're welcome. I'm sorry this happened to you. It must have been terrifying."

Until now, Naomi had done a pretty good job of keeping it together, but the nurse's sympathy cut through the gratitude she felt to be alive to the lingering horror inside her. She had come so close to being raped and murdered.

She swallowed the lump in her throat, fought to hold back tears. "It's not what I was expecting from my Colorado vacation."

"It's certainly not what we put in our tourist brochures." Lolly rested a reassuring hand on her forearm. "You just rest, and push the call button if you need anything."

Naomi was exhausted, but the emergency room was no place to catch up on sleep. A woman arrived who was about to have a baby, her cries making Naomi swear she would never have kids. She'd just managed to drift off, when Dr. O'Brien stepped into her little exam room.

Dressed in blue scrubs, his long blond hair in a ponytail, he couldn't have been much older than she was. He was tanned from lots of time outdoors and ripped, too. "How's that arm?"

"It's sore."

He took a look at it, touched it. "Can you feel any pain?"

Naomi shook her head.

"I'm ordering IV antibiotics, and we'll give you a tetanus shot, too. You had a lot of dirt in the wound, and I want to be careful."

"Thank you."

"Your CT scan came back normal—no skull fracture or bleeding. The headache is a concussion, the result of your fall into the ravine. It will take time to heal, but heal it will. The X-rays showed a broken tibia. Also, one of your tendons was torn from the bone and took a flake of bone with it. You're going to have to have surgery."

"What?" She couldn't afford that. She had health insurance, but it was useless. She had a deductible of almost twelve grand before it would pay a penny. "Can't I just wear a cast for a long time or something?"

"Nope." Dr. O'Brien turned and typed something into a computer keyboard, calling up her X-rays, which filled the monitor. "Your tibia is slightly displaced. You can see that it doesn't quite meet up with the rest of the bone. Also, there's no way that tendon is ever going to reattach itself. The surgeon will align the two parts of your tibia with some hardware and then put the tendon back with more hardware."

The full impact of her situation struck home, leaving her dizzy, panic making her pulse spike. She'd come to Colorado to celebrate her success, and this trip was going to strip her of every penny she had in savings. Everything she'd worked so hard for might be ripped away from her because those *bastards* had attacked her. She would be in debt for years. She couldn't let herself end up on the streets again.

Dr. O'Brien noticed her distress. "It's going to be all right."

"No, it isn't. I can't afford any of this—the rescue, the ambulance, the ER, and now surgery."

Dr. O'Brien gave her an understanding smile. "The good news is that the rescue was free. The Team doesn't charge."

She stared at him. "Really?"

Something beeped.

He pulled a pager out of his pocket, scanned the message. "All rescues are free, regardless of who's at fault. That is our hard and fast rule. If we were to charge people, they might not call until the situation was dire. That would lead to loss of life. I'm a primary Team member—though I rarely get out of the ER these days."

That explained the tan and the biceps.

"So those people today—"

"They were all volunteers." He stuck the pager back in his pocket and pushed the call button for the nurse. "As for the rest of it, you're the victim of a violent crime. Colorado has a program that helps cover the medical costs of people who are victims of violent crimes. The victim's advocate from the Sheriff's Department will tell you about that when she comes to visit. Now, let's get your arm stitched up. Are you squeamish about needles?"

"I don't know." She'd never gotten stitches. She'd never even had an IV.

Then Lolly stepped in and helped Dr. O'Brien set up a tray that included a wicked curved needle that looked like an enormous fish hook.

Holy shit.

They were going to use *that* on her?

"Okay, so maybe I am afraid of needles."

Lolly walked around to the other side of Naomi's bed and took her right hand. "Just close your eyes and breathe nice and even. You won't feel a thing."

Chaska called the office to say he wouldn't be in today, then waited by his pickup for McBride, who was inside the Scarlet Springs Police Department, arranging things with the locals. He sent a quick text message to Winona to tell her what he was doing.

She texted back right away.

Be safe. I hope you find the bad guys.

So did he.

He'd never thought of himself as a violent man, but the image of Naomi lying in the dirt, semi-conscious, blood-spattered and in pain, made him want to take these bastards apart. Men who hurt women didn't deserve to keep their balls.

McBride emerged, wearing black BDUs, a black T-shirt, and black body armor that said *U.S. Marshals Service* in big white letters on the back. He had a mean-looking M4 in one hand and a spare set of body armor in the other. "This is for you."

He tossed the body armor to Chaska.

"Are you serious?" It was heavier than it looked.

"Dead serious. The perps are armed. Need help getting it on?"

He hoped not. "I'm a mechanical engineer."

A minute later, the vest was in place and the Velcro secure.

"Let's go."

Chaska followed McBride to his Ford SUV, climbed into the front passenger seat, and buckled his seatbelt. "Where are your FBI buddies?"

"They're off with a sheriff's deputy to question the victim." McBride kicked the vehicle into drive and headed out of the parking lot.

Chaska's rush of irritation was instantaneous. "Couldn't they wait?"

McBride shook his head. "We need to find these assholes before they kill or assault anyone else. You don't like the FBI."

It was a statement, not a question—and it was true.

"I don't trust feds. My grandfather helped occupy Alcatraz in 1969 and Wounded Knee in 1973."

McBride nodded, apparently needing no further explanation. "I had the sheriff's department cordon off Ms. Archer's campsite to preserve whatever sign they hadn't already trampled."

"Good call."

They arrived at the campground twenty minutes later to find it evacuated and a handful of squad cars parked near Naomi's campsite, including a K-9 unit. Deputy Marcs waited by the yellow tape with five other deputies, one holding the leash of a big bloodhound. They all wore body armor and carried rifles. Chaska recognized most of them from his work with the Team.

Deputy Marcs smiled. "You let him rope you into this, Belcourt?"

"I want to find these guys so they can get what's coming to them."

McBride introduced himself then outlined the plan. "We had rain last night, and I don't want to risk losing these bastards' trail. I watched Belcourt track a couple of years back. He found the real trail while the tracking dog was misled and followed the scent in rainwater in the wrong direction. Thanks to Belcourt, we were able to save a young woman's life."

It had been fortunate for the asshole who'd drugged Winona and abducted Lexi that he'd been dead by the time they'd found him. Chaska would have ended him.

McBride motioned toward the campsite. "Belcourt, it's all yours."

Chaska ducked below the yellow crime-scene tape, his gaze on the ground. Deputies had trampled the hell out of the place, but as he walked carefully through the site, what had happened here was slowly spelled out in dirt and duff.

He crouched near the fire pit, her account of the story written in sign all around him. "Naomi said she tossed burning embers on one of them. These bits of charcoal scattered here would be consistent with that. Over there, you can see that someone was knocked to the ground and struggled to get up. That's a palm mark. These two depressions are probably knees or the tips of his boots. There's the piece of firewood she hit him with. Part of it is charred, which is consistent with her story. And these dark spots on the dirt—blood. His nose or forehead must have been bleeding."

McBride knelt beside him. "I wonder if the dogs can get a scent off that."

"It's worth a try."

McBride motioned for the bloodhound to be brought up. While McBride spoke to the officer with the dog, Chaska followed the men's footprints toward the forest.

A moment later McBride joined him. "Got something?"

"They followed her." He pointed with his chin. "That way."

Naomi looked at the photos Special Agent Price handed her. She recognized the two men immediately, the smirk on Arlie's face making her stomach knot. She handed the photos back. "That's them."

"You're sure?" Special Agent Price held them out again as if he thought she hadn't looked at the photos long or hard enough.

Naomi drew back her hand, refused to take them. "Yes, I'm sure. I was forced to cook for them and listen to them for at least an hour."

Didn't these agents believe her?

"Why didn't you call for help on your smartphone?" Agent Biggs stood at the foot of her hospital bed.

"I already answered that question. It was in my tent with my backpack. I couldn't get to it."

"Did they ask you to drive them anywhere—maybe hint at where they were headed?"

"No—nothing like that."

"You said they had planned to steal your vehicle. Did they tell you that?"

"Not exactly. Arlie told Clem that my Honda would come in handy. I figured they were going to take my keys and steal it—or force me to drive them."

"How did you know they were fugitives?"

"Do I have to answer all your questions twice? You might not have noticed, but I'm in the hospital." She wasn't in a lot of pain, thanks to the drugs they were giving her, but she was weary to the bone, her body aching for sleep.

Special Agent Price spoke up. "Sometimes the smallest details make a big difference in an investigation. When we ask a question more than once, we often get slightly different answers with details that were overlooked before. I'm sorry about what you've been through, but we want to find these guys and lock them up before they can hurt anyone else. You're lucky to be alive, Ms. Archer. They would have sexually assaulted you, maybe even abducted you. In the end, they would have killed you."

The weight of that pressed in on Naomi, turning her stomach. "Thanks. I feel so much better now."

The door to Naomi's hospital room opened, and a tall woman in green scrubs entered, carrying a clipboard. "Hi, Naomi. I'm Doctor Thorne. I'm going to be your anesthesiologist. I have some questions I need to go over with you before your surgery. If you gentlemen could please step outside…"

"We were about to go." Special Agent Price took a card out of his suit jacket pocket. "If you think of anything else—any details that might be helpful—call."

"I will." She took the card, and the two men turned to go. "Wait! Arlie and Clem said something about an abandoned ranger cabin. That's where they'd been hiding."

Special Agent Price shared a look with his partner, then gave Naomi a nod. "Thanks. Good luck with your surgery."

At the word *surgery*, Naomi's heart gave a hard knock.

When they'd left, Doctor Thorne stepped up to Naomi's bedside. "You know, I've always wondered why they call themselves 'special agents.' All FBI agents are *special* agents. Apparently, there are no ordinary agents in the FBI, but no one's special if everyone's special."

For the first time all day, Naomi laughed.

"I made you smile. Good." Dr. Thorne asked her a dozen health-related questions, which Naomi did her best to answer. "Everyone is hammering you with questions. Is there anything you'd like to ask me?"

A half dozen questions raced through Naomi's mind, butterflies filling her stomach. How much pain would she be in afterward? What were the chances that something could go wrong? What if she woke up in the middle of the operation?

She'd never had surgery before and the idea of being helpless and unconscious terrified her. "How long will I be out?"

"This is a pretty simple procedure. You'll probably be under for about thirty minutes and in the recovery room for maybe an hour." Dr. Thorne reached over and gave her hand a squeeze. "I'm going to take good care of you. I promise. I need you to read and sign these consent forms."

Naomi took the pen and clipboard, wincing at the soreness in her shoulder. She hoped she wasn't signing away her life.

Chaska followed the men's tracks as they moved away from the campsite, the bloodhound a few paces ahead of him. One of the men he was tracking wore boots with a heavy tread—maybe hiking boots—while the other wore what looked like cowboy boots with a small piece missing from the heel of the right foot in the shape of the letter D. They'd jumped up and run after Naomi, her smaller tracks spaced far apart as she'd run for her life.

The bloodhound followed the men's scent downhill.

Chaska stopped, turned to McBride. "This is a waste of time."

"What do you mean?"

"They ran after her, but we know they didn't catch her. If they were right behind her like she said they were, that means they couldn't have had time to slash her tires or try to hotwire her car. They must have given up trying to find her, turned back, and then tried to steal her vehicle. When they failed, they slashed her tires."

That was the only way the pieces fit together.

McBride seemed to consider this. "Solid analysis. Let's search the periphery, find which way they headed when they left the site."

The bloodhound quickly found the place where they'd come out of the forest. Chaska backtracked a few yards from there to the spot where the two men had stood and watched Naomi, disgust fueling his anger as he glanced back toward her campsite. From here, they would have been able to see every move she made without being visible themselves.

Chaska glanced around. "They came from that direction."

But where had they gone after Naomi had gotten away?

While the bloodhound sniffed the periphery, Chaska circled the camp slowly, doing his best not to step on sign, looking for that heel with the missing D-shaped chunk. He found what he was looking for not far from Naomi's tent—tracks leading out of camp. "This way."

With the bloodhound in the lead, they moved fast, following the tracks through a long stretch of ponderosa pine forest. Chaska kept his gaze on the ground. In places, the duff—mostly old pine needles—was so deep that there were few tracks to follow, and that was where the bloodhound was especially helpful. At one point, the tracks crossed a dirt road, then disappeared into a grove of chokecherry bushes.

A black search helicopter passed overhead, tree branches dancing in the rotor wash, the noise it made eliminating any chance that they'd take these guys unawares.

McBride held a hand to his earpiece, then spoke into his mic. "Copy that."

"News?"

"The victim told Price that the suspects said something about hiding in an abandoned ranger cabin. The chopper spotted a structure up ahead."

A few minutes later, they saw it—an abandoned cabin, its log walls bleached by the sun.

"The scent trail leads right up to it," said the bloodhound's handler, who'd drawn the dog up beside him.

McBride nodded and motioned for everyone to stop. "Keep out of sight."

But rather than approaching the cabin, they waited for other law enforcement teams to arrive. It seemed to take an eternity.

Chaska pointed out what ought to have been obvious. "We don't know for sure that they're still there. With that helicopter flying overhead, they must know we're closing in on them."

"True, but I won't risk them opening fire, killing a few of us, and getting away in the confusion." McBride studied him for a moment. "You're not going in."

Chaska covered his disappointment. What had he imagined—that he would go charging in, his pistol drawn like some kind of action hero? "I knew that."

"No, you didn't." McBride grinned. "You've been a huge help, but I can't let you go any farther."

Chaska found himself standing with the bloodhound and its handler while McBride and a dozen sheriff's deputies and deputy marshals got into position.

"Did you learn this growing up—you know, cutting sign?" the dog's handler asked. "I thought McBride was full of shit when he brought you into this, but I can see how it comes in handy."

"Thanks—and, yeah. I learned from my grandfather." The old man had been determined to make sure Chaska and Winona had a true Lakota upbringing, and both of them would forever be grateful.

"What tribe?"

"Oglala Lakota nation." Chaska watched as McBride gave the signal and the officers moved toward the cabin.

When Naomi woke up in the recovery room, it took her a moment to remember where she was and why she was there, her mind fogged by anesthesia and morphine. Arlie and Clem. That terrible night in the forest. Winona and Shota. Chaska.

A nurse came to stand beside her, touched a hand to her right arm. "Hey, Naomi. How are you feeling?"

"My leg hurts."

"I bet. Let's get you more morphine. They'll hook you up to a morphine pump when we get you upstairs, and then you'll be able to control your pain relief yourself."

The nurse returned with a syringe and injected something into Naomi's IV, and she drifted off. But it wasn't peaceful sleep.

In her dreams, she was falling and falling, fear chasing her.

Chapter Four

Naomi woke as she was wheeled into a hospital room. She was still groggy on anesthesia and pain meds, the world coming together in random pieces. Bright lights. A window with a view of mountains. People in blue scrubs.

"Hi, Naomi. I'm Ellie. I'll be your nurse for the next few hours. We're going to take good care of you." Ellie hooked her up to the morphine pump and explained how it worked. "When you need pain relief, push this button. Easy enough?"

Naomi nodded, more alert now.

"It sounds like you've had a rough time of it. I'm very sorry."

"Does everyone here know what happened to me?"

Ellie fiddled with Naomi's IV line. "My fiancé was one of the Team members who helped in your rescue—Jesse Moretti. Also, Scarlet Springs is a very small town."

"I remember Jesse."

Ellie gave a little laugh. "He'll be gratified to hear that."

"Is that where I am—Scarlet Springs?" She remembered driving past the town on her way up to the campground.

Ellie adjusted the blood pressure cuff that Naomi hadn't noticed on her arm. "Yep. Scarlet Springs, population less than fifteen hundred."

The town where Naomi had lived as a child had been smaller than that. She had spent her entire life wanting to escape. "Is it a good place to live?"

"I love it, but then I grew up here." Ellie gave her a warm smile. "The doctor should be in shortly to talk with you about the surgery. Also, you have a visitor."

"A visitor?" Naomi's heart gave a sick thud. "I don't know anyone here."

Had someone tracked down Peter and Ruth?

"Remember Winona? She came to check on you."

"Winona?" Naomi found herself smiling, relieved. "She's here?"

Ellie patted Naomi's arm. "I'll send her in."

A moment later the door opened, and Winona entered. "Hey, there."

Naomi recognized her, and yet she'd been so out of it earlier that it was almost as if she were seeing Winona for the first time. "Hey."

Winona's shoulder-length black hair was tucked behind one ear, her brown eyes warm. It took her a moment to notice what Winona was carrying.

Naomi stared. "Flowers?"

No one had ever brought her flowers.

Winona set the vase down on the bedside table, gerbera daisies in pink, white, and yellow keeping company with white and pink roses in a vase of pink glass. "It must be hard to be in the hospital so far from home."

"Thanks—and thanks for finding me out there. I don't know what would have happened if you and Shota hadn't come along."

She probably would have died.

"You're welcome." Winona sat in the chair next to the bed. "How do you feel?"

Naomi wasn't sure how to answer. In the past twenty-four hours, she'd run for her life from two escaped convicts, been shot in the arm, broken her ankle falling into a ravine, stayed awake most of the night in pouring rain afraid the bastards would find her, only to wake up and find out she'd been saved by a wolf. All in all, not her best day. "I'm okay—a little groggy. They had to operate on my leg."

She tried to shift it, winced at the sharp jolt of pain.

"How long are they keeping you in the hospital?"

"I'm not sure." Naomi knew that she and Winona were essentially strangers—two people brought together by bad circumstances. Still, she felt at ease with her, as if she'd known her for a long time. "Where's Shota?"

"He's back home. He's got an enclosure behind the wildlife rehabilitation center that I run. I live next door, so his enclosure is kind of my backyard."

"You're a vet?"

"I specialize in rehabilitating wildlife."

"Is that how you ended up with Shota?"

"I had just started my wildlife residency when a game warden arrested a man for illegally transporting gray wolf pups into the state. There were two females and one male. They were close to death when we got them—hypothermic, dehydrated, starving. We took care of them around the clock, but the two little females died.

"Shota survived, but he was socialized to accept people and couldn't be released into the wild. I couldn't bear to see him end up in a zoo. I offered to give him a home. I had to jump through a few hoops, but I finally got permission."

"It's legal here? Wait. Of course, it is." Naomi had seen pastures with llamas and ostriches on her drive through Colorado. "Marijuana is legal here, so why not wolves?"

Winona laughed. "Some Colorado cities ban wolves and wolf-hybrid dogs, but not Scarlet."

"Has he ever bitten you?"

"No. Chaska and I—we're his pack. He likes you. I've never seen him—"

Someone knocked on the door, and a man in blue scrubs entered. "Hi, Naomi. I'm Doctor Renshaw, the orthopedic surgeon. How are you feeling?"

"A little groggy and sore. My leg hurts."

"I bet." The doctor explained the surgery at some length, then told her they planned to keep her overnight for observation because of her concussion. "The surgery went well. Your leg should heal without problems. I used glue on your incision so you can take showers. You might need a little physical therapy, but you'll be back to hiking within a few months. I promise. You'll need to visit an orthopedic surgeon in about ten days for a checkup. He can remove those stitches in your shoulder, too.

You won't be able to put weight on that leg for about six weeks, and that means no driving."

The reality of her situation rushed in on her. "How will I get home? I drove here. My Honda is still up at my campsite—if it wasn't stolen."

God, what a disaster!

"You could fly back and return for your vehicle later," the doctor suggested. "Or ask a family member to fly out and drive you and your vehicle home."

She didn't bother to tell him that she didn't have family. "Yeah."

What was she supposed to do now?

She forced a smile onto her face. "Thank you. I appreciate your help."

"I'm sorry your vacation was interrupted. Let the nurse know if you're not getting adequate pain relief. If all goes well, we'll release you tomorrow morning. In the meantime, get some rest." The doctor walked out of the room and shut her door.

Naomi drew a deep breath, fought to rein in a growing sense of panic. "I should be grateful. Last night, I was sure that I was going to be raped and killed. Today, I'm wondering how I'm going to get home again and how much all of this is going to cost."

And then it hit her.

"My tools!" *Damn it!* "I brought some of my jewelry-making tools along. If those bastards stole my SUV, they took my tools, too. That's thousands of dollars."

How was she going to recover from this? Would car insurance cover that?

Winona closed a warm hand over hers. "I know this must be overwhelming. Chaska is working with the U.S. marshals, trying to track them."

"He is?" Naomi remembered Chaska's dark eyes, the intensity of his gaze, the reassuring calm of his voice. "Isn't that dangerous?"

I won't let them hurt you, Naomi.

"My brother is an adrenaline junkie."

"I hope he's safe." She hoped all the people hunting those bastards were safe.

"What are you going to do?"

Naomi's thoughts spun, muddled by morphine. "I guess I need to find a hotel."

She could stay there until her stitches were out and then…

"Why don't you stay with Chaska and me? We have a spare bedroom. I'll take you to your appointments, and you can see Shota. You can figure out the rest later."

Naomi stared at Winona, astonished once again by her kindness. "You truly wouldn't mind?"

"It would be fun to have you there, and it would save you money."

Naomi studied Winona for a moment, saw nothing in her eyes but kindness. "Okay, if you're sure—and thank you."

McBride turned onto Fourth Street and pulled to a stop in front of the two-story Victorian house Chaska shared with his sister. "You were a big help out there today. Thank you."

"You're welcome." Chaska couldn't hold back his frustration. "My help didn't amount to much in the end, did it?"

They hadn't caught the bastards. The cabin had been empty.

"I wouldn't say that. If you want to meet some of the Shadow Wolves, let me know. I'll set something up. They could use a good man like you."

It was a powerful compliment, especially coming from a man like McBride, who understood a few things about Native culture.

"Thank you." Chaska climbed out.

"Can I get in touch with you if I think we need your help again?"

Chaska had no problem with that. "Sure. I can't make any promises."

McBride grinned. "Good enough. Have a good night."

"You, too."

"I'm off to talk to the victim about her vehicle."

That would be a fun conversation.

Chaska walked up to the house, body tense with frustration. What he needed was a good couple of hours at the rock gym, doing laps up a 5.11 route until his muscles screamed and his mind was empty.

He stepped through the front door and found his sister cleaning the downstairs bathroom, rubber gloves on her hands. A mop leaned against the bathroom door, Linkin Park blasting over the speakers. Winona was home early, and she was cleaning.

Something was up.

She jumped when she saw him. "Oh! I didn't hear you."

He believed that. "Is the music loud enough? I'm not sure all of our neighbors can hear the lyrics."

She stopped scrubbing the sink. "How did it go out there? Did you get them?"

"No." He walked to the iPod stereo and turned down the music, not wanting to have an entire conversation by shouting. "We tracked them to a cabin, but they'd been gone for hours. We picked up their trail again, but it ended at a long-term parking lot next to a pile of window glass. McBride thinks they found a car that had keys in it, busted the window, and stole it. The owner is probably backpacking in the Indian Peaks Wilderness and has no idea the car is gone. That's why nothing has been reported stolen."

"So, you have no idea what kind of car it is or what its license plate number is."

"From the tire tracks, it must be an SUV. We won't know more than that until the owner gets back and finds it missing."

"I'm sorry. That must have been frustrating."

"Yeah." He pointed to the mop with a jerk of his head. "What's this about? Is Old Man coming for a visit?"

Grandfather was almost ninety, but he still got around. He liked to drop in on them once in a while to see how his two youngest grandchildren were doing.

Winona went back to scrubbing the sink. "Naomi had a displaced fracture and had to have surgery on her leg. The doctor says she can't put weight on it for six weeks, and that means no driving. She doesn't know how to get home and doesn't have any family to help her. She's really not in any shape to figure it all out right now. I told her she could stay here with us in the meantime."

"Naomi is going to be staying here—with us?"

"Mr. Listens Well—that's my brother. Yes, with us. She asked about a hotel, but that didn't seem right."

No, that wasn't right, not when they were here to help her. So, why was Win avoiding his gaze?

Chaska knew his sister. "What's really going on here?"

She rinsed the sink, turned her sponge on the tub, squirting a homemade mix of vinegar and dish soap on the porcelain and getting onto her knees to scrub. "Do you remember what you said right before Shota ran off, right before we found her?"

He thought back. "I said I wasn't going to ask Nicole out."

"No." Winona glared at him over her shoulder. "You said you were going to wait until the right woman came along. Then you said, 'Creator can feel free to put her in my path anytime.' Remember?"

Aiii.

So that's what this was about.

Chaska crossed his arms over his chest. "You're matchmaking again."

"Naomi needs help, and we need to see where this goes. You were led to her."

"Yeah, by Shota's sense of smell."

It had been a long time since Chaska had believed in anything that couldn't be proven by science. He still smudged and made a spirit plate at every meal, but that was just tradition for him, a way of staying connected to his roots as a Lakota. That didn't mean he held any spiritual beliefs. Yet, even as he rejected the idea that Shota's finding Naomi was anything but completely random, he found himself remembering Naomi's bruised and beautiful face—and her courage.

Winona went back to scrubbing. "All I know is that the moment you said what you said, Shota took off. Old Man doesn't believe in coincidences."

No, he didn't.

Grandfather saw the world through different eyes than Chaska or Winona or even most Lakota these days. He was a traditional, what old-timers would call a true Lakota. For him, what had happened today would seem full of spiritual significance. And now Winona thought perhaps Creator had sent Chaska his half-side. If Old Man heard about this and how it had all happened, he'd probably start planning a wedding.

He would also be angry with Chaska for invoking *Wakan Tanka*—the Great Mystery—the way he had.

Chaska tried not to take the frustration he'd been carrying all afternoon out on Win. "It's the right thing to help her, but don't try to turn this into something it isn't. I doubt Naomi needs anyone meddling in her private life right now. Besides, we know nothing about her. She might prefer women."

"I won't meddle."

"Right." Chaska grabbed the mop. His father would never have done housework, but Chaska couldn't leave it all to Winona. She had a job, too, and worked every bit as hard as he did. "Where do you want me to start?"

So much for working off his temper at the rock gym.

"They didn't steal my Honda?" Relief washed through Naomi.

"They slashed the tires, and they tried to hotwire it but didn't know how. Unfortunately, your steering column and the electrical wiring is a stripped mess. You might be able to find someone local to repair it for you."

Yes, but how much would that cost?

Then she remembered. "What about the tools in back? Were they still there?"

The officer—a chief deputy U.S. marshal named Zach McBride—was still wearing body armor. "We went through the vehicle before we had it towed to the police yard. There was a tool set in the back, as well as some personal gear—a camera, some clothes. Your tent was there, too, but they had destroyed it. I did find this."

He held up her backpack, set it carefully on the bed beside her. "They took your food and your camp stove and slashed your sleeping bag."

She reached into the front mesh pocket and pulled out her cell phone. "At least I have the important stuff. How do I get my vehicle back?"

"Right now, it's part of a crime scene. When the forensic team is sure they're done with it, the Scarlet Springs PD or my office will get in touch with you. There's no cost to you to have it released from their impound yard. You can have it towed to a garage for repairs at that point."

She took in what he told her, unable to keep herself from feeling overwhelmed by it all. "I appreciate what you've done for me today."

"There's no doubt in my mind, Ms. Archer, that your quick thinking and willingness to fight back saved your life. The two men who attacked you are guilty of pretty much every violent crime on the books." He didn't say more.

He didn't have to. Special Agents Price and Biggs had already filled her in on that score. Besides, Naomi had watched news coverage on the TV and heard about their criminal records. It had been hard to see Arlie and Clem on the screen. Killers. Rapists. Thieves. She'd had to turn the TV off after just a few minutes.

Fear snaked through her belly. "Do you think they'll come back for me?"

McBride shook his head. "They're probably doing everything they can to get far away from here. Their last known location is the mountains above Scarlet Springs. There's no way they're going to come back just to finish with you. You can rest easy on that score. Has the victim's advocate been to see you?"

Naomi nodded. "She helped me fill out paperwork for that fund that covers medical expenses for crime victims."

Oh, how she hated having to think of herself in that category—a victim.

"Good. When are you flying back to Rapid City?"

"I don't know. I haven't figured it all out yet. I'm staying with Winona and Chaska Belcourt for a while."

McBride frowned. "You're personal friends with them?"

She shook her head. "I only met them today, but they offered me a place to stay."

"That's decent of them." Deputy Marshal McBride stood, reached into his front right pants pocket, and pulled out a business card. "If you run into any problems, give my office a call. In the meantime, those two have moved to the top of the Most Wanted list. We're going to find them, Naomi. I promise you."

His gray eyes looked into hers, his sympathy bringing her strangely close to tears.

"Thank you."

"You're welcome. I hope you won't judge Colorado by this terrible experience."

"Everyone I've met—except those two—has been very helpful and kind." She thought of Chaska again and how he'd stayed with her.

"I'm glad to hear that. I hope you feel better soon."

Naomi watched McBride go, then pushed the button for more pain relief, and drifted to sleep.

Chapter Five

Naomi sat on her hospital bed, staring at the bags of clothes and toiletries that Ellie had set on the blanket before her. She swallowed the lump in her throat. "I can't believe you did this."

Inside the bag, there was a beautiful white sundress with tiny purple flowers, a flowing cotton skirt in turquoise blue, tank tops in white, yellow, and black, some bikini underwear, a pair of denim shorts, and a sleeveless sleepshirt in butter-soft yellow cotton. There were toiletries, too—a toothbrush, toothpaste, floss, a comb and brush for her hair, shampoo, conditioner, lotion, sunscreen, lip balm, and even a nail care kit.

Why were they being so kind to her?

"We can't very well discharge you naked, can we?" Ellie shared a smile with Lolly, the nurse who'd cared for Naomi in the ER.

Naomi had forgotten until this morning that the paramedics had cut off her clothes. The rest of her belongings were in the back of her SUV, which was in the police impound yard. "I'd been wondering what I was going to wear. I was going to ask to borrow a pair of scrubs."

Ellie tugged on her blue scrubs shirt and wrinkled her nose. "Trust me. You don't want one of these."

Naomi drew out the pair of shorts, saw on the tag that they were a size six. "How did you know my size?"

"I peeked at your clothes," Lolly said, pointing to the plastic hospital bag that held the tattered remains of the clothes Naomi had been wearing when she'd been admitted.

"It's not much, but it ought to get you through the next couple of days," Ellie said. "If there's anything you don't like, the name of the store is on the bag. Winona will know where to go. You can tell the woman who owns the shop who you are. You won't need a receipt to exchange them. She'll remember."

This was too much. "What do I owe you?"

"Owe us?" Lolly looked affronted. "Nothing at all, sweetie. Just take care of yourself."

What had Naomi done to deserve any of this? "I can't just accept—"

"Sure, you can." Ellie patted her arm. "People in Scarlet Springs take care of one another. We all feel terrible about what happened to you. No one here is going to let a guest to our town hobble around on crutches naked."

That made Naomi laugh. "I don't know what to say. Thank you."

After that, Ellie disconnected Naomi from the morphine pump, removed her IV, and helped her take a shower, getting her settled on a bench and covering her ankle and left shoulder with waterproof dressings so that her wounds wouldn't get wet. Naomi had never showered sitting down before, but she got the hang of it. The hot water felt so good, soap and water washing away dirt and fear, making her feel like herself again.

She wrapped a towel around her hair and another around her body and pushed the call button for Ellie, who came quickly. Ellie steadied her while she got to her feet—or her foot—and walked beside her while she hobbled out of the bathroom on her crutches. The motion hurt the injured muscle in her shoulder, but not unbearably. "I think I'm starting to get the hang of these."

"How was the shower? Do you feel better?"

"*So* much better." It was bliss to feel clean again.

Ellie stayed while Naomi got dressed, then handed her two pain pills and a cup of water. "The doctor has prescribed Percocet, enough to get you through the next couple of weeks. We can pick up the prescription at the hospital pharmacy on your way out. Take it on time. It's important to stay ahead of the pain. I'll print your discharge instructions, and we'll get you out of here."

An hour later, Naomi sat in a wheelchair, wearing her new sundress and holding her belongings in her lap, while Ellie wheeled her out to the exit and Winona walked beside her, carrying her crutches.

"I'll get the car." Winona handed Naomi the crutches and hurried out to the parking lot.

Naomi looked up at Ellie. "Thanks again. Everyone here has been so kind."

"You're welcome. No one should go through what you went through. It's a pleasure for us to help."

Winona pulled up in a green Subaru Forester and parked, then climbed out to help Naomi into the front seat.

Ellie helped, too. "Watch your foot. There you go. You did it."

Naomi lowered the window. "Thanks for everything."

Ellie waved as Winona put the vehicle into gear and left the hospital behind.

The drive to Winona and Chaska's home gave Naomi her first look at Scarlet Springs. There was a small downtown area with boutiques, coffee shops, and restaurants, as well as a strip mall with a grocery store, a dry cleaners, and an ice cream shop. She'd seen at least two marijuana dispensaries—something she wouldn't find back home. There was a fossil and geode store and a place called the New Life Institute.

"What do they do there?"

Winona smiled. "They freeze people's heads after they die in hopes that they can one day be brought back to life. I hear it's very expensive."

"Oookay."

Scarlet Springs wasn't just small. It was also a little … *weird.*

Winona slowed down as they made their way through a roundabout where a big, bearded man was begging for change.

Naomi stared. "Is he wearing buckskin?"

"That's Bear," Winona said. "He's lived in the mountains west of town for as long as anyone can remember. He's a big guy and probably seems scary, but he has a child's heart and mind. We do our best to take care of him."

Bear waved as Winona passed, calling to her. "'Whoever is righteous has regard for the life of his beast.' God bless you, Winona Belcourt."

Naomi caught a glimpse of a big smile on the man's bearded face before Winona turned down a side street. "Did he just say your name?"

"Bear and I are friends. He comes into the sanctuary now and again with orphaned or injured wildlife. He knows the names and faces of every person in town. I'm not sure how he remembers everyone, but he does." Winona pointed with a nod of her head. "There's my clinic."

A one-story U-shaped building stood on the corner behind a sign that read "Aspen Wildlife Sanctuary," a grove of aspen trees out front.

"It's yours?"

Winona nodded. "I started it after I finished my residency with the help of grants and support from the people of Scarlet."

Naomi was impressed. "What kind of animals do you treat?"

"Everything from hummingbirds to mountain lions and black bears." Winona turned the corner and pulled into the driveway of a beautiful two-story Victorian house. "Here we are."

The roof was steeply gabled with a little tower rising to a spire on one corner, the lacy trim painted white. A wrap-around porch held a few chairs and a wooden swing, bird feeders, and baskets of flowers hanging from arched supports. A tall cottonwood stood in the front yard, strips of yellow, white, black, and red cloth tied to one of its branches and fluttering in the breeze.

Naomi couldn't help but smile. "It looks like a gingerbread house."

Winona laughed. "Don't let Chaska hear you say that. He wanted a cabin, something a little more masculine. He got over that when he saw the workshop out back. We merged this parcel and the land the clinic stands on to build Shota's enclosure. Let's get you inside."

While Winona carried Naomi's things, Naomi made her way up a brick walkway to the covered front porch and then took the stairs one at a time, still uncertain on her crutches. Winona held the door as she stepped inside.

"Wow."

The interior of the house was bright and airy, sunlight reflecting off the polished wood floors. The entryway led to a wide staircase with a wooden banister. To her left, there was a sitting room with a big stone fireplace. To her right, there was what looked like a study with a drafting table and lots of books.

"That's Chaska's office. When he's not climbing, he's designing climbing gear or propulsion systems for satellites."

Satellites?

"He must be super smart."

"He thinks so." Winona gave a laugh then gestured toward the back. "I put you in the guest room behind the kitchen. You'll have your own bathroom with a shower, and you won't have to deal with the stairs."

"Thanks so much."

The big, sunny kitchen had a checkerboard floor of black and white tile. The white cupboards looked like they were original, with carved detail that must have been done by hand. The appliances were all new, their aluminum surfaces gleaming. A simple dining table of polished maple sat together with six chairs in the adjoining dining room.

"This is lovely."

"Too bad neither of us likes to cook."

"Really?" Naomi loved to cook.

"Here's your room." Winona waited for Naomi to enter. "The bathroom is just through there."

The room was small but clean and bright. The twin bed had a plain, white coverlet, a green Pendleton blanket with white buffalo on it folded neatly at the foot. A pine nightstand with a lamp sat beside the bed, a wooden rocking chair in one corner. Green drapes that looked like they'd been sewn by hand hung by simple fabric tabs from a metal curtain rod. Then Naomi saw it.

A medicine wheel.

It hung on the wall across from the bed. Except for its size and the bald eagle feather hanging from its center, it looked like the one Naomi wore around her neck.

"My grandmother made that as a gift for Chaska when he left home."

The quillwork was exquisite. "It's beautiful."

Naomi didn't want to get drawn into a discussion about her heritage, so she changed the subject. "Thanks so much for taking me in like this."

Winona smiled. "You're welcome. I need to get back to the clinic. I've got a baby raccoon waiting for surgery. She was hit by a mountain biker and has a broken leg."

Naomi could sympathize. "Poor little thing."

"She'll be fine. Just rest and make yourself at home. We can go shopping tonight to get anything you might need, okay?"

"Thanks, Winona." Naomi watched her go, then stretched out on the bed, resting her leg on a pillow. Before she knew it, she was asleep.

Chaska waited for the microwave to finish cooking his frozen burrito, his gaze moving over the printed memes and comics taped to the break room cupboard doors. Someone had added a few new ones this morning.

"Holy shit!" read one that featured an image of a man with a horrified expression on his face, telephone in hand. "You used Imperial units?"

Chaska chuckled. Yeah, that stupid mistake had cost NASA a Mars Lander.

"Engineering: If you're not tired, you're not doing it right," read another.

The microwave beeped.

Chaska took out the plate and carried it, together with a cup of coffee and a jar of salsa, to the table. While he ate, the system schematic of the propulsion module for the Comet project ran through his mind. With a propellant load of 90 kilograms of hydrazine, the system was intended for the final orbit trim of the new Comet ST-5, a joint project of scientists at the University of Colorado-Boulder and NASA. RMSA—the company Chaska worked for—had been contracted to build some of the electrical systems as well as the launch and propulsion systems. Scheduled for launch in three years, the Comet ST-5 would spend its life hanging out at a Lagrange point monitoring space for comets and asteroids. It was Chaska's job to find a way to build a system that was responsive enough to get the satellite precisely where it needed to be in space without increasing overall weight or blowing the hell out of the project budget.

He'd taken a couple of bites when Casper, his supervisor, walked in with the new hire, who was in the middle of his orientation day. The kid was fresh out of college—some fancy school back east—but the freckles on his face made him look younger. He wore a suit and tie, Greek letters engraved on his tie pin. A frat boy. Apparently, the kid was unaware that the dress code was strictly jeans and T-shirts.

"Hey, Belcourt, I'd like you to meet Sheldon Moore. He'll be taking the vacant seat on the avionics team. We've got high hopes for him."

Chaska stood, shook the kid's hand. "Chaska Belcourt."

Sheldon gave him a toothy bro grin. "Hey."

"Chaska here is our propulsion systems genius. He's also a world-class rock climber and designs gear for search and rescue operations in his free time. He could be making bank off patents, but he lets other people use his designs."

That part about being a world-class climber was an exaggeration, but what Casper had said about the patents was probably true. Chaska didn't care about the money. He designed the gear to make rescues safer and easier, not to line his pockets.

"Yesterday, he was out on a rescue," Casper said. "Belcourt here not only found the girl and saved her life, but he helped agents track the bad guys."

Sheldon looked confused. "Track?"

"He's Lakota. Grew up on the reservation. Pine Ridge, right?"

Chaska nodded, wishing his boss would shut up.

Casper missed the cues, kept talking. "We try to be flexible with his schedule so that he can participate in rescues. He's earned that privilege."

"Cool." The kid made an awkward attempt at a high-five, which Chaska did not reciprocate. "Way to go, chief."

Chief?

Nice.

In his teenage years, Chaska might have responded to an insult like this with rough words or fists, but time had given him more control over his temper. Now, he chalked up shit like this to ignorance. "I think you misheard my name. It's Chaska, but you can call me Belcourt."

"Let's let Belcourt get back to his lunch. We've got a Monday development deadline and a meeting with the NASA team." Casper guided Sheldon out of the break room, his voice drifting back to Chaska. "Can you find your way back to my office? We should talk, but I need to have a word with Belcourt first."

The kid's first day with the company might well be his last.

"Sure. Yeah."

Casper stepped back into the break room. "I'll talk to him. He's young. He didn't mean anything by it."

"They never do." Chaska sat again and finished the last few bites of his burrito, his mind shifting back to the Comet ST-5. His cell phone buzzed.

A text message from Win.

I just left Naomi at our place. Will be home as soon as I can. Grab something for dinner on the way home?

Naomi.

Chaska had forgotten that she would be staying with them. It was good and right to give her a place to rest and recuperate. Their grandmother had taught them to welcome strangers into their home and to offer help and protection to those who needed it. But Chaska knew there was more to his sister's invitation to Naomi than old-fashioned Lakota notions of *wacantognaka* — generosity.

You were led to her.

No. No way. Naomi had been lying in that exact spot for hours before Chaska had spoken those foolish words. It was just a coincidence.

Chaska pushed it from his mind and got back to work.

Chaska unlocked the front door and carried the food to the kitchen, the house silent. He thought no one was home until he caught a glimpse of Naomi in the back bedroom. He walked to the bedroom door to say hello—and froze.

He'd thought she was beautiful when he'd first seen her, but now…

She slept with her face turned toward him, her lips parted, her breathing deep and even. Dark hair fanned out on the pillow around her, long lashes resting against her bruised cheeks, a bandage on her wounded shoulder. Her dress had ridden up to her thighs, revealing strong, smooth legs and soft skin. Her injured ankle was wrapped in a compression bandage and propped on a pillow, her feet delicate, her toenails painted a frosty shade of peach.

Is there anyone I can call for you—your family, a significant other, an employer?

No. No one.

He wondered how that could be true. How could a woman as brave and beautiful as Naomi have no man in her life? How could it be that there was no one—friends, family, neighbors—who would want to know what had happened to her, no one to help her get home again?

Life wasn't easy, but walking the path alone made it much harder.

Chaska's family was far from perfect, but when Winona had been attacked and drugged, there'd been a half dozen pickup trucks parked out front the next day. Their aunties had cooked more food than they could eat—*wohanpi*, buffalo burgers, fry bread, plum cakes, corn with walnuts. Their cousins had gotten underfoot trying to help. Old Man had held an *inipi* ceremony, pouring water, leading the songs and prayers for Winona. Chaska's friends on the Team had done their best to help, too. Hell, everyone in Scarlet had pitched in, doing what they could to support Winona and Lexi, who'd been badly hurt, enfolding both women and their families in well-intentioned chaos.

It didn't seem right that anyone should face a situation like this alone.

Chaska looked at Naomi's sweet face, whatever doubts he'd had about having her stay here gone. She wasn't alone—not any longer. She had Winona, and, yes, Chaska, too. They would travel this part of her journey with her, doing whatever they could to help her get back on her feet and home to Rapid City.

It was only when she stirred and he thought she was about to wake up that he realized he'd entered her room and was standing next to the bed, staring down at her.

Aiii. You idiot. What are you doing?

She'd just been attacked by two men. The last thing he wanted to do was startle her or make her feel unsafe.

He turned and walked quietly from the room, shutting the door behind him.

Chapter Six

Naomi awoke with a whimper, her leg throbbing, her shoulder aching. She glanced at the clock on the nightstand and realized she'd slept off her last dose of painkillers and was now two hours behind on the next. Carefully lifting her leg, she sat on the edge of the bed, her mind in a fog. Where had she left her pills?

She reached for her crutches, got to her feet, and made her way over to the rocking chair, where she'd put the bag that held everything from the hospital. She found the bottle of painkillers in the bottom of the bag together with the receipt. She took two pills from the bottle and popped them into her mouth, holding them there as she walked to the closed bedroom door and opened it. She stepped into the kitchen in search of a glass of water—and stopped short.

Chaska.

She forgot about the pills and swallowed hard, tablets dragging their way down her throat, leaving a bitter taste.

She recognized him. Of course, she did. And yet...

How could she not have noticed how *beautiful* he was?

He was tall, over six feet, a black T-shirt stretched over well-developed pecs, his arms lean and muscular. Thick, dark hair hung almost to his waist, long lashes framing intense brown eyes. His face looked like it had been sculpted by an artist—a proud nose, high cheekbones, a wide mouth with full lips.

This was the man who'd stayed with her, who'd promised to protect her, who'd helped save her life. He was the most stunning man she'd ever seen.

His dark brows drew together, and he took a step away from the refrigerator, where he'd been busy putting groceries away, toward her. "Are you okay?"

She searched for words, her thoughts scattered. "I came to get a glass of water."

He walked toward a cupboard and pulled a glass out for her. "The glasses are here, silverware in the drawer down here, plates and bowls over there. Do you want ice?"

"Yes, please—and thanks."

He pressed the glass against the dispenser in the refrigerator door, filling it first with crushed ice and then with water. He turned to hand it to her, his brow furrowing again. "Why don't you sit down?"

Right.

She couldn't carry the glass and walk with her crutches at the same time. She hobbled awkwardly over to the table. How clumsy she must look. "It's going to take me a while to get the hang of this."

"You're doing well for your first day." He set the glass on the table and drew out a chair for her, holding it while she sat.

Oh, God. He even *smelled* good, the warm scent of sage making it hard to think.

"Thanks."

"You're welcome." He went back to what he'd been doing, sticking something in the fridge, his back to her. "Winona will be home in a few minutes. I grabbed a roast chicken for us. I hope you're not a vegetarian."

"Me?" *Yes, you. Who else could he be talking to?* "No. I'm not."

She drank, washing the bitter medicine taste down her throat. She set the glass on the table, her mind searching for something to say. "I never got the chance to thank you for staying with me, for taking care of me, for calling the rescue team. If Shota hadn't found me..."

He turned away from the fridge, leaned up against the center island. "You did the hardest part yourself—getting away from those men, staying alive. You're a brave woman."

She stared at him, taken aback by his praise. "I wasn't brave. I was terrified."

He nodded as if he understood. "That's what courage is—doing something that needs to be done even though you're afraid."

She'd never thought about it like that before.

Chaska ate his supper, listening while the women talked, his gaze drawn repeatedly to Naomi's face. There was a vulnerability about her, something fragile that tugged at him, set off some primitive instinct to protect her. She'd had to be strong to escape those men the way she had, and yet there were shadows in those blue eyes.

He wished they'd found the bastards. It would have given him immense satisfaction to watch McBride take them down and haul them away in chains. Prison was too good for them. In the old days among the *Oceti Sakowin*—the Seven Council Fires—a man who'd done what those men had wanted to do to Naomi would have been given a knife and commanded to walk away from the village and end his own life. If he hadn't had the courage to do it, the warriors of the village would have finished him.

Rape wasn't a crime against an individual woman or her family alone. It was a crime against nature because it was through women that life came into this world. That's what Chaska's grandfather had taught him.

Chaska found Winona watching him.

"You look angry. Are things not going well at work?"

He didn't want to ruin Naomi's supper by bringing up her ordeal, so he searched for an excuse. "We have a new kid at the office—a frat boy type with a suit and Greek letters on his tie. He called me 'chief.'"

Winona gave a disgusted *hmph*. "Are you going to tell Casper?"

"Casper was standing right there. He ordered the kid to his office. I guess we'll see if the guy still has a job tomorrow."

Winona turned to Naomi, who was looking down at her plate. "Chaska is lucky to work for a company that at least tries to do the right thing."

Naomi looked over at Chaska. "You're an engineer, right?"

He nodded. "I work for RMSA—Rocky Mountain Space and Avionics. I design propulsion systems for satellites."

"That's what Winona told me. You must be super smart."

Winona laughed. "He'd be the first to agree with you there."

"Funny." Chaska glared at his sister. He wasn't sure he liked the idea of her running a PR campaign behind his back, telling Naomi about him.

Winona ignored his pointed glance and turned to Naomi. "What do you do?"

"I make jewelry."

Chaska hadn't been expecting that.

Win looked surprised, too. "What kind of jewelry? Beads?"

Naomi had just taken a bite of chicken. She shook her head, chewed, waiting until she had swallowed to answer. "I work mostly with silver and semi-precious stones, but sometimes gold, too."

She tucked her dark hair behind her ear. "I made these."

A silver raven, its wings outstretched in flight, dangled from her earlobe set off by small, irregularly shaped turquoise stones. The detail was amazing.

"*You* made those?" Winona leaned closer. "They're beautiful."

Naomi smiled. "Thanks."

It was the first genuine smile Chaska had seen on her face, and it took the breath from his lungs.

"I have a website if you want to see more."

Winona's smartphone appeared in her hand. "What's the web address?"

"It's my name and then dot com." Naomi spelled her name for Winona, who typed the URL into her phone's browser.

Winona read aloud. "Naomi Archer: Jewelry inspired by the Black Hills. Oh, wow! Look at this, Chaska. This is fantastic."

Win stood and walked around to his side of the table, bending down to share the images on her screen with him.

He found himself sharing his sister's amazement. Jewelry wasn't his thing, but he knew a good deal about metalworking, enough to understand that Naomi had true skill. "You're good."

Winona scrolled down the page, images of ravens, eagles, coyotes, wolves, bears, flowers, feathers, and different animal tracks rendered gracefully into silver rings, earrings, bracelets, pendants, tie clips, and belt buckles.

"Oh, wow!" Winona turned the phone to show Naomi what they were looking at.

The silver bracelet was inlaid with lapis lazuli, mother of pearl, coral, and onyx to create a tiny scene of a raven flying in front of a setting sun.

Naomi's face lit up. "That's one of my signature pieces. They're one-of-a-kind pieces for people looking for something special. I really love working in mosaic."

Chaska shook his head. "I take that back. You're not just good. You're an artist."

Her face flushed at his compliment, her lips curving in a shy smile that made his pulse skip. "Thank you."

Naomi looked into Chaska's eyes, his words warming her. She'd learned a long time ago not to take other people's opinions about her work seriously, but what he'd just said had touched her.

Winona turned off her smartphone and went back to her seat. "How did you get into jewelry-making? Did you study it in college?"

"Oh, I couldn't afford college. I only have a GED." Naomi hesitated to tell them more. She couldn't tell them the whole truth without talking about her heritage, so she settled on the partial truth. "Ever since I can remember, I was fascinated by jewelry. I waited tables to earn the money for jewelry-making classes—metalsmithing, inlay, repoussé, enameling, stone setting, wax casting, PMC."

"PMC? What's that?"

"Precious metal clay. I'd be happy to show you how it works once I get my tools and things back. They're still in my SUV."

She had no idea when the police would release her vehicle.

"So, you took classes and…" Winona waited for the rest of the story.

"I took all the classes I could, buying the tools as I went along. When I felt ready, I started selling my pieces."

"People must have gone crazy for it," Winona said.

Naomi couldn't help but laugh. "It was an uphill battle just to be noticed. There are so many artisan jewelers, all of us competing for clientele. I set up tables at trade shows and farmers markets when I could afford it. I thought I was going to end up waiting tables forever."

She told them how the buyer for a western jewelry catalog had come by her table at a trade show in Phoenix. "She invited me to submit images of my work and suggested I get a website. The catalog picked me up and started carrying my work. My clientele grew. I finally launched a website, and things really took off after that."

Winona set her fork aside and dabbed her lips with her napkin. "I love stories like that—about people who find success doing what they love. When I left home to go to college in Fort Collins, a lot of people were against it. Chaska had already moved away, and they didn't want me to go, too. But I knew that it was what I was meant to do. Is that how it was for you?"

Nothing about Naomi's life had been simple—except for her love of jewelry-making. "Yes, that's exactly how it was for me, too."

Chaska had sat, listening, until now. "We are all born with a gift, and part of the journey is finding out what that is and learning how to share it."

Naomi liked that. "Your gift is engineering?"

"I used to think so." He told her how he'd moved to Colorado to go to college but had seen people rock climbing and decided to try it. "It's like engineering in motion. It's geology and physics and engineering wrapped together. Every climb is a different equation, a different problem that has to be solved. Putting my abilities to use for the Team and helping to save lives—that means a lot more to me than building propulsion systems."

"My brother has designed a lot of the gear the Team uses during rescues," Winona said. "He's always in his workshop, trying something new."

Chaska's gaze fell on an empty saucer that sat in the center of the table, his brows knitting in a frown. He took some chicken from the serving dish and set it on the plate, together with a tiny amount of potatoes and salad.

"Is that for Shota?"

Chaska chuckled. "It's a spirit plate."

Winona explained. "We share a little bit of everything we eat during the day with the spirit world. It's a way of showing our gratitude, of being mindful of the abundance in our lives."

"Don't the animals just eat it?"

Winona nodded. "Yes, but that doesn't matter. It's the offering that counts."

Naomi didn't know much about Lakota customs or culture.

"Where do you get your blood?" Winona's question—inevitable as it was—sent a jolt of adrenaline through Naomi.

Why did it always come to this? Everyone assumed that everyone else came from normal families like they did, but it wasn't true. Not everyone was comfortable making small talk about their families—or lack thereof.

Naomi tried to deflect the question with a joke. "I get it from the same place as everyone else—my bone marrow."

As the words were out, she regretted them. They sounded less like a joke and more like she was being a smart ass. Chaska and Winona had been so kind to her. They'd shared a meal with her, given her a place to stay. They had saved her life. The last thing she wanted to do was offend them. But why did her heritage matter?

Winona didn't laugh. She didn't even smile, her gaze flicking to her brother. Chaska watched Naomi for a moment, his dark eyes inscrutable. Then he got to his feet and carried the spirit plate out the back door.

Chaska spread out the work he'd brought home on the drafting table, the door to his office closed. Winona occasionally brought Shota inside for a while after dinner, but Chaska couldn't share his workspace with a hundred pounds of energetic wolf. Shota could destroy everything in a room in a few minutes if he felt like it, and there was nothing here that Chaska was willing to lose. Monday's meeting with the NASA team was coming up fast, and he needed to make progress. Still, he couldn't get his mind to focus on propellant loads, pressurant subsystems, and cavitating venturi, and he didn't have to be a genius to know why.

Naomi.

He'd spent only a few hours in her company—not counting helping with her rescue—and yet something about her got to him. He had met lots of beautiful women in his life, but until Naomi, he hadn't met a woman who could knock the breath from his lungs with a smile. She was talented, too, her work showing not just skill but artistry. And there was that strange combination of courage and vulnerability.

His reaction to her was probably just the result of having helped to save her life. He'd never had contact with anyone he'd helped rescue afterward. He'd never watched them struggle with the aftermath of almost losing their lives. Whatever he was feeling would surely fade as she recovered.

Where do you get your blood?

I get it from the same place as everyone else—my bone marrow.

The woman confused him. Her art showed a deep respect for all life—the four-legged, the winged ones, even the metals of the earth—but her response to Winona's question had been flippant. And yet it hadn't been disregard he'd seen on her face—it had been fear. Her pupils had dilated, and she'd inhaled—a sharp little gasp—as if she was having a full-on adrenaline reaction.

Of course, Chaska had met people who felt the way she did—people for whom Native heritage was a burden or didn't matter at all. He couldn't understand that. Blood mattered. Chaska would be nothing if not for his ancestors and his *tiospaye*—the broader community of his relatives.

You were led to her.

Yeah, right.

He willed his mind off Naomi and focused on his calculations, managing to get nowhere before the sound of wolf nails clickety-clicking on the wood floor in the hallway broke his concentration.

Shota scratched and whined at the door.

Not wanting to replace the door *again*, he set his calculator and pencil down.

It was pack time.

Winona had taught him that every interaction with Shota required Chaska to maintain his dominance and to see things from Shota's point of view—a wolf's point of view. They couldn't risk Shota challenging them for leadership of their little pack. Even though Shota had been neutered as a pup and had been hand raised by Winona, he was still a wolf with all the predatory drives and physical strength of his wild relatives.

Chaska got his head in the game, then opened the door and stepped out, shutting the door behind him.

Shota fell onto his side, showed his belly, his tail thumping on the floor, acknowledging Chaska's status as alpha male.

Chaska bent down, rubbed Shota's belly, tugged at his ears, grabbed his muzzle, rough-housing with him. "Where are your toys?"

Shota jumped up, dashed into the living room, and grabbed his new rubber chicken from his toy box. He shook the chicken in his jaws, unleashing a cacophony of high-pitched squeaks, making Winona and Naomi laugh.

Chaska found the women in the living room, his sister on the floor holding a battered length of knotted rope, Naomi in the reclining chair, her injured leg propped up, her crutches leaning against the wall. Nothing had passed between him and Naomi, and yet he could feel the pull of her from across the room.

What was wrong with him?

"What do you feed a wolf?" Naomi asked.

Winona stood. "I'll show you."

The moment Winona walked to the freezer, Shota lost all interest in his rubber chicken. He pranced and whined while she got his supper ready.

"I mix his food myself. It's mostly raw or frozen venison and elk that we buy from the butcher or get from road kill. I mix it with kibble for vitamins, bones for minerals, and vegetables for—"

Chaska's Team pager went off. He pulled it from the pocket of his jeans, scrolled through the message.

Climber Stuck on Cenotaph Spire.

He almost felt relieved. He needed to get out of here.

A chill shivered down Naomi's spine. Someone was in trouble, their life in danger, just as hers had been.

"Is it serious?" Winona asked her brother.

"Someone's in trouble on Cenotaph Spire," Chaska called back to his sister as he disappeared down the hallway, his footsteps sounding on the stairs a moment later.

Naomi glanced out the window, saw that the sun had begun to set. "It's going to be dark soon."

It had been dark as pitch when she'd fallen into that ravine, Arlie and Clem shouting for her, chasing her.

Winona dropped a large chunk of frozen red meat mixed with kibble and carrots into a steel bowl and set it out for Shota, who lay down and began to gnaw. "The Team gets called out all hours of the day and night. You wouldn't believe the trouble people get themselves into. Some college kids once hauled a keg of beer up to the top of the First Flatiron and got—"

"Where are my Team T-shirts?" Chaska reappeared wearing only a pair of black athletic pants, his upper body gloriously bare.

"Maybe they're in the dryer where you left them last night," Winona offered, a teasing tone to her voice.

As he strode through the room, Naomi couldn't help but stare at the shifting slabs and ridges of muscle—his strong arms, that six-pack, those pecs, and …

Scars.

Pinched bits of flesh marred his skin of his hairless chest in an almost symmetrical pattern, three scars on each side. Were they scars from chicken pox or some other kind of sickness? No, they were too big for that, too regular.

Chaska hurried through the kitchen toward the back of the house, leaving Naomi to stare after him. When he returned, he'd pulled a familiar yellow T-shirt over his head. He headed toward the front door. "If all goes well, I should be back in a couple of hours."

A moment later, Naomi heard the door shut.

"How often does the Team get called out?"

Winona set a big steel bowl of water next to Shota's food bowl and left the wolf to its dinner. "In the summer, they can get called out three or four times a day. Things quiet down in the winter—for the most part."

"Do people ever die?"

Winona nodded. "Sometimes they're called out to evacuate bodies—suicides, avalanche victims, people who were killed in a fall."

"That must be hard." Naomi couldn't imagine it.

Winona nodded. "They save many more people than they lose. I think that's what keeps them going despite the difficulties. There are so many times when they are a person's only chance of getting home alive."

Naomi wanted to ask about the scars but didn't want to offend Winona again. In the end, her curiosity got the better of her. "Can I ask you a question?"

"Yes."

"The scars on Chaska's chest—how did he get them?"

For a moment, Winona was silent, as if thinking how best to answer. "Our grandfather is a hereditary Sun Dance chief. Chaska followed the path of a sun dancer for a time. Part of the ceremony involves piercing as a sacrifice."

Naomi had never heard of the Sun Dance—outside of stories about Butch Cassidy and the Sundance Kid or the famous film festival. She hadn't realized the name came from a Native ceremony. "It looks painful."

"It's not something we talk about with outsiders."

Outsider.

Naomi had heard that word before. She wasn't sure what Winona meant by it now—whether she meant that she'd told Naomi all she was willing to tell her because Naomi was an outsider or whether she meant to say she was trusting Naomi with this information despite the fact that Naomi was more or less a stranger.

Maybe she means that it's hard to trust you because you didn't trust her when she asked about your heritage.

Some part of Naomi wanted to answer that question now, to trust Winona with the truth and hope that she and her brother were different than the people she'd met at the Native American art and craft shows she'd tried to join.

Look, hot stuff, if you're not a registered tribal member, you're not a Native American at all. Pack your shit, and get out.

Naomi opened her mouth to speak—but nothing came out.

Chaska was wrong about her. She wasn't the least bit brave.

Chapter Seven

Chaska downclimbed with Hawke and Moretti, the three of them acting as a secondary belay for Sasha Dillon, Mitch Ahearn, and Nicole while they lowered the uninjured climber safely to the ground. The kid had tried to free solo Harebell, the only route on the Spire. He'd been near the top—only about fifty feet off the ground—when he'd started shouting for help, paralyzed by fear.

The kid's voice drifted up to Chaska, sounding more defensive than grateful. "I don't know why I freaked out. I could've done it myself."

"Don't worry about it," Sasha reassured him. "It's better to get help and be safe than risk a critical fall."

The youngest member of the Team and one of the best sports climbers in the world, Sasha Dillon was the Team's celebrity. She lived off sponsorships, climbing around the world and using Scarlet Springs as her home base.

The guy moaned. "God, how humiliating. I was just rescued by two girls and an old guy."

Chaska's feet had just touched the ground when he overheard this. "One of those *girls* is a world-champion sports climber, and the other has been rescuing climbers like you for the better part of five years. That old man beside you—he helped invent this sport. Show some respect, man."

Nicole shot Chaska an appreciative glance—making Chaska wonder whether he should regret his words. He did not want to lead her on.

The guy looked at Sasha, and his eyes went wide, as if he'd finally realized who she was. "Fuck. Sorry, man."

"Don't worry about it." Nicole unclipped her harness. "We've encountered sexism in men we've rescued before."

Chaska bit the insides of his cheeks to stop himself from laughing, his gaze meeting Hawke's and Moretti's, who were also fighting not to laugh.

"I don't owe you anything, right?" There was a stiff, cocky tone to the guy's voice now, humiliation apparently having morphed into resentment. "I'm free to go?"

Ahearn stepped out of his harness. "We don't charge for rescues, but this was a clear reminder to climb within your ability."

Without a word, the guy turned and stomped off down the trail.

"You're welcome," Hawke muttered, shaking his head.

Sasha laughed. "What a fragile ego."

"Okay, okay." Ahearn shouldered a coil of rope. "Leave the poor guy alone. Let's stow the gear and head home."

Chaska knew right then that they were going to hear from Megs about this. As the Team's director, she didn't tolerate unprofessional behavior from members.

They worked together to get the ropes, harnesses, and other gear back onto Rescue One, the truck's rooftop lights turning nighttime into day. Bats flitted overhead, drawn in by the insects who were attracted to the light.

"How's Naomi?" Moretti asked.

Chaska tried to ignore the way his pulse skipped at the sound of her name. "She seems to be doing well. Win has spent more time with her than I have."

Moretti started folding ropes into a large rope bag. They would be washed, dried, and inspected inch-by-inch before being used again. "Ellie told me you and Winona invited her to stay with you while she recovers."

Chaska shoved his harness in a nylon stuff sack with the others. "She was going to stay in a hotel, but Winona wouldn't have it."

Hawke tossed his harness to Chaska. "Your sister has a big heart."

That was the truth.

"Doesn't she have friends or family to help her out?" Nicole asked.

Chaska didn't want to share something he'd been told in private, but he figured this was public knowledge by now. "I guess not."

"That's not right." Sasha pulled her rack of gear over her head, set it down on the vehicle's tailgate, carabiners and cams clinking. "Everyone should have someone."

Hawke gave a snort. "What a nice world that would be."

Moretti zipped the rope bag, set it inside the vehicle. "Ellie thought maybe you could talk to her and see how she felt about Joe holding a fundraiser for her at Knockers. You know Joe would do it."

Knockers was Scarlet Springs' one and only brewpub and the hub of the town's social activity. Its menu was good, but its indoor climbing wall was even better. Named after the legendary Tommyknockers, spirits that lived in the abandoned mines above town, it was owned by Joe Moffat—or Caribou Joe, as locals called him. Joe went above and beyond to give back to his community.

"That's a great idea." Taylor slipped off his climbing shoes and stepped into a pair of Tevas. "The state will probably pick up most of her medical expenses, but she's going to have to get her vehicle repaired, too, and find some way to get both herself and her car home again."

It *was* a good idea, but the decision wasn't theirs or even Joe's to make. "I'll talk to her and see how she feels about it."

Naomi ran for her life, her heart slamming in her chest. Shrubs and tree branches grabbed at her, threatening to trip her, slowing her down, Arlie's voice chasing her through the darkness.

"Get back here, you little bitch! I think she broke my nose."

A gunshot rang out, pain slicing through her shoulder.

She'd been shot!

And then she was falling.

Naomi sat bolt upright, chased from sleep by terror. She tore off the covers, shot to her feet—and collapsed onto the floor with a cry as her weight hit her broken leg, fear and pain bringing tears to her eyes. "Shit!"

How could she have forgotten?

Heart pounding, she sat there for a moment, the nightmare still dragging at her, her body shaking, the pain in her ankle almost unbearable.

A voice came from the other side of her door, made her jump.

"Naomi? Are you okay?" It was Chaska.

She tried to get her good leg beneath her, but her injured one was bent in an awkward position that made any movement excruciating. "I fell."

"Do you need help?"

She tried again to stand but only succeeded in hurting herself. "Yes."

The door opened, and Chaska stepped inside, wearing only climbing pants, his chest and feet bare. He stepped over to where she sat and knelt down beside her, his brown eyes dark as he took in her predicament.

She could only imagine what she looked like sprawled on the floor in her nightgown, all bruises and bandages, her hair a mess. She found herself babbling an explanation. "I had a bad dream. I was running from them and … I just forgot. I tried to get up, but …"

How could she have been so stupid?

He nodded as if what she'd said made perfect sense to him. "Let's get your leg straightened out, and then I'll help you up. I can't guarantee it won't hurt. Ready?"

She nodded, steeling herself.

"Try to relax. Let me do the work." He took her calf and lifted her ankle off the floor. "Turn toward your right side a little. Just like that."

She did as he asked, squeezing her eyes shut against the pain and fighting not to moan, her fingers digging into the wooden floor.

And then it was over, her injured leg straight now.

In a single motion, Chaska scooped her into his arms and lifted her off the floor.

Startled, she reached around his neck and held on, his skin warm and smooth beneath her palms, his body hard, the scent of sage surrounding her.

"I won't drop you." He set her down on the bed and sat near her feet. "Can I get you anything?"

"No—and thanks. I bet you never had to rescue anyone from the floor before."

He reached out, wiped the tears from one cheek with his thumb, his touch leaving a trail of heat. "You're crying—and shaking like a leaf."

She hugged her arms around herself. "The nightmare. It seemed so … *real*."

He stood, pulled the Pendleton blanket from the foot of the bed, and wrapped it around her, his hands lingering on her shoulders. "What you've been through would give anyone nightmares. It will be with you for a while."

His quiet understanding, offered without judgment, cut short her next thought, which had been to blame herself. Somehow, he made it seem okay, as if what she'd done hadn't been stupid at all.

She reached down with both hands to rub her shin, the pain in her ankle still sharp. "I hope I didn't re-break it."

He slid his hand over her shin as if examining her, stopping just above her bandages, his touch sending sparks across her skin. "Unless you felt or heard something snap, you're probably okay, but you might want to call your doctor in the morning."

"How did the rescue go? Is everyone okay?"

"We got the climber down. He wasn't hurt, so it went quickly."

"I'm glad."

A breeze caught the curtains, made them dance, cool mountain air wafting through the room. For a moment, neither of them spoke, silence stretching between them. It wasn't like any silence Naomi had known. It wasn't awkward or uncomfortable despite the strangeness of the circumstances—an attractive man she barely knew sitting bare-chested on her bed in the middle of the night. Nor did she feel rushed to fill the space with idle conversation. Time passed in heartbeats.

When at last he spoke, his voice was soft and soothing. "You were alone out there in the forest, but you're not alone anymore. You have me and Winona and Shota. You've got the entire town of Scarlet Springs behind you. The people are talking about doing a fundraiser for you to help you get your life back to normal again. I was going to ask you about that in the morning."

"A fundraiser?" Tears pricked Naomi's eyes at this news, gratitude at war with that same sense of unease she'd felt at the hospital when Ellie and the other nurses had shown up with clothes for her. "Why would they do that?"

"The people of Scarlet take care of their own."

"But … I'm not even from here."

Chaska gave a soft chuckle. "Try telling them that."

Chaska lay in his boxer briefs on his bed, staring up through the darkness at the ceiling, his arm bent behind his head. Ten minutes ago, he'd been beat, ready for sleep. Now, he felt wide awake, his body buzzing with sexual energy.

Naomi.

He'd been on his way from the laundry room to his bedroom when he'd heard her hit the floor and cry out. He'd opened the door to find her there, tears on her cheeks and in obvious pain, her dark hair in tangles around her shoulders. He'd done his best not to hurt her, but he'd had to do it without his brain. It had stopped working the moment he had touched her.

He could have set her down on the bed and kept his distance, but he hadn't. Yeah, he'd wanted to make sure she was okay, to offer her some comfort, but he could have done both of those things while standing on his feet. He'd *wanted* to be close to her because … *damn.*

He closed his eyes, images of her filling his head, his cock already hard. Her sweet face. Her dark hair in tangles. Her nightgown slipping to reveal the graceful line of her collar bone, the soft curve of her shoulder, the valley between her breasts. The silky skin and feminine shape of her legs. He'd wanted to hold her and kiss her, to bury his face in her hair, to inhale her sweet scent.

It was nothing more than biology, simple neurochemistry, the attraction of male to female, but knowing that didn't make the urge easier to ignore.

He wanted her.

Oh, no. No. Bad idea.

She was vulnerable right now, a guest in his home. He had promised her safety, a place to rest and recover. No, he wasn't a gentleman in any sense of the word. Even the concept was foreign to him. But he *had* been taught to respect women and honor visitors. That rarely included trying to get between their legs.

Unless, of course, she felt the same attraction…

Would you listen to yourself, kola*?*

Naomi was a guest. She would be heading back to Rapid City soon anyway, so what was the point?

He reached inside his boxers, took hold of himself, and gave his body the release it wanted.

Naomi woke to find sunlight streaming through her window, Chaska and Winona already gone. There was a note from Winona on the kitchen counter.

Call me when you're up. ☺

Naomi typed in the number Winona had left, adding Winona to her contacts.

No answer.

She left a message, then made herself a bowl of cornflakes. She'd just stuck the empty bowl into the dishwasher when her phone rang.

It was Winona. "How are you feeling? Chaska said you fell last night. He thought you might want to call your doctor."

Her leg felt better today than it had last night. "I'm fine."

"I thought you might want to visit the clinic, get a tour. We've got lots of baby fawns, a little burrowing owl, a pair of fox kits, some mountain lion cubs—"

"I would *love* that." Winona thought she had to ask?

"I'll come get you. I don't want you to try to walk here by yourself. It's not far, but it's kind of rocky."

Naomi hurried to get ready for the day and had just finished dressing when Winona arrived, wearing a white lab coat over her green scrubs. They walked together out the back door, Winona staying close beside Naomi as Naomi hobbled along on her crutches. The backyard seemed surprisingly small for the size of the house—just a small patio with a gas grill, two reclining patio chairs, a raised vegetable bed, a few rose bushes, and a large shed. Then Naomi remembered that they'd set aside part of the property for Shota's enclosure.

Winona pointed to the shed. "That's Chaska's workshop. That's where he does his machining, his mad-scientist work."

"I would love to see the kind of tools he uses."

For some reason, this made Winona laugh. "I'm sure he'd be happy to show you."

Naomi could sense the affection Winona felt for her brother. "The two of you are really close, aren't you?"

Winona looked confused by the question. "He's my brother."

Naomi had never been close to Peter and Ruth's sons. To them, she'd always been an outsider and a female.

Winona led her out the back gate and called to the wolf. "Hey, Shota."

How could Naomi have mistaken him for a dog?

The big animal stood behind two heavy chain-link fences—an outer one that was about five feet tall and an inner one that must have been fifteen feet high. The enclosure ran up the side of the mountain and included a den and lots of toys—balls, a wading pool filled with water, and . . .

Was that white thing a bone? Yes, it was.

Signs in red and white warned people away.

BEWARE OF WOLF

This wolf is a wild animal and

will bite or attack if provoked.

Do not try to enter pen or

stick anything through the fence

you don't wish to see ripped apart.

Okay. That was direct.

For all of his fierceness—and Naomi was certain Shota could be fierce—he whined like a puppy when he saw Winona.

"I try to get outside to play with him a few times a day. He gets lonely." She stopped for a few minutes to talk with him, reaching inside to pet him.

"Have you thought about getting him a friend?"

"We've talked about it—a wolf-hybrid or a big dog—but we've found a kind of balance with Shota. It's hard for a captive adult wolf to accept new pack members. It might work out, or it might end with Shota or one of us getting hurt."

The back entrance of the clinic stood not thirty feet from Shota's enclosure. Winona scanned her ID and held the door open for Naomi. "Tell me if you need to sit or if you're too tired to go on. I don't want to wear you out."

Winona showed Naomi the intake area where she examined new arrivals, then led her past two small operating rooms to bigger treatment rooms on the other side of the hallway, telling her how the clinic operated. "Spring and summer are our busiest seasons because that's when animals have their young. We get a lot of orphaned babies—fawns whose mothers were hit by cars, baby raccoons that got washed downstream, that sort of thing. Our goal is always rehabilitation and release, though sometimes that's impossible."

"If you can't release them, are you forced to put them down?"

Winona put a hand over her heart, a horrified expression on her face. "Oh, no. We only euthanize animals that can't be saved. If we can't release them, we keep them here until we find a safe home for them."

A woman with long red hair walked toward them, a sleeping red-haired baby in a carrier on her chest, a basket full of baby bottles in one hand. She smiled at Winona before her gaze came to rest on Naomi. "I'm Lexi Taylor. You must be Naomi."

It was both strange and kind of nice that people knew who she was. "I would ask how you know that, but …"

Lexi laughed. "Scarlet is a *really* small town. Also, my husband, Austin, was part of the Team that brought you in."

"Oh, yes. The paramedic. I remember. Please thank him."

"Lexi is one of my volunteers," Winona explained. "She and little Emily help out a few times a week."

"I bribed my way in, but Win has been nice enough to let me stay."

"I let Lexi stay because she's good with the animals." The two women shared the kind of smile that marked them as good friends.

The baby, Emily, stirred against her mother's chest, looking like a strawberry in her little red dress.

"She's adorable." Naomi felt an overwhelming impulse to touch her. "May I?"

Lexi nodded.

Naomi balanced herself on her good leg and ran a hand over the baby's silky hair. "She's so tiny—and she looks just like you. How old is she?"

"Emily just turned four months last week."

"Let me take those." Winona took the basket of bottles from Lexi.

"The milk is for the fawns," Lexi explained. "It's feeding time."

"Fawns? Oh, God, can I watch?"

"You bet." Winona turned and walked down a side hallway.

Lexi leaned in as if to share a secret. "Be careful. The levels of cute around this place are almost lethal."

Chapter Eight

"I got to feed the fawns. God, they were cute. Their little tails flicked back and forth the whole time they were feeding, and the little sounds they made…"

Chaska ate his spaghetti and listened while Naomi described her day at the wildlife clinic, unable to take his gaze off her. Her face was alive with excitement, and there was a light in her blue eyes he hadn't seen before. Spending time with the animals had been good for her.

"The little burrowing owl looks like a potato with legs. I would love to take photos of him or try to sketch him. I've never seen one before."

Winona reached for another piece of garlic bread. "You're welcome to come back and bring your camera or your sketchpad anytime."

"I think they're with all the stuff in my SUV."

Chaska had a surprise for her, but that could wait. He didn't want to interrupt her. "What was your favorite part?"

"Oh, that's hard. I loved all of it. The bald eagle. She was *huge*. Or maybe the mountain lion cubs. I had no idea that mountain lions purr."

"They *are* cats." Winona was clearly enjoying Naomi's excitement as much as he was. She turned to Chaska. "Bear brought in a fish today. He came in carrying it in a bucket. It had a hook and fishing line caught in its gill, and he was afraid he'd hurt it. I managed to get the hook out, and he left, carrying it in that bucket, planning to dump it back where he'd found it."

"You met Bear?" Chaska watched Naomi's response.

One could tell a lot about a person by how they treated those who were different.

Naomi dabbed her lips with her napkin, nodded. "He's so sweet—like a little boy. He was beside himself with worry about that fish. It touched me to see how much he cared. Does anyone know where he came from?"

Okay, so she passed that test.

Chaska shook his head. "He's been here as long as anyone can remember. No one is sure how old he is, how he got here, or how he became the way he is. We all try to watch out for him, but he knows more about living off the land and surviving in these mountains than anyone I've met."

Naomi seemed to consider that. "Do you think he knows where he came from?"

"I asked him once," Win said. "He told me that he was born in the mountains and that his family is waiting for him in Heaven. That's all he knows."

"That must be hard for him." The light in Naomi's eyes dimmed.

"He seems to take it in stride."

Naomi's gaze dropped to her plate, her fingers tightening around her paper napkin. "I don't know anything about my parents—who they were, where they came from, whether they're still alive. My mother left me in an alley next to a dumpster in Martin right after I was born."

She spoke the words without self-pity, simply stating a fact, but the weight of what she said came down on Chaska—hard. No wonder she'd reacted the way she had to Winona's question about blood. Like an arrow striking bone, that question must have pierced the heart of a grief she'd carried her entire life.

Chaska met his sister's gaze, saw her shock and regret, unanswered questions rushing through his mind. What kind of woman could abandon her newborn? Who had raised Naomi? Given that she'd been found in Martin, which sat roughly halfway between Pine Ridge and Rosebud, had the authorities even bothered to check the two reservations when they'd searched for her mother?

Naomi looked up at the two of them, defiance on her face. "You asked about my blood. I have no idea what I am. All I know is that my mother left me with this. It was tucked inside my blanket."

She took the leather cord that hung around her neck, drew the medicine wheel from inside her tank top.

What would Old Man say at a moment like this? If only Chaska had one-tenth of his wisdom…

He nodded to show that he'd understood her, waiting to speak until he was certain he could do so without emotion. "What you are, Naomi, is a survivor. *Who* you are is entirely up to you."

She gave a little laugh. "Yeah. Right."

What did that mean?

Winona reached over, touched her hand to Naomi's arm. "We don't care where your blood comes from."

Naomi's chin came up. "Then why did you ask?"

Naomi sat in the rocking chair in her room and checked her online sales with her smartphone, trying not to notice the hole she'd punched in her own heart, her eyes not really seeing the data on her screen.

Why had she told them? What had she been thinking?

She hadn't told anyone where she'd come from in a very long time. She didn't like talking about it, and she didn't want anyone's pity. If Chaska and Winona were like the Native people she'd met at art shows, they would lose all interest in spending time with her. If they were like the young women she'd waited tables with, they would pity her or ask lots of questions that opened up dark places inside her. They were good people, and they had already done so much for her. But even good people could be disappointing.

You ought to have stayed in a hotel.

She could still do that. She could pack up and take a taxi to the inn that Lexi's family owned. She'd feel better if she were paying her way. She hated being dependent on anyone for anything. It made her feel vulnerable, weak. She had learned long ago that the only way *not* to get hurt was to have no expectations of others.

What you are, Naomi, is a survivor. Who you are is entirely up to you.

That wasn't true.

What a person became depended in part on what others *allowed* them to be.

She'd been told who she was her entire life. Men at the restaurants where she'd waited tables thought of her as a set of breasts and a vagina, while those at Peter's church saw her as a womb and submissive helpmeet. White people saw her as Native or Latina. Native people learned that she wasn't a registered member of any Indian nation and told her she wasn't one of them.

The only person Naomi had ever been able to rely on was herself.

A knock came at the door. "Naomi?"

Naomi closed the browser on her phone and drew a breath, steeling herself against what was bound to be an awkward conversation. "Yes?"

The door opened, and Winona stepped inside. "Are you okay?"

Naomi couldn't look her in the eyes. "I'm fine."

"Chaska has a surprise for you."

A surprise?

Chaska appeared in the doorway, carrying her tool box in one hand, her camera bag and tripod in the other. "I think these belong to you."

She gaped up at him. "You brought my stuff."

She hadn't been expecting this.

"I stopped by the police impound yard on the way home." He set the camera down on the bed and the tool box on the floor near her feet. "They're done with your vehicle, so I took your stuff and had it towed to Frank's garage. It's the only repair shop in town, but he does good work."

"Thank you. Do you have his number? I'd like to get an estimate."

"There's no need. The town has got you covered. Some folks from Scarlet are paying for parts, and Frank and his crew are donating the labor."

Naomi shook her head. "I can't let you do that."

"Why not?" Winona looked genuinely confused. "People want to help."

Naomi tried to explain, her emotions at an edge. "I don't mean to sound ungrateful, but it's not their problem. *I'm* not their problem."

A thoughtful frown came over Chaska's face, and he dropped onto one knee so that he was eye-level with her. "What you told us today proves that no one can know what another person has lived through. We don't know you well, and you don't know us. But we *do* know what happened to you at the campground, and people want to make it better for you. No one expects anything from you. We all just want to help."

Then his lips quirked in a grin. "This is Scarlet Springs. It's how we roll."

Could it really be that simple?

Winona took Naomi's hand, her fingers warm. "If you really don't want our help, no one will force you to accept it."

"Except Frank." Chaska stood, crossed his arms over his chest. "I doubt he'll take your money."

"Really?"

The warmth in his eyes made her breath catch. "Really."

Something beeped—Chaska's pager.

He drew it out of his pocket, scanned the display. "Megs is calling a meeting—a debriefing for last night's rescue. She's going to bite my head off."

"What did you do?" Winona asked.

"Told off the victim."

"Uh-oh." Winona shook her head. "Megs is going to kick your butt."

"You want to come along?" Chaska asked. "You can see The Cave—the Team's headquarters—and meet some of the people who helped with your rescue."

"I don't know. If you're really in trouble …" Naomi didn't want to find herself in the middle of a shouting match.

Chaska chuckled. "She won't really kick my butt. Megs is just … She's Megs—climbing legend and hard-ass."

Naomi told herself that this would be a great chance to thank the entire Team for saving her life, but some part of her knew the truth. She'd told Chaska and Winona about her roots—or lack thereof —and they still wanted to spend time with her.

How could she say no to that?

The Cave was only a block away, but they drove for Naomi's sake, taking Winona's Subaru, which had more passenger room. Chaska steadied Naomi while she climbed down, then followed her inside the open bay doors.

Team members milled around, talking and joking with one another, their voices filling the cavernous space. Taylor and Hawke left the rope they'd been inspecting when they saw Naomi and came over to say hello.

Naomi remembered both of them. "Thanks for all you did for me."

She held out her hand, but Hawke gave her a hug instead. "I'm glad to see you looking so well."

Taylor did the same. "Lexi told me you were up and about. It's good to see you."

The two men went back to inspecting ropes.

Naomi glanced around her, her gaze moving over the gear that hung from racks on the walls—skis and snowshoes, litters, ice tools, rock climbing equipment, orange medical kits. "This place is huge."

"It's the old fire station." Megs stepped out from behind Rescue Two, clipboard in hand, gray hair pulled back in a ponytail. "Belcourt, I see you brought backup. Good to see you, Win. Naomi, I'm Megs Hill."

Naomi's lips made a little "o," her eyes going wide for a moment in a way that Megs couldn't miss. "You're the Team's director."

Megs' eyes narrowed. "Has Belcourt been telling you stories?"

Uh-oh.

But Naomi covered well. "He said you're a climbing legend."

"That's all he said?" Megs patted Chaska's cheek, a knowing smile on her tanned face. "She's quick on her feet. Finish your tour, Belcourt, and let's get this debriefing underway."

Chaska showed Naomi around the bays, opening Rescue One so that she could see the gear and the medical supplies. "This is the vehicle they brought out on your call. We keep both trucks loaded and operational at all times."

"Do you ever have both out at the same time?"

"More often than you'd think."

"If you don't get paid for rescues, where does all this gear come from?"

"We're a nonprofit. We get a lot of support from the climbing community, along with some corporate sponsorships and local and state grants. Let's head to the operations room." He opened the door for her—and found himself stuck holding it for everyone else.

"That's mighty gentlemanly of you, Belcourt." Hawke clapped him on the shoulder as he passed.

Chaska gave Naomi a quick tour of the ops room, with its radio set-up. The other Team members saw her, their gazes following her. Those who didn't know her were quickly and quietly filled in by those who did. It wasn't often that someone they rescued came for a visit.

Naomi didn't seem to notice the attention, her gaze fixed on the big floor-to-ceiling 3D topo map of the area. "Where was I?"

Sasha bounced across the room, blond ponytail swinging, her face all smiles and sunshine, and pointed to a place on the map. "You were found right here. I'm Sasha."

"Were you there?"

"Yep, but I wouldn't expect you to remember any of us."

Megs' voice carried over the conversation, bringing it to an end. "Now that you're all reacquainted, let's cut the chatter and get started."

Her words brought snickers. Team members had no need to get reacquainted. They probably spent more time with each other than they did with their families.

Megs started roll call. "Mitch Ahearn. Chaska Belcourt. Harrison Conrad … is still in Nepal."

"How's he doing? Have you heard from him?" someone asked.

A troubled expression came over Megs' face. "No word."

Naomi looked over at Chaska, curious.

He leaned down, spoke quietly. "Harrison Conrad is our lead alpinist. He was climbing Everest for the second time in May when his two climbing buddies, prominent climbers, were killed. Conrad survived. No one had heard from him since he left base camp."

"That must have been terrifying."

"Sasha Dillon. Eric Hawke. Dave Hatfield. Creed Herrera. Jesse Moretti. Malachi O'Brien … is working in the ER tonight."

"He took care of me," Naomi whispered.

"Isaac Rogers ... is on the john. Need help in there?"

Rogers' shouted expletives made everyone laugh.

Megs finished roll call and set her clipboard aside. "This is a debriefing for last night's rescue. We had a climber stuck on Cenotaph Spire and got him down pretty quickly. It was all routine, all textbook. I asked all primary members to be here tonight because of what happened *after* the rescue. Anyone care to confess?"

"We got sassy," Nicole said.

"I'm the one who started it," Chaska said. "I take responsibility."

"Way to go, Belcourt," Herrera mumbled with feigned disgust.

Ahearn took over from there, recounting what the guy had said—and what Chaska, Nicole and the others had said in response. "The guy was an asshole. I'll give you that. But it's not our job to put him in his place."

This opened the door for Megs, who spent the next five minutes reminding them all of the high professional standards required to remain a primary Team member. It wasn't enough to be an expert climber and EMT. Team members had to behave in a way that reflected well on the institution.

"Belcourt, it's not your job to defend the women or Ahearn here, who *is* an old man, by the way."

Laughter.

Ahearn shrugged.

"Turner, it's not your job to take down the patriarchy. I know how sexist the climbing community can be. I was dealing with these testosterone-addled idiots before you were born. Be as sassy as you want to be on your own time, but when you're wearing a Team T-shirt, keep your very clever comments to yourself."

Megs paused, glanced around. "Am I understood?"

Heads nodded.

"Good. Let's try not to have this discussion again this year." Megs turned to Chaska. "We've got a guest tonight. Belcourt, would you do the honors?"

Chaska motioned to Naomi. "This is Naomi Archer. Some of you were part of her rescue Tuesday morning. She's staying with Win and me for now."

"Hey, Naomi. Happy to see you doing well."

"Nice to see you again, Naomi."

"Welcome to The Cave."

Chaska could tell that Naomi felt a little overwhelmed. He tried to imagine it from her point of view—coming face to face with people who had saved her life when she'd been helpless and mostly unconscious.

She looked around the room, her voice tight as if she were fighting tears. "Thank you for all you did for me. You came out of nowhere and saved my life."

She was answered with a chorus of *you're welcomes.*

An image of Naomi lying unconscious and wounded flashed into Chaska's mind, and for the first time it struck him how terribly close she'd come to dying alone out there—a terrible end for a woman who'd been left by a dumpster as a newborn.

You were led to her.

Maybe he had been.

Naomi spent most of Friday sleeping, so tired that she was awake only long enough to take pain pills, go to the bathroom, and eat.

"You're healing," Winona said when she came home for lunch to find Naomi dragging herself into the kitchen for a glass of water. "Your body is working hard. You probably overdid it yesterday."

"I guess so."

She woke Saturday morning rested but strangely anxious, a sick feeling in the pit of her stomach, worries chasing one another through her mind before she opened her eyes. Would the State of Colorado approve her application for compensation? Would they be able to fix her Honda? How long could she stay here before Chaska and Win would grow tired of her? When would they catch Clem and Arlie?

She found Chaska and Win in the kitchen. They had just returned from a run in the forest with Shota and were waiting to eat breakfast with her.

"Do you like waffles?" Win asked. "Because I love waffles."

Chaska leaned back in his chair, a resigned look on his face. "What my sister is saying is that she wants me to make waffles."

"I love waffles, too."

Chaska got to his feet. "Okay, then. Waffles it is."

Naomi found it hard to keep up with their banter, and more than once missed something one or the other of them said to her. "I'm sorry. I guess I'm distracted."

After breakfast, Winona left to check the animals at the clinic. "It won't take long. Then we can talk about what you'd like to do today."

Chaska poured Naomi and himself another cup of coffee. "Come. Win refilled the hummingbird feeders this morning, and they've drawn a crowd."

Chaska wasn't kidding.

Naomi sat on the wooden swing, sipped her coffee and watched dozens of tiny, glimmering hummingbirds dart from feeder to feeder, unable to keep the smile off her face. There were so many of them that their wings made a buzzing sound like a swarm of bees. "They look like flying jewels."

"*Tanagila*—that's the Lakota word for hummingbird."

Naomi repeated it. "I wish I'd thought to grab my camera."

"I'll get it for you." Chaska disappeared inside.

Their house was on a hillside, giving Naomi a view of Scarlet and the surrounding mountains. She inhaled the fresh air, took in the beauty of the place, some of her anxiety easing away.

Chaska returned carrying her camera bag and her tripod. "I wasn't sure what you'd need, so I brought everything."

"It's beautiful out here." Naomi took her camera out of her bag, set the shutter speed to 1/4000, and then attached her flash. "You must love sitting out here in the evening and looking out at that view."

Chaska sat beside her. "I don't often take the time."

Naomi took a few photos and checked the images. Not fast enough. The wings were blurred. She adjusted her shutter speed to 1/8000 and snapped a few more shots. "Much better."

"Show me."

"Sure." Naomi scrolled back through the photos, holding her camera so that Chaska could look at them.

"You're an artist with a camera, too. These are good."

Heat rushed into Naomi's cheeks at the compliment. "It's just science."

She indulged herself then, taking photo after photo—rufous hummingbirds with their glossy orange-red throats, broad-tailed hummingbirds with their iridescent green backs, Costa's hummingbirds with their shiny purple crowns. For a time, she forgot about her worries, her mind focused only on the birds—and the man beside her.

She could feel him there, as if his body were touching hers even though there were several inches between them. He watched her, asked questions, his attention focused entirely on her. It felt … intimate.

"Let's see what I got." She scrolled through her shots, Chaska leaning over so he could see, too, his arm stretched across the back of the swing behind her, his praise warming her. "I might have to start making hummingbird jewelry."

"Win would probably buy it all."

Naomi was pleased with the photos, especially the last few. "This is why I came to Colorado—to see wildlife, take photos, sketch."

She told him how she'd first seen the mountains from that Denver hotel room and how she'd dreamed for five years of returning.

"I'm sorry things turned out like this." He was quiet for a moment. "Win knows what you're feeling. Two years ago, she was almost killed."

Naomi gaped up at him. "What?"

She listened while Chaska told her how a bank robber had come into Winona's clinic, aimed a firearm at her head, and forced her to give him medical care.

"He'd burned his hand on the explosive dye pack that banks put in bags during robberies, and the burn had gotten infected. She did her best to help him. He was afraid they'd give him away—Bear was there, too—and threatened to kill them both.

"He decided gunshots were too loud and grabbed a vial of ketamine—that's an animal tranquilizer—and injected them with it. She saw how much he'd given her and knew she would die of an overdose unless help came. My sister slipped into unconsciousness expecting not to wake up again." A muscle clenched in Chaska's jaw, and Naomi could sense the rage he still carried inside him.

"God, Chaska, that's awful." She reached over, slid her hand over his.

Heat arced between them like a static shock, and Naomi might have pulled her hand away if he hadn't taken it, entwining his fingers with hers.

"Lucky for them, Lexi walked in. She managed to get a call off to the police before the bastard took her hostage. He stole Win's car, drove Lexi into the mountains, and tried to hide in a mine shaft. The place collapsed, and he was killed. Lexi was almost killed, too. Taylor, Hawke, and I got her out. But thanks to Lexi, the police arrived in time and took Win to the ER. She was home the next day."

Naomi started to say that she couldn't imagine how scary that had been, but that wasn't true. She *could* imagine it—and it horrified her. "How awful for all of you. I'm so glad Winona was okay—and Bear and Lexi, too."

"The town came together for us. I think everyone in Scarlet brought a casserole." He chuckled, a deep, warm sound. "Our relatives drove down from Pine Ridge. Our grandfather held an *inipi* ceremony—a sweatlodge—to help Winona heal. Even with all of that, those first weeks afterward were tough for her. I know this is difficult for you. You don't have to pretend with us. If you need to talk, my sister and I are here to listen. You're not alone."

His words, so unexpected, put a lump in Naomi's throat, tears blurring her vision. "Thanks. I … I am trying to be strong."

Chaska released her hand and cupped her cheeks, his thumbs wiping her tears away, dark eyes looking into hers. "Hey, you *are* strong."

Then he leaned down and kissed her.

Chapter Nine

Chaska hadn't meant to kiss her. Oh, but now that his lips had touched hers, he didn't want to stop. She tasted sweet, her body soft and pliant. Any doubts he had about her wanting this were swept away when she arched against him, her arms sliding behind his neck.

Oh, hell, yes.

Lust hit his blood in a rush, his pulse spiking, the soft press of her breasts against his ribs making him burn. He reined himself in, did his best to take it slowly, giving her time to get used to the feel and taste of him. He caught her lower lip with his lips, tugged on it, traced its fullness with his tongue.

She shivered, whispered his name. "*Chaska.*"

Wanting more, he slid his fingers into her hair, angled her head, and took her mouth with his. She yielded, letting him shape the kiss, her arms drawing him closer, as if she, too, couldn't get enough.

His tongue found hers, stroked it, teased it. She responded with strokes of her own, her fingers dug into the hair at his nape, her breath mingling with his. His cock strained against his jeans, his blood thrumming hot and fast through his veins.

This wasn't like any other first kiss he'd known. How did she do this to him?

He drew back, looked into her eyes for the answer, and saw the same confusion there, her pupils dilated, her breathing rapid.

He claimed her lips again, but this time he didn't hold back. With just enough presence of mind to be careful of her injured shoulder, he crushed her against him, plundered her mouth, groaning when she kissed him back with the same ferocity. Her body moved against his, and he knew she wanted him, too.

He fisted a hand in her hair, forced her head back, and went for the sensitive skin of her throat, kissing her, licking her, nipping her with his teeth.

She whimpered, her pulse pounding against his lips.

"Where are you guys?"

The screen door opened, making Naomi jump.

"Oh! Oh, sorry!" Winona ducked back inside, but the moment was lost.

Damn.

Naomi tried to pull away, but they weren't teenagers who'd been caught doing something naughty. Chaska wasn't about to let this end on an awkward note.

"Hey, it's okay." He held her until the tension left her body, then pressed his forehead against hers and looked into her wide blue eyes. "Don't think I've gotten enough of you, because I haven't."

He let her go and stood and walked with as much dignity as a man with a raging hard-on could back inside the house and into his office. He closed the door, leaned back against it, his pulse still racing.

What the hell had just happened?

Naomi took the top off her silver pot with tongs and set it down on the concrete where it could finish cooling. She picked up the earrings she was making and held them out for Winona to see. "The real aspen leaves have burned away."

Winona looked unimpressed. "They're still white."

"Let's get back inside, and I'll show you."

Winona took the fired PMC leaves from Naomi and held the door open for her as she made her way back inside the house and into the kitchen.

Winona hadn't yet said anything about what she'd witnessed on the porch this morning. She didn't seem to be upset about it either. This was a huge relief to Naomi, who had no idea what she would say should Winona confront her.

Chaska had kissed her, really truly kissed her, and it had been … *perfect.*

Naomi had been kissed plenty of times, but never like that. Her heart beat faster just thinking about it. The shock of his lips against hers. The hard crush of his body. The pleasure-pain of his teeth against her throat.

Don't think I've gotten enough of you, because I haven't.

Heat rushed into her face, her heart skipping a beat.

She'd never met a man like Chaska. He wasn't just incredibly handsome and ripped. He was also smart and compassionate. He cared about his sister. He cared about the strangers whose lives he saved.

What does he see in a woman as ordinary as you?

Naomi had no idea.

She sat at the table, took the leaves from Winona, and forced her mind off Chaska and back on what she was doing. "Now I'll make a hole for the jump rings."

She took a pin vise out of her toolbox and made a little hole at the base of each of the three leaves—two for earrings and a spare in case one of the others broke—explaining what she was doing as she went along.

"They're so thin. I'm amazed they don't break."

"Once they've been fired, they're pretty tough." She took a small needle file and smoothed the edges of each little hole. "Now for the fun part. Can I have a little bowl of sudsy water?"

Winona got the water for her and set it on the table. "Now you wash it off?"

"More or less." Naomi reached for her brass brush and scrubbed away the remains of the clay, using the water to make sure she didn't release dust for them to inhale.

Beneath the wire bristles, silver appeared.

A bright smile spread across Winona's face. "It's so pretty. It has all the little details of the aspen leaf."

Naomi finished the first leaf and handed it to Winona, then scrubbed the other two. When that was done, she reached for a curved burnisher and rubbed it over the surface of each leaf. "This is called burnishing. See how it brings out the details?"

"Chaska, you should see this!" Winona shouted over her shoulder.

At the sound of his name, Naomi's pulse took off again.

Chaska didn't answer. After Winona had caught them kissing, he had locked himself inside his office, saying he had a lot of work to get done before Monday.

Naomi tried not to feel disappointed. The man was a rocket scientist, after all. He had more important things to do than watching her play with PMC paste.

When the three leaves were burnished, she took two jump rings out of a little plastic box, reached for her needle nose pliers, and attached the jump rings through the holes she'd made in the bases of the leaves. "I could add stones now or create some kind of ornamentation. I could add multiple leaves to a single earring or stick them together before I fire them to make something long and elegant."

She attached wires to the jump rings, then on impulse held out the earrings for Winona. "They're not fancy, but they're yours."

Winona stared at her wide-eyed. "Really?"

Naomi nodded. "You and your brother have done so much for me, and I know things haven't always been easy for you. Chaska told me what happened to you and Lexi and Bear a few years ago."

The flicker of surprise on Winona's face made Naomi regret bringing it up like that, but in the next moment, Winona smiled again. "*Pilamayaye.* Thank you."

She took the earrings and put them on, silver gleaming against her dark hair. "How do they look?"

Naomi tried to turn off the inner critic that told her she ought to have added turquoise stones or peridot beads. Besides, the earrings really did look good on Winona. "Beautiful."

A door opened down the hallway, and Chaska appeared, long hair hanging down his back, lips that had kissed her silly curving in a grin. "What's the noise about?"

Winona stood and brushed her hair to the side. "Naomi made these for me."

Chaska leaned in, dark brows drawing together in apparent confusion. "She made them for you? You mean just now?"

Winona handed him one of the earrings and gave him a detailed description of how Naomi had done this, making it sound far more interesting that it was.

He listened, studying the silver leaf in his palm, then looked up at Naomi, the intensity in those dark eyes making her breath catch. "Good trade."

Chaska logged out of his work VPN, satisfied with the progress he'd made this afternoon. He had a report to write before Monday morning's meeting with NASA, but he could handle that tomorrow.

He found the women on the back porch.

"Shhh!" Win whispered when he stuck his head out the back door.

Naomi lay on the reclining patio chair next to Winona, sound asleep, face turned toward them, her lips parted.

Winona stood, walked back inside, the earrings Naomi had made her dangling from her earlobes. "We were talking, and the next thing I knew she was just out. It must be the concussion—or maybe the pain pills."

"It's probably both."

Winona walked into the kitchen to get herself a glass of water, but Chaska stayed near the door where he could keep an eye on Naomi. He didn't want to leave her out there, asleep and alone, not during tourist season when the crime rate shot up. More than once he'd had to chase drunken idiots out of their yard and away from Shota's enclosure.

"Sorry I interrupted the two of you. If you don't want to talk about it, I understand." The excited gleam in Winona's eyes told Chaska she very much hoped he wanted to talk about it.

"There's not much to say. I kissed her. I plan to kiss her again if she's willing—not that it's any of your business."

Winona did a silent happy dance, water glass high in the air, a wide smile on her face. "Every time I mentioned you this afternoon, she blushed."

He glared at his sister. "Don't meddle, Win."

"I won't." She blinked up at him through innocent brown eyes.

Chaska wasn't buying it. "I'm serious. Don't interfere."

"Okay, fine." She shrugged. "I should try to find reasons to be out of the house more often to give you two time alone together."

He was about to point out that this would be interfering but stopped himself. The idea of more time alone with Naomi sounded good to him.

"You told her about John Charles Ready."

Chaska cringed inwardly to hear the bastard's name spoken aloud. "I didn't mention him by name, but, yes, I told her what happened. I didn't want you to have to tell her, but I thought it might help her to know that you understand at least some of what she's going through. I hope that's okay."

"Of course, it's okay—and thanks." She took a drink, then gave a little laugh. "When did my big brother start being wise?"

"When did my little sister turn into a smart mouth? Oh, wait. She was born that way." He grabbed the newspaper off the kitchen table and bopped her on the head with it, then stepped quietly outside and sat in the chair across from Naomi.

Naomi sat in the backseat of Winona's SUV while Chaska drove them through Scarlet to some pub called Knockers. "This isn't some kind of belly-shirts-and-boobs place, is it?"

Chaska and Winona laughed.

"It's named after the tommyknockers," Winona said.

"Tommy … who?"

Chaska met her gaze in the rearview mirror. "Tommyknockers are spirits that live in the mines. This area was settled by Cornish miners, and tommyknockers are one of their legends."

"They might not be legends," Winona said. "Lexi believes a tommyknocker saved her life when she was trapped in that collapsed mineshaft. She goes up there every once in a while to toss in bread or pastries for him. There are other stories from people around here who say they've seen one."

"That's kind of … creepy." Naomi would avoid going near any mine shafts.

Chaska made a left turn, passing the little strip mall with the grocery store before turning right into a crowded parking lot. "I'll let you two off at the door and then park."

He shut off the engine and helped Naomi to the ground, his hand holding hers longer than was necessary. "You're going to like it here. I promise."

How did he know she was feeling nervous?

He and Winona had told her after she'd woken up from her nap that no one cooked supper on Saturdays at their house. They always ate at the pub, a favorite hangout for Team members and other locals. Naomi hadn't been excited. After years of waiting tables and serving food and drinks to men who thought they were paying her a compliment when they grabbed her ass, she much preferred to eat at home.

While Chaska parked the car, she and Winona went inside. People crowded the entryway, making it hard for Naomi to pass through with her crutches, music coming from a live band forcing her to raise her voice to be heard. "Excuse me. Pardon me."

Winona helped, calling some people by name.

A woman with long blond dreadlocks and a nose ring saw them and headed straight for them, clearing a path. "Make room here, folks, please."

She had a beautiful face and bright green eyes, her arms covered with tattoos of twining skulls and roses. "Hey, Win. The Team's back at the usual table. You must be Naomi. Welcome to Knockers. I'm Rain, hostess and general manager."

Rain led them through the pub around a corner toward the back, her easy smile and familiarity with her guests marking her as a pro. "You just missed Sasha trouncing some tough guy from California who thought he could show her the ropes. Oh, man, it was sweet!"

Naomi was about to ask what she meant by that when she saw.

A climbing wall.

It took up the entire rear wall of the pub. Nearby, Team member sat together, cheering and ribbing Jesse Moretti who was working his way upward. He reached the top, did a fist pump, and was slowly lowered to the floor.

That explained why Chaska had come wearing climbing pants and a T-shirt.

"Hey!" Sasha saw them and waved. "Move over, guys. Make room for Win and Naomi. That means you. Yes, *move.*"

Megs and Ahearn were there, too. So were Creed Herrera, Isaac Rogers, Nicole Turner, Eric Hawke and…

"Ellie!"

Ellie saw Naomi and got to her feet. "How are you feeling?"

"Better."

Ellie spoke with Rain, who helped Naomi get settled at the end of one of the tables with an extra chair so that she could elevate her leg. "Do you need ice or a cushion?"

Ellie answered before Naomi could say a word. "Yes, to both."

"You got it." Rain disappeared into the crowd.

Naomi turned to Winona. "Wow. This place is not what I was expecting."

"Wait till you try Victoria's Chicago-style deep-dish pizza."

Eric Hawke called down the table to Naomi. "Vicki is my wife. I used to come here a lot. Now I spend my whole life here just hoping to catch a glimpse of her. She runs the pizza part of the business."

"He's such a whiner." A beautiful dark-haired woman in a chef's coat walked up to the table and kissed Eric's cheek. "Does someone need attention?"

Eric grinned. "Always."

"What's your favorite part of a woman's body?"

"Her mind." Chaska was in a hell of his own making.

On his left sat Nicole, who'd traded places with Herrera to get closer to him. She'd had one too many margaritas and was doing her best to get him into her bed, asking suggestive questions, getting a bit too close, touching him.

On his right sat Naomi, who had grown quiet and was trying to pretend she wasn't miserable. She was polite to everyone, even Nicole, but Chaska already knew her well enough to see the hurt in her eyes. She hadn't eaten all of her pizza, either.

Farther down the table sat Megs, who had noticed all of this and was watching, an amused grin on her face. "What do you think, Belcourt? Can a man have too much of a good thing?"

Chaska glared at her.

What the hell was he supposed to do?

He needed to talk to Nicole. He needed to tell her that he wasn't interested, but he didn't want to hurt or humiliate her, not here in front of the rest of the Team. He needed to talk to Naomi, too. He needed to tell her that he and Nicole were just friends, but he couldn't do that in front of Nicole.

He was tempted to solve the whole problem by taking Naomi in his arms and giving her a deep, hard kiss, but he wasn't sure how she would feel about that. They had only shared one kiss, and that had been in private. Besides, he didn't want to disrespect either woman—or take the coward's way out.

"Hey, Nicole, would you be my belay slave?" Winona had been doing her best to run interference with Nicole, but so far it hadn't worked. "I really want to try that new five-ten route."

Nicole shook her head. "Sorry, Win. I'm past the two-drink limit."

Winona looked apologetically at Chaska.

Nicole leaned closer to him. "Dance with me."

Up on the stage, newgrass band Gold Dust Creek had just started a high-energy number that had couples streaming to the dance floor.

Okay, fine.

"Let's go." He met Winona's gaze, hoping she would understand, then walked with Nicole out to the dance floor.

Rather than breaking into a two-step like everyone else, he drew her toward the far edge, where no one from the Team could see them. "We need to talk."

Nicole swayed a little in his arms, let herself fall against him. "Why are you so serious all the time?"

He set her back on her feet. "I like you, Nicole, but you and I are never going to be together. You're a great climber and a good person, and I have a world of respect for you, but I'm just not interested. I would never hook up with a fellow Team member."

She stopped dancing and looked up at him, hurt on her face. "You don't even want to sleep with me?"

"You're pretty, Nicole, but I'm just not—"

"Are you gay? If you are, that's fine. I just want to know. Guys usually don't turn me down, but then you're not like other guys, which is why I like you so much."

"No, I'm not gay." Not that it ought to matter.

He'd been raised to respect those who were *winkte*.

Her gaze dropped to the floor. "Okay. I get it. Thanks."

She turned and walked away.

Shit.

Chaska walked back to the table wishing there'd been an easier way.

Chapter Ten

Naomi fought not to look toward the dance floor, a sick feeling in her chest. Then again, why should a man as good-looking, smart, and successful as Chaska be interested in her? Yes, he'd kissed her—an amazing, mind-blowing kiss—but she knew from experience that physical passion meant nothing to most men. She had no claim on Chaska, no right to the disappointment and jealousy she was feeling.

Winona leaned closer so as not to be overheard. "My brother isn't interested in Nicole. She's had a thing for him for a while, but he doesn't want to hurt her feelings. I'm sure that's why he's dancing with her. He wants to let her know the truth without embarrassing her in front of everyone."

Why was Winona telling her this? "What Chaska does is his business."

Win seemed to hesitate. "*You* are the only woman my brother has been attracted to in a very long time."

Naomi stared at her. "You're not serious."

"Oh, yes, I am. If Chaska knew I'd told you … "

At that moment, Nicole reappeared—alone and visibly upset. She grabbed her jacket and drawstring backpack off her chair and walked away.

Winona jumped up and followed her. "Are you going to be safe getting home?"

"I'm good," Nicole called back, not bothering to stop or turn around.

Chaska intercepted her, said something to her, then looked over at Winona and Naomi. "I'm going to drive Nicole home. I'll be back in a few."

His gaze caught Naomi's, and what she saw in his eyes made her pulse skip.

Winona nudged her. "See?"

What had been a terrible, awkward evening suddenly seemed brighter.

"Your brother is a good man," Megs said from the other end of the table.

Naomi could think of a dozen ways that Chaska could have handled this tonight, all of them less thoughtful, less caring, than what he'd chosen to do.

And to think you were feeling jealous.

Rain appeared at Naomi's side. "You didn't like your pizza, sweetie?"

"I guess I just wasn't hungry." She'd lost her appetite when Nicole had slid her hand up Chaska's thigh.

"I'll box it up for you. Joe, the owner, would like to meet you." Rain disappeared with Naomi's pizza.

Naomi had been watching her throughout the evening and was impressed. Rain was a true professional, someone capable of rising above the chaos of a restaurant to meet the needs of her customers.

A moment later, a tall man with a thick beard and a man bun walked over to the table, people waving to him as he approached.

"Hey, Joe."

"Howdy, Moffat."

"What's up, Joe?"

"It's a pleasure to meet you, Naomi." Joe shook Naomi's hand and sat in Chaska's chair. He was a handsome man, perhaps in his mid-forties. His face was tanned from a life lived outdoors, and there was just a touch of gray at his temples. "I'm Joe Moffat, the owner of this place. Are you enjoying yourself?"

She was now. "Yes. Thanks."

"You are an incredibly brave woman. I know I speak for most of Scarlet when I say how sorry we are about what happened to you."

Was that really how these people saw her—brave?

"That's very kind of you."

"I came to tell you a couple of things. The first is that your meal tonight is on the house—yours, too, Winona, and your brother's."

Winona looked delighted. "Thanks, Joe."

Naomi opened her mouth to object, but Joe held up a hand to stop her.

"This is my place, and I get to treat people to dinner when I want to," he said. "Also, has anyone talked to you about the fundraiser?"

Winona shook her head. "We mentioned it, but that was it."

Joe told Naomi how he and some of the locals wanted to raise money to cover whatever expenses weren't paid by the victim's compensation fund. "This was a major disruption of your life, and we'd like to help you get back on your feet."

His kindness was making it very difficult not to cry.

Keep it together!

"I really appreciate the offer, but there are lots of people in this world who are worse off than I am. None of you owe me anything."

He gave a nod. "True enough. It's your decision, of course, but it would mean a lot to us to help set this right."

Chaska walked back to the table, drew out the chair Nicole had vacated and sat next to Joe. "What's up, Joe?"

"Naomi and I were just talking about the idea of a fundraiser." Joe turned back to Naomi. "I'm betting you're a pretty self-reliant person. You had to be to escape those guys the way you did. But sometimes it's okay to accept help from people, especially when it comes with only the best wishes and no strings attached."

Chaska chimed in. "I think the fundraiser is a great idea."

Naomi would have the money she needed to get safely home again—and she would see that people could be kind without expecting something in return.

Naomi considered what they'd said, then nodded. "Okay—though I feel guilty asking anyone to help me."

Chaska reached over, took her hand. "You're not asking. We are."

They spent the next ten minutes working out the details—how staff would put up posters around town to get out the word, how Joe would contact the paper, how he'd try to book the Timberline Mudbugs that night. Naomi's eyes went wide when Joe estimated her portion of the receipts to be at least fifteen thousand dollars.

"If there's money left over after your bills are paid, you can always donate it to the Team," Joe said. "I'm sure they'd be grateful."

"I love that idea."

"That's a great idea!" Megs shouted.

That made Naomi laugh.

Somewhere behind his beard, Joe was grinning. "Thanks for letting us pitch in, Naomi. I hope you enjoy the rest of your stay here in Scarlet. Let Rain know if you need anything."

"Thanks, Joe." Chaska got to his feet when Joe stood and shook the man's hand.

Ellie came and sat down where Joe had been sitting, Jesse following her. "You've just met Caribou Joe. What do you think?"

"He seems like a really good guy. Why do you call him Caribou Joe?"

Eric got to his feet and moved down the table to be closer. "He owns the defunct Caribou silver mine in the mountains west of here. A hundred and fifty years ago, his ancestors more or less owned this town and all the people in it. My great-great-granddaddy worked for his great-great-granddaddy. Hey, Belcourt, want to get some vertical time?"

Hell, yes, he did.

He glanced down at Naomi. He hadn't spent much time talking with her tonight, first because of Nicole and then because of Joe. "Mind if I—"

"I would love to see you climb."

As he walked away, he heard Win whisper, "You're going to love this. My brother is an *amazing* climber."

Yeah, that was probably meddling, but he was okay with it.

Naomi watched, awestruck, while Chaska climbed the wall, moving with a kind of grace and power she'd never seen before. Some of the holds were tiny, with just enough room for his fingertips or the tips of his toes.

Others forced him to hang by two fingers or his closed fist. It looked like some kind of vertical dance or a poem made of motion and muscle, and yet she knew his moves weren't rehearsed or part of a routine.

It was sexy as hell.

And to think he'd kissed her today, kissed her like he'd meant it.

"Here comes the crux move." Megs sat beside her, explaining things Naomi didn't understand, answering her questions. "He has to dyno to finish the route."

"What's a dyno?"

"You're about to see."

Chaska hung for a moment, both hands on a large hold, feet dangling in mid-air. Then he launched himself upward using only the power of his arms, his entire body airborne for a second before he caught another hold with his right hand. For a moment, Naomi was sure he would fall, his feet searching for purchase. The toes of one foot caught a tiny hold—and the table exploded with cheers.

"Way to stick it, man!"

"Great dyno!"

"Sick!"

A few moves later, Chaska reached the top of the wall.

More cheers.

"Belcourt is a strong climber, but he's also extremely level-headed." Megs had to raise her voice to be heard above the din. "I've seen him take a few whippers—serious falls—that would have made most of us scream. He didn't make a sound."

"It's true." Winona took a bite of the ice cream she'd ordered for dessert. "He doesn't get scared. When I climb with him, I can see him doing the math in his head."

Chaska switched places with Sasha, who had been his belayer—a term Naomi now understood.

"There's my girl." Megs watched Sasha rope in, pride on her face. "She's been the world's top-ranked female sports climber for three years running."

Naomi had been looking forward to seeing her climb. "That's what I've heard."

"My brother is good." Win took another bite of her ice cream. "But Sasha—she's an artist."

Naomi immediately understood what Winona meant. Chaska had climbed with strength and grace, but Sasha moved as if gravity had no hold on her. She was fast, smooth, elegant, flowing upward as if she were unstoppable.

She reached the crux, exploded, missed the handhold—and fell.

Naomi gasped, but Chaska caught Sasha's fall, leaving her suspended mid-air.

"Damn!" Megs laughed. "I think she's tired. She's been at it all evening."

There was a chorus of disappointed *awws* mixed with laughter.

"How many margaritas was that, Sasha?" Eric called to her.

Sasha motioned for Chaska to lower her to the ground. Far from being upset, she was laughing, apparently as easy-going as she was skilled. When her feet reached the floor, she gave Chaska a hug, and the two of them started untying themselves.

"How did the Team get started?" Naomi was certain there must be a story.

"I was climbing with friends on El Diente. This was back in the day before climbing was big and before there were search-and-rescue teams equipped for technical backcountry rescues. Our buddy Dean took a tumble not far from the summit and broke his ankle. Ahearn and I helped him get to a safe place, left him with food and water, and went for help. But there was no one prepared for that kind of rescue, no one who could respond immediately. The sheriff's department said they'd head out for him in the morning. That night, the San Miguels were hit by a freak July snowstorm. By the time we reached him the next afternoon, Dean was dead, killed by the cold. I swore on his grave that nothing like that would happen again."

Naomi saw on Megs' face the grief—and guilt—she still carried with her. "You took tragedy, and you turned it into something good."

Megs nodded. "We've saved thousands of people—a couple hundred every year—but I still wonder if Dean would be alive if we'd made a different choice."

Chaska walked up to the table, a grin on his face, sweat trickling down his temples and staining the front of his T-shirt.

"Way to go, Belcourt."

Naomi looked up at him, unable to keep the smile off her face. "You were amazing."

"Yeah?" He reached for his water and drank. "You ready to go home?"

There was something in the way he said it, something in those dark eyes, that made it hard for her to breathe.

"Yeah."

Winona glared at her brother. "Can I please finish my ice cream?"

Chaska stepped out of the shower, towel-dried his hair, then walked from the bathroom to his bedroom, the women's voices drifting up from the living room below. He'd be going to bed soon, so he skipped the boxers and slipped on a pair of old jeans and a T-shirt, then made his way downstairs.

Winona had already put Shota in his enclosure for the night. She got to her feet when she saw Chaska and stretched, even managing a yawn. "I'm heading to bed. We're short a volunteer, so I'll be spending a lot of the day tomorrow at the clinic."

Right.

It was a good thing that Naomi didn't know his sister as well as he did. She wasn't a very good liar.

Winona grabbed a glass of water from the kitchen and headed down the hallway toward the stairs. "Good night."

"Good night," Naomi called after her.

Chaska walked into the kitchen. "Can I get you anything—water, soda, tea?"

"Do you have herbal tea?"

He heated water on the stove, let her choose the flavor, then set the mug on the end table beside her. "What did you think of Knockers?"

Are you nervous, kola?

Yeah, he was.

"It wasn't what I was expecting." She turned in her seat and put her feet on the floor so that he could sit on the sofa beside her. "Rain is a pro. She was on top of everything. The food was good, too, though I wasn't very hungry. I think it's cool that the place has a climbing wall. Joe really seems to understand the people in his community. That's probably why Knockers is successful."

He hadn't been expecting a professional assessment, but then he remembered. "You waited tables for a long time."

"It felt like an eternity." Naomi picked up her tea, blew across it, took a sip. "None of the places I worked were as nice as Knockers. I doubt Joe lets his customers grope the wait staff."

"It happens once in a while, usually during hunting season. Joe might not look tough, but under all that facial hair and plaid, he's ripped. I've seen him throw big men—bikers, hunters, tough guys—out the front door like he was taking out the trash. Locals are pretty good about helping, too, and no one—and I mean *no one*—messes with Rain."

Naomi took another sip, set her mug down. "I really liked watching you climb."

"What did you like about it?"

Color rushed into her cheeks.

That was interesting.

"I've never seen anyone move like that. You looked really graceful and powerful at the same time."

Yeah, this wasn't hard on his ego.

"Your hands must be so strong." She reached over and slid her hand, fingers outstretched, beneath his, raising his hand his up as if she were examining it.

Heat arced between them, the shock of it bringing his entire body alive, from blood to bones. "It's more about legs than arms."

"What about that dyno thing?" She moved her hand slowly, making Chaska aware of how sensitive the skin of his fingers and palm truly was—and how small her hand was compared to his.

"Oh, well, yeah." There was that. "Most of the time you try to hang from the skeleton of your upper body while using your legs for strength moves. Climbing is all about strength-to-weight ratio. That's why women can climb as well as men."

"How long, um… did it take you? To learn how to climb, I mean." Her breathing had changed, her words coming slower, as if she couldn't quite concentrate on what she was trying to say.

He laced his fingers through hers, stroked her thumb with his. "I made the Team in about a year, but, uh, I was climbing every day."

Now *he* was having trouble thinking, her scent and the softness of her skin derailing his concentration.

"Why did you kiss me this morning?" she asked, her voice almost a whisper.

"Because then, like now, I wanted to." He turned toward her, slid a hand into her hair, and lowered his mouth to hers.

God, she was sweet, her lips warm and ripe, but he needed better access.

He managed to stop kissing her long enough to turn her in his arms so that she lay back across his lap, her legs stretching the length of the sofa. "This is better."

He claimed her mouth again, catching her little whimper, her arms sliding behind his neck, drawing him closer.

Bzzz-Bzzz Bzzz-Bzzz

Damn it.

Since only family was likely to call this late at night, he had no choice but to take this. "Sorry."

Still holding her, he set her upright, got to his feet, and retrieved his phone from the kitchen. The display on the screen read *ZACH MCBRIDE.*

"What the…?" He answered. "Belcourt here."

"I understand that Ms. Archer is staying with you."

"That's right."

"Given what she's been through, I didn't want to risk waking her, so I thought I'd call you. I wanted to let you both know that we found the two suspects in the mountains west of Crestone."

That was only about four hours south of Scarlet.

Shit.

"Go head." He glanced over at the sofa and found Naomi watching him, wariness in her eyes as if she somehow knew what this call was about.

"An alert citizen recognized them when they went into Crestone for supplies and called in their vehicle with the plate number. A park ranger spotted the vehicle at a campground west of town. We moved in, and there was a firefight. Clem McConnell was killed. Arlie Harding crawled into the forest and got away."

Damn it!

"I appreciate your letting us know."

"There's more. The vehicle they'd stolen had several newspapers on the dashboard, all featuring articles about their attack on Ms. Archer. One had a photo of her, pulled from DMV files in South Dakota. Harding and McConnell had circled her image, and someone had drawn a penis on her face."

Chaska fought to control his rage and revulsion. He didn't want to make this harder on Naomi. She was going to be upset enough as it was when she learned that her photo had run in at least one paper and that these bastards had defiled her image.

Sick sons of bitches.

"What do you plan to do at this point?"

McBride was a chief deputy US marshal. He'd damned well better have a plan.

"I told Ms. Archer that I didn't think she was in any danger from these two. I'm more concerned now. I've already spoken with the Scarlet Springs police chief and the Forest County Sheriff's Department. They will be stepping up patrols in and around your home. We've got checkpoints on the roads. All law enforcement are on high alert. We've got teams, including a K9 unit, standing by for a search at first light."

"I appreciate the call. Please keep me posted."

"Do you want me to talk to Ms. Archer in the morning?"

"No. I think it's best if I handle that." Chaska ended the call, saw the fear in Naomi's eyes.

How was he going to tell her this?

Chapter Eleven

Naomi hugged her arms around herself, her pulse pounding in her ears, her head swimming. "What do you mean when you say they *defaced* it?"

Chaska's brow bent in a frown, a muscle clenching in his jaw. "They drew … They drew a penis on it."

Naomi let out a laugh, the sharp sound surprising even her. "Well, that's desperate. Was it good for them?"

Chaska drew her into his arms, stroked her hair. "I know you're scared, but he's on the run with McBride, the marshal's service, the FBI, and every cop in that county hot on his tail. He doesn't have a vehicle. He doesn't have any friends or money or food. They're going to find him."

"But you said McBride thinks he might come after me."

"That's not what I said. McBride is just being cautious. I think it surprised him that the two were still in the state, and he wants to do all he can to make absolutely certain that you're safe. He's not the only one."

Chaska drew back, tucked a finger beneath her chin, lifted her gaze to his. "The local police are on alert. The sheriff's department knows. I'm here, too, and I'm not going to let him hurt you. He has no idea where you are, and if he did show up in Scarlet and start asking about you, we would hear about it."

She heard Chaska's words, but they couldn't penetrate the ice inside her. "How am I supposed to sleep tonight? You and Win are upstairs, and I'm down here by myself. Win told me that wolves don't bark at intruders. If Arlie breaks in, he could slit my throat, and you wouldn't even know."

That didn't sound hysterical at all.

"That's not going to happen."

"Do you have an alarm?"

"A burglar alarm? In Scarlet?" Chaska shook his head and was quiet for a moment. "Let's move you and all your stuff into my room, and I'll take your room. I think you'll feel safer up there. Win and I can help you with the stairs."

"You … you don't mind?"

"I'd sleep better knowing you feel safe."

Why was he being so kind to her?

She knew the answer as soon as she asked the question.

He's a good man.

Hadn't Megs said that tonight?

"Let's get you upstairs and settled. I'll come back down for your stuff."

"Okay."

In the blink of an eye, Chaska scooped her into his arms and stood.

She gave a little shriek, threw her arms around his neck.

He chuckled, carried her toward the stairs. "I'm not going to drop you. You're not heavy. You're not even a workout. I had to carry Conrad on my back for three miles during rescue training once. He is one big guy—six-four, hairy, and probably two-twenty. *That* was tough."

Naomi leaned her head against Chaska's shoulder, closed her eyes, let herself relax into his strength, the sharpest edge of her panic smoothed by the feel of his arms around her. He made her feel safe, protected. Had any man made her feel that way before?

No. Never.

He climbed the stairs with no difficulty, not even out of breath when they reached the top. He pointed to a closed door to their right with a jerk of his head. "Win is through that door. I'm over here. The bathroom is across the hall there."

He carried her into his dark room, set her carefully on his bed, and then turned on the light. "I'll be back with your stuff in a moment."

He disappeared out the door.

She found herself sitting on a queen-sized bed. She wasn't surprised to see that his room was neat and clean. The bed was made, covered with a gray quilt with a red, white, and black arrowhead pattern, the rustic headboard constructed of polished aspen logs. A small lamp with a rawhide lampshade stood on a nightstand of pine. There was a tall chest of drawers to her left. A black leather sofa sat in front of a row of windows, an abalone shell with a sage bundle resting in the center of the coffee table in front of it. The gray blinds were already drawn, shutting out the darkness.

The walls were mostly bare. A dream catcher hung above the windows, and there were three wreaths on the wall across from the foot of the bed. They looked like they were made of sage that had been wrapped in bands of red cloth, long ribbons in yellow, white, black, and red hanging dangling from the bottom.

The space was understated, masculine, very Chaska. It even smelled like him—sage and spice.

Then she noticed the photograph of an elderly man on the night stand. She scooted closer, reached for it.

"That's Old Man—my grandfather."

Naomi picked up the photo, studied it. "Are you close?"

Chaska set her belongings on the floor at the foot of his bed. "Yeah. He and my grandmother did more to raise us than our parents. He's a Sun Dance chief, what old-timers call a true Lakota. He lives by the old ways."

"That's what Winona told me. You have his eyes."

Chaska had heard that before. "That's what my grandmother used to say."

Naomi set the photo carefully back on his nightstand, the care that she took with it touching Chaska. "Is she … Is she gone?"

"She made the journey to the spirit world a few years back." It had hurt more than Chaska could have imagined to let her go. She'd been like a mother to him and Winona. So much of who they were had come from her.

"I'm sorry."

"Thanks." Chaska didn't want Naomi worrying about him. "Do you think you'll be comfortable in here?"

"Oh, yes. Thank you."

"If it helps you sleep at night, I'm happy. I'm going to go get your stuff out of the bathroom and bring—"

"Chaska, who are you talking to?" Winona appeared in the doorway in her pajamas. "Oh! I … uh … I'm sorry."

Naomi's eyes went wide.

"It's not what you think, Win." Chaska fought not to laugh.

"It's not?" Win sounded disappointed.

Chaska told his sister about the phone call from McBride. "Naomi didn't feel safe downstairs by herself. I offered to switch rooms with her."

"That's awful." Winona sat next to Naomi. "That would shake me up, too."

Chaska left the women to talk and made his way downstairs. Winona could comfort Naomi far better than he could. He had no idea how it felt to be female, to know that one was physically weaker than most men. He'd grown up bigger and stronger than most boys on the rez and had never once been afraid for his physical safety.

He checked the guest bedroom once more to make sure he hadn't missed anything, then went into the bathroom and grabbed her stuff. He made his way back upstairs to the main bathroom, the women's voices drifting out into the hallway.

"For the first few months after it happened, I kept expecting the man who'd done it to walk in again, even though I knew he was dead," Winona said.

"Arlie *isn't* dead. He's out there somewhere. He drew a dick on my face. I'm sure he's the one who did it. He was the one who kept trying to grope me."

"Disgusting pig."

That was kinder than the words Chaska would use to describe the son of a bitch.

He went downstairs one last time and grabbed Naomi's tea and her crutches, then made his way back to his bedroom to find Winona changing his sheets, Naomi standing on one leg beside the headboard. The two women had fallen silent the moment he'd hit the landing, the oh-so-innocent look on Winona's face a dead giveaway.

His sister had been meddling again.

He set the tea down on his nightstand and handed the crutches to Naomi, fighting to rein in his irritation. "Thanks, Win. I've got it. You head back to bed."

Winona must have sensed his frustration with her because she didn't argue.

"Right. Yeah. Okay." She walked around to the other side of his bed and gave Naomi a hug. "I'm right down the hall if you need anything, okay? I'll help you get settled in here in the morning."

"Thanks, Win." Naomi made her way to the sofa and sat.

Chaska picked up where Winona had left off, smoothing the flat sheet over the fitted sheet and tucking it in at the foot of his bed.

"It must be wonderful to have a sister who loves you so much."

"Most of the time." Then he remembered that Naomi would never know whether she had siblings. "I didn't mean that. I'm very lucky, and I know it. But she's stuck on the idea of you and me getting together, so take everything she says about me with a grain of salt."

"Oh. Okay."

Chaska looked over in time to see Naomi's expression fall.

Shit.

What had Winona said to her?

He walked to the sofa, sat down beside her. "I moved all of your things from the downstairs bathroom to the upstairs bathroom."

"Thanks. What about my pain pills?"

"I brought them up, too." He walked over to her backpack, stuck his hand in one of its pockets. "Where do you want me to put them?"

"The nightstand would be perfect. I could use a glass of water, too, please."

"Sure thing." He went back downstairs, filled a glass with ice water.

When he reached his bedroom again, she was looking out one of the windows.

"I heard Shota howl."

"He does that sometimes. The coyotes start it, and there goes the neighborhood. He joins in. It can go on for hours. I'm sure the entire town of Scarlet can hear him. So far, they haven't kicked us out."

"I don't know why they would. What an amazing sound—haunting and beautiful at the same time. Primal."

That's what he'd always thought, but he'd never had the words.

She turned away from the window, made her way over to him. "I feel really guilty kicking you out of your own bed."

"You didn't kick me out. I'm giving it to you."

He ran his thumb over her cheek and kissed her. "Sleep well, Naomi. No one is going to hurt you while you're in this house."

He left her to get ready for bed and went down to the kitchen, where he lit the braid of sweetgrass, blew out the flame, wafted smoke over his head, and prayed for the first time in a decade.

Tunkasila, Creator, guard this house and keep Naomi and Winona safe.

Naomi woke the next morning to see sunlight streaming in around the blinds. She sat up, stretched, the terrible news of last night, and the panic she'd felt, seeming far away. She lay back and let herself remember the good parts of last night—Chaska kissing her again, Chaska holding her, Chaska giving her his room, carrying her up the stairs.

You are the only woman my brother has been attracted to in a very long time.

Warmth blossomed in her chest—and then vanished.

She's stuck on the idea of you and me getting together, so take everything she says about me with a grain of salt.

Clearly, Chaska didn't plan on getting together with her—outside of the occasional kiss. Why else would he have told her that?

It doesn't matter.

Had she really believed that a man as amazing and handsome as Chaska could fall in love with her? For a woman with no education, no money, no family, that would be like winning the lottery, and Naomi had never had that kind of luck.

She reached for her crutches and made her way to the bathroom, where she brushed her teeth and took a shower, voices at times drifting up from the kitchen below. She couldn't tell what Chaska and Winona were saying because they were speaking Lakota. At times, it sounded like they were arguing.

Were they arguing about her?

It's none of your business.

She dressed in a black tank top and her new denim shorts, then made her way to the stairs—and froze. She looked down, felt almost dizzy. Eighteen stairs. Last week, this would have seemed like nothing, but now…

Damn.

The only stairs she'd done had been the front porch steps, but that had been on the way up. This was going down.

She thought about calling for help, but that would be wimpy. She remembered what Ellie had told her and tried to tuck both crutches under her left arm so that she could hold onto the railing with her right hand. Just when she thought she had it, one of the crutches slipped and went tumbling down the stairs.

The sound of running feet.

Chaska was there first, shirtless in a pair of jeans, Winona still in her pajamas a few steps behind him, relief coming over their faces when they saw her.

Win put a hand on her chest. "Oh, thank goodness! I thought you'd fallen."

Chaska picked up the crutch. "I think you dropped something."

Naomi was *such* an idiot. "I've never gone down stairs with crutches before."

"I guess it's a good time to learn." Chaska walked up to stand on the step immediately below her and handed her the crutch, long, dark hair spilling over one shoulder. "Is this how they taught you to do it?"

She had a hard time answering because right now her mind was more focused on the man and muscle standing inches away from her. "Um, yes."

"Just take it one step at a time. I'll be here to catch you if you fall."

"Won't I just knock you down the stairs, too?"

A grin flashed across his face, making her pulse skip. "Not a chance."

She drew a breath, steeled herself. "Okay."

He stepped back to give her room. "Take it one stair at a time."

One hand on the banister, the other holding her crutches, she moved the crutches down to the next step, then brought her good foot down.

"You've got this."

She moved slowly downward, Chaska staying a couple of steps ahead of her. By the time she reached the bottom, she felt like a pro. "I did it—well, thanks to you."

"I didn't do anything." Chaska stepped aside, walking beside her back to the kitchen. "Did you sleep well?"

"Yes. How about you?"

"Like a rock."

Naomi had a bowl of cereal, while Winona and Chaska finished their coffee, whatever they'd been arguing about put aside for now.

Winona refilled her coffee mug. "Chaska and I thought you could spend the morning at the clinic with me so that he can get some work done. Then, this afternoon, you can go on a drive through the mountains with him."

Naomi stopped, the spoon inches from her mouth. "In the mountains? But isn't *he* up there somewhere?"

Chaska took his smartphone out of his pocket, typed something into his browser, then turned it so that she could see it. "We're here, and Crestone is four hours south of us. We won't be going that direction. There are lots of things to see around here. Trust me. I would never put you in danger. Besides, I'll be carrying."

It took her a moment to realize that "carrying" meant "carrying a gun."

The warmth in his gaze confused her. *Was* he interested in her?

Did it matter?

She hadn't come here for romance.

He slipped his smartphone back into his pocket. "You came to Colorado to see the mountains and photograph wildlife, right?"

She nodded.

Chaska's expression grew serious. "Don't let that bastard steal this from you. You've worked so hard."

She *had* worked hard, harder than anyone could know. "Okay. If you think we'll be safe…"

"I *know* we will."

Chapter Twelve

His lunch eaten, Chaska scooted closer to Naomi so that he could see the images on her camera.

"This is the burrowing owl." She had that same bright smile on her face that she had Thursday after spending the day at the clinic. "He bobbed his head and made a rattlesnake sound when I sat down to sketch him."

"You sketched him? Show me."

"Oookay." She set the DSLR down on the table and reached for a sketchpad, opening it and flipping past several pages to find the owl. "They're not very good."

"Wait. Hey. Slow down. Go back to the beginning."

She did as he asked, showing him a sketch of a raven. "I use the sketches to inspire jewelry, so they're not meant to be art or anything."

Art or not, Chaska was impressed. With a few strokes of pencil, she had managed to capture the essence of a raven in flight—the flare of its flight feathers, the stretch of its wings, the curve of its body. The next drawing showed a raven tumbling through the air, playing with the wind, the next a raven sitting on a fence post, the wind tousling its feathers. Page after page of drawings—mostly ravens—left him wondering how Naomi had gotten the idea that she wasn't skilled at this.

"I don't care what you say. These are good. Where did you take art classes?"

"I haven't—just jewelry-making classes."

Okay, *that* blew his mind. "You have natural talent then."

"I loved to draw, even as a kid."

"You must really like ravens."

"I watched them a lot when I was a little girl." She smiled, but there was sadness in her eyes now. "They were free to fly wherever they wanted, free to do whatever they wanted. The couple who adopted me tried to keep them out of their corn, but it never worked. I wanted to be one of them. I wanted to fly away, to play with the wind like they did, to be as free as they were."

"Were the people who adopted you strict?"

She hadn't used the word *parents*, so he didn't use it either.

She seemed to hesitate. "They weren't just strict. They were religious fanatics. Peter had his own church where his word was God's word."

There was nothing Chaska despised more than a hypocrite. "That's convenient."

"Isn't it? He truly believed that God spoke through him, that he was among the chosen. His little congregation believed it, too. Ruth was his submissive helpmeet. On the outside, they looked like the perfect family—a husband and wife with nine children, one of whom they'd adopted.

"But Ruth bludgeoned people with the power that came with being Peter's wife. And Peter took absolute control over every aspect of the lives of his congregants. He told them what to wear, how to talk, what to sing, when to plant, what to grow, when to harvest, how many babies to have, what to name those babies, how to raise their kids. He decided who could get married and when, marrying girls who were fourteen and fifteen years old to much older men as a reward for joining his church. I'm sure it wasn't legal, but no one intervened."

"It sounds like a cult, not a church." It made him sick to think her childhood had been lost to that kind of … insanity.

Naomi gave a little laugh. "When you grow up with it, you don't see that. It's just how the world is. You believe it because all the adults around you believe it and you're a child. Of course, I don't believe any of it now. I don't believe in anything."

Chaska knew what it felt like to be disillusioned, to feel betrayed by one's parents, to lose one's beliefs. "Why did they adopt you if they had so many children?"

"Peter always said he felt called to adopt me the moment he heard about me on the TV news. He and Ruth told me over and over again how lucky I was that my birth mother abandoned me. Otherwise, I might have been raised by heathen Indians." Naomi's gaze shot to Chaska's. "I don't want to offend—"

He pressed a finger to her lips. "Don't apologize. The words aren't yours. I take it they weren't Native?"

"They were white. I don't think Ruth ever really wanted me. When she got angry with me, she would hit me or pinch me and call me a dirty Indian brat. I grew up thinking there was something wrong with me."

Chaska had heard stories like this from old-timers who'd been taken from their parents and forced into government schools. His grandfather had repeatedly had his mouth washed out with soap for daring to speak Lakota.

But Naomi went on. "I asked her once why God would make a whole race of people who were beyond redemption. Could it be that God had made a mistake?"

"That seems like a fair question. What did she say?"

"She slapped me."

Chaska bit back a stream of profanity. "Did no one stand up to them?"

She shook her head, a faraway look in her eyes. "Anyone who questioned them was verbally berated in front of the others, told to repent, and banished from the church if they refused."

Chaska had to know. "Is that what happened to you?"

Chaska's mind filled with all kinds of ideas—about what might have happened to an innocent sixteen-year-old girl in a place like that, about the hardships she must have faced on her own at such a young age, about the loneliness she must have felt.

"Not exactly. I ran away when I was sixteen after Peter told me he'd found a husband for me. The man was old—older than Peter. I just couldn't. When I refused, he beat me. So the next night, I took my medicine wheel out from beneath the floorboard where I'd hidden it and ran away."

"How did you survive?"

She'd been so young and inexperienced.

"I was walking along the highway in the dark when a big truck pulled up. A woman named Gloria offered to give me a ride. 'You better come with me, or the wolves will eat you up,' she said. I was so naïve that I thought she meant real wolves. She drove me to Sioux Falls, helped me get a job waiting tables at a truck stop, and rounded up some normal clothes for me so that I didn't have to walk around looking like an extra from *Little House on the Prairie.* That night, she let me sleep in her truck."

Thank you, Tunkasila, *for Gloria.*

"Things got better after that, though it wasn't easy. It was a truck stop, so I had access to showers. I tried getting into a women's shelter, but they didn't take girls under eighteen. I slept on the floor in the restaurant storeroom until I could afford to get a little apartment. I had so much to learn—my job, how to use a microwave, how to use a computer, how to drive, how to use a TV remote and cell phone, how to deal with men who thought that any waitress within reach was fair game. I didn't know anything about technology or how normal people lived. It was like waking up and finding myself in another world. Everything I'd been raised to believe had been a lie."

"You are incredibly strong, Naomi." He reached over, ran his thumb over her cheek, sorry that his questions had erased her smile and brought her fears to the surface again. "You know what I say?"

"What?"

"To hell with Peter and Ruth. You are free of them. Let's go enjoy the afternoon."

Naomi sat in the front seat of Chaska's pickup truck, looking out the window at the astonishing beauty that surrounded them. He took her first to Caribou, the site of the old mine that Joe owned, showed her the ghost town where many of the mine's workers had once lived, and helped her out of the truck so that she could photograph the little cemetery with its touching grave markers.

"So many children."

"Life in the mountains was hard back then."

When she'd taken all the photos she wanted, they climbed back into the truck and drove to a place called Moose Lake.

"Are there moose here?" she asked.

She'd never seen a moose before.

"I've seen a few moose here. Maybe we'll get lucky. The trail is fairly level, so you ought to be okay."

He carried her camera bag, going slowly so that she could make her way around rocks and exposed tree roots. "Let me know if you need to rest."

Soon, she was stopping every few feet, not to rest, but to take photos. A plant that Chaska called kinnikinnick. Delicate blue and white columbine. Purple wild iris.

It wasn't easy taking photos without being able to stand on both feet, and more than once Chaska steadied her so that she could operate her camera with both hands.

They sat on a log bench on one side of the lake in the shade of an aspen grove, reeds and cattails at the water's edge offering red-winged blackbirds and dragonflies a perch. A light breeze blew across the water, making small ripples.

"It's so peaceful here."

From across the lake came a strange cry.

Naomi looked toward the sound. "What was … oh, God!"

A black bear cub. No, *two* bear cubs.

She grabbed her camera bag, so excited that she nearly dropped her macro lens as she switched it out for the telephoto.

"It's okay. You've got time. They're not going anywhere. Their baby brother is stuck in a tree."

Three bear cubs?

She drew a breath, finished making the lens switch, then held the camera up to her eye, smiling when she spotted the third cub. He was lighter than the other two, more caramel than black, and he was stuck halfway up a pine tree, bawling his little heart out.

Naomi started shooting, moving with her crutches to get a better view.

"There's Mama."

Naomi lowered the camera. "God, she's big. Are we safe here?"

They were only a hundred yards away.

"She's not going to swim across the lake." Chaska stood beside her, a hand at her elbow in case she lost her balance. Sunlight glinted off his hair, turning it a rich shade of brown, his face so striking that she found herself wanting to photograph him.

Naomi turned her attention back to the bears, shooting photo after photo as the mother ambled over to the tree and tried to coach her cub down. "What will she do if he can't make it?"

"He will. Watch."

But still Baby Bear didn't climb down, his two siblings tumbling and playing near the base of the tree. Then Mama Bear had had enough and started up the tree herself.

Naomi couldn't believe what she was seeing. She stopped shooting and just watched as Mama reached her youngster, gave one of his rear paws a nip, then climbed down again, encouraging him with little growls. Baby Bear followed her. In a moment or two, it was over, the three cubs rolling and playing together, Mama foraging near a thicket of chokecherry bushes.

Naomi made her way back to the bench and sat, watching for a good long time, Chaska beside her, until the not-so-distant rumble of thunder caught their attention. Dark storm clouds had moved in from the west behind them, the wind picking up and driving the storm their way.

"Better put away your camera. We need to go."

"I love thunderstorms."

"I love the thunder, but not the idea of being struck by lightning. Every couple of years the Team gets toned out to bring down someone who's been struck."

"Really? Wow."

They headed down the trail but didn't get far before fat raindrops began to fall. Then the sky opened up, and it poured, lightning splitting the heavens, thunder echoing among the mountain peaks.

Laughing, Naomi did her best to go quickly, but the trail soon became muddy and slick, slowing her.

Chaska stepped in front of her and bent down. "Give me your crutches, and climb onto my back."

"Are you serious?"

"I carry eighty-pound packs when I go on rescues. I can handle you."

Camera bag slung over her shoulder, she did as he said, wrapping her arms around him, his body hard, the firearm he carried concealed at his hip pressing against her leg. He stood upright and started toward the parking lot again, thunder crashing around them, the sound almost metallic.

"The thunder is so loud!" She had to shout to be heard above wind and rain.

"You're at nine thousand feet elevation," he called back to her.

A doe bounded across the trail in front of them, disappearing into a thicket of young junipers, her fawn a few feet behind her.

"Look!" Naomi pointed.

Chaska grinned, whether because of the doe and her fawn or because he thought she was being silly, Naomi couldn't say.

A blue flash of lightning. The roar of thunder. The fresh scent of ozone.

She laughed, feeling more alive than she could remember, the thunder seeming to crash right over their heads. "That was close!"

"Too close." Chaska moved much faster than Naomi had been able to, and soon the parking lot came into view. He set her down near his truck, unlocked the door, and put her camera bag on the seat. "Get in!"

He helped her up, stuck her crutches behind the seat, then jogged around to the driver's side and climbed in. They looked at each other and laughed, both breathing hard, spattered with mud, and soaked to the skin, strands of wet hair clinging to their cheeks.

And then he was kissing her.

This was nothing like the kiss they'd shared on the front porch. That had been gentle and sweet. This was rough, wild, fierce, his mouth ravishing hers, his fingers digging into her wet hair, one strong arm dragging her closer.

No man had ever kissed her like this, and, oh, it was perfect. The storm raged around them, but Naomi was barely aware of it, the thrum of rain on his truck not enough to drown out the pounding of her pulse. He smelled of pine and tasted of rain, the feel of him hard beneath her splayed palms.

Desire licked through her, made her bolder. She kissed him back with everything she had, biting down on his lower lip, teasing its fullness with her tongue, drawing his tongue into her mouth. He moaned, held her tighter, wresting control of the kiss from her, doing to her what she'd just done to him—and more.

She couldn't get enough of him. She tugged on his T-shirt, slid a hand up the wet skin of his belly, the hard feel of his abs sending shivers of excitement through her. She shifted her position, trying—

She cried out.

Pain.

"Your leg?"

She nodded, answering through gritted teeth. "I hit it against something."

"Shit. Sorry. I think you hit it against the brake pedal."

Concern on his face, he helped her get settled back in her seat, her leg in front of her, then leaned over and kissed her cheek. "This wasn't the right place for this. Next time I kiss you, we're going to be alone so that no one can interrupt us, and we're going to have lots of room."

Her heart gave a little knock at those words, the pain in her ankle subsiding.

Then she said to him what he'd said to her on the porch. "Don't think I've gotten enough of you, because I haven't."

His lips curved in a slow, sexy smile. "Good."

When the storm cleared, Chaska drove Naomi along the Peak-to-Peak Highway, pulling off the road at the best overlooks so that she could take photos. They stopped in Estes Park for hot dogs, ice cream cones—and, of course, saltwater taffy.

"Win would kill me if she knew I'd been in Estes and hadn't brought her taffy."

Something had shifted between them since this morning. Naomi seemed more at ease than she had since he'd known her, and there was an intimacy that hadn't been there before, her small hand reaching for his more than once.

Well, he didn't mind that, not one bit.

Estes was teeming with tourists, so they stopped in only one shop—a jewelry boutique.

"They carry my stuff." She made her way to the display case. "One day, I'd like to have a shop like this. I'd sell a mix of my stuff and work by other artisans."

"You should sell your sketches, too, and your photographs."

She laughed as if this were an absurd idea. "I don't know about that."

"I do."

Her gaze moved over the earrings, bracelets, and belt buckles in the glass display case. She showed him the work of silversmiths she knew, then pointed. "That's mine."

It was a silver bracelet, and it was exquisite, semi-precious stones worked into a mosaic image of a coyote howling in front of a full moon, the edges filigreed flowers.

"I don't think you have one like this." The sales clerk, a young woman, stepped forward, opened the case, and retrieved the bracelet. "This is an exclusive by Naomi Archer. It's one of a kind."

"I *am* Naomi Archer."

"You're … Naomi?" The young woman's eyes went wide. "Wow. Wait here! Just wait a second."

She disappeared and returned with an older woman, the manager or perhaps the shop's owner.

"Naomi Archer?" The older woman shook Naomi's hand. "I just love your work. It's exciting to have you here in my store."

Chaska watched while the three women talked jewelry, pleased to see Naomi getting the attention she deserved. Her work truly *was* amazing. Why couldn't she see that? Okay, so he'd bet that being left to die by her mother and being raised by religious lunatics who'd adopted her because God told them to but who didn't really love her had something to do with that.

I grew up thinking there was something wrong with me.

It hurt Chaska to think that belief might still live inside her.

Naomi seemed to float all the way back to his truck. "Did you hear them? They said people come in asking for my stuff."

"I'm not surprised." He opened the door for her and helped her up.

He drove back toward Scarlet, listening as Naomi talked about the boutique she dreamed of owning and how she'd even thought of moving to Colorado.

"Are we going home?" There was a note in her voice that told him she wasn't sure she wanted to go back just yet.

"Nope. We've got one more stop." He turned off the highway onto Sugarloaf Mountain Road, drove to the trailhead, and parked. He grabbed a daypack from behind his seat, checked to make sure it still held a space blanket and first aid kit, then added her camera and two bottles of water. "The trail is rocky and steep, so I'm going to have to carry you on my back."

"Are you sure this is a good idea?"

"It's two miles there and back, so it's no big deal." He gave her the daypack, helped her adjust it, then bent down. "Ready?"

It was a much tougher hike with a hundred twenty pounds on his back, but it was good training. There was no telling when he might have to do this to save a life. By the time they reached the summit, he was breathing hard.

"Oh, God, it's beautiful up here!"

"It's one of the best places in the county to watch the sunset." He carried her to a rocky area, then set her down, helping her to keep her balance while she hopped to a wide, flat rock and sat.

"What is this place?" There was awe in her voice.

"Sugarloaf Mountain." He sat beside her, took the daypack, handed her the camera, then pulled out a bottle of water and drank. "I'd hoped you would like it."

"Like it?" She looked over at him, eyes wide. "It's breathtaking."

"That's Mount Meeker, and that's Longs Peak. We've done a lot of rescues on Longs. Over there are the Indian Peaks that surround Scarlet. To the south, there are Boulder's mountains—Green Mountain, Bear Peak, South Boulder Peak."

She switched lenses, adjusted the settings on her camera, and shot a few photos. But as the sun began to set, she put the camera down. "Some things you just have to see with your own eyes."

A chilly breeze blew from the west, and she shivered.

"Hand me that blanket in the pack."

She did as he asked.

He opened it, scooted closer to her, and wrapped it around the two of them, the symbolism of it striking him as he put his arm around her shoulders. In a Lakota wedding, the man and woman were wrapped together just like this in a blanket to symbolize their union.

You were led to her.

Okay. Why fight it?

To the west, the sun dipped behind the mountains, turning the horizon a stunning shade of pink, transforming clouds into hues of blazing gold.

He felt her tremble and looked to see tears streaming down her face, the last rays of the sun casting her skin in a pink glow.

"It's beautiful."

While she watched the sunset, clearly awestruck, he found himself watching her. "Yes. Beautiful."

Chapter Thirteen

They arrived home to find a black SUV with government license plates parked in front of the house.

Naomi's pulse spiked. "Do you know them?"

"It's McBride." Chaska parked in the driveway, then reached over to give her hand a squeeze. "No matter what he's here to tell us, it's going to be okay."

She climbed out and made her way across the lawn to the front steps, Chaska close beside her carrying her camera bag. They found McBride sitting in the living room, armed and wearing body armor, Winona in the chair across from him, Shota leashed and sitting beside her, eyeing McBride warily.

McBride got to his feet when they walked in.

So did Shota.

The wolf pushed past McBride to greet them, giving Naomi's hand a lick, then flopping onto his side at Chaska's feet.

"How was your day?" Winona looked relieved to see them.

Naomi answered. "It was wonderful."

Until now.

"Give me just a minute, McBride." Chaska rubbed the wolf's belly, tousled his fur, grabbed his muzzle, speaking to him in Lakota.

"I'll feed him and get him settled for the night." Win got to her feet, took Shota's leash and led him out of the room.

"That's a beautiful animal. Winona tells me the wolf led them to you, Ms. Archer. That's an amazing stroke of luck."

"Yes, it was." Naomi sat beside him, propped her crutches against the sofa, her heart beating a little too fast. "You have news?"

Why else would he be here?

"I do, and I wanted you to hear it from me."

That didn't sound good.

McBride grinned. "We got him."

Relief washed through Naomi in a wave, her eyes going shut, the breath leaving her lungs in a rush. She inhaled, opened her eyes. "How? When?"

"Our search teams located him hiding in an abandoned vehicle several miles west of Crestone. We surrounded him, and that was it. He tried to rush one of our officers, probably hoping we'd shoot him. The officer decked him instead."

Naomi's stomach sank. "He's … he's still alive?"

If he was alive, he might escape again, and then…

"Any chance he'll escape again?" Chaska stood at her end of the sofa, arms crossed over his chest, his gaze on McBride.

McBride shook his head. "Not a chance. He's in lockdown—disciplinary segregation. I can understand why you're worried, Ms. Archer, but I wanted to bring him in alive for a reason. Suicide-by-cop would have been the easy way out. I want him to *pay* for the two correctional officers he killed in Texas—and for what he did to you."

Naomi heard the suppressed anger in McBride's voice and knew that he meant what he'd said. "What will happen to him?"

McBride explained that Texas would have Arlie extradited so that he could face trial there. "I'm betting he'll get the death penalty. He was already serving a life sentence, so until then, he'll spend his days in maximum security. The state of Colorado will have to wait for a long time to prosecute him for the crimes he committed here."

Naomi didn't care about that as long as Arlie was behind bars. Then it hit her. "It's over."

"Yes, it's really over." McBride got to his feet, reached for Naomi's hand, shook it. "You deserve the lion's share of the credit, Ms. Archer. Because you fought back, because you got away from them, we learned they were in Colorado and were able to bring them down. You're a brave woman."

Naomi stood, balancing on one foot, and gave McBride a hug. "Thank you. Thank you for not giving up. Thank you for catching them."

He hugged her back, his body armor rock hard. "You're welcome."

Chaska walked McBride to the door, leaving Naomi to sort through the maelstrom of her emotions.

Chaska took a shower to wash off the mud and sweat. He dried himself and slipped into a pair of jeans and a clean T-shirt. He found Winona alone in the kitchen drinking a cup of tea. They had argued this morning about her meddling in his relationship with Naomi, and it had gnawed at him all day.

Winona spoke first. "She showed me her photos of the bears. It sounds like you two had a great afternoon. I think she's in the shower now."

Chaska walked over to his sister, rested his hand on her shoulder, and switched to Lakota. "I'm sorry about this morning. I was wrong to be angry with you."

"No, you weren't. Sometimes I push too hard. I like her, and I can't stop feeling that this is meant to be—the two of you together."

He weighed his words carefully. "I believe we were meant to find her. Whether she and I have a future ahead of us—who can say? But you were right to think we need to see where this leads."

Chaska had no real choice at this point anyway. He was drawn to Naomi in a way that was more than physical, more than sexual. He wouldn't get her out of his system by sleeping with her. He knew that already. Somehow, his emotions had gotten tangled up in her. He couldn't let go of whatever there was between them—not yet.

He sat with his sister, listening while she told him about her day. Then he heard Naomi make her way from the bathroom to his bedroom. "I'm going up to her. Please, don't come into my room."

"Not even if I hear screaming?" Win gave him her best innocent look.

Chaska glared at her. "Especially not then."

He wished his sister a good night, then took the stairs two at a time, and knocked on his bedroom door. "Naomi? Can I come in?"

He heard her gasp, heard a crutch hit the floor.

"Are you okay?"

"Yes. Come in."

He opened the door, felt a jolt of raw lust.

She sat on the edge of the bed holding her bathrobe shut with both hands, her comb on the floor beside her fallen crutch, wet hair hanging over one bare shoulder. It was obvious that she'd rushed to put on the bathrobe because it was inside out, and her left arm wasn't entirely in the sleeve.

"You got big news tonight." He closed the door behind him, walked over to her, and drew the sleeve up to her shoulder, letting his fingers brush against her skin. "How are you feeling?"

"Relieved. Some part of me can't seem to grasp that it's over."

"I bet." He bent down, picked up her comb, then sat beside her and started working the tangles from her hair. "Sometimes it takes the mind a while to catch up."

"I suppose I should start making plans to go home." She tilted her head toward him, wet strands passing through the comb like silk, the feminine scent of her shampoo teasing him. "I don't have to worry about him tracking me down in South Dakota now."

He hadn't realized she'd been afraid they would do that.

He moved to sit behind her, drawing her hair together so that it hung down her back, combing through it with his fingers. "How long had you originally planned to stay in Colorado?"

"Just one week." Her eyes drifted shut as his fingers curled against her nape. "I would have driven back today."

Damn.

He wasn't ready to let her go.

He moved closer, drew her back against his chest, his hands cupping her shoulders. "If you really need to get back, we'll find a way to make it happen, but there's no rush. You're welcome to stay here as long as you like—for another week, until you can drive, whatever you need."

"Chaska?" She leaned back against him, her head resting against his chest.

He inhaled the clean scent of her skin. "Mmm?"

"We're alone, and there's lots of room here."

He bent down, nuzzled her ear. "Are you saying you want me to kiss you?"

"*God, yes.*"

And more.

It wasn't like Naomi to initiate things. She'd grown up in a world where silence and shame shrouded the topic of sex, where even being caught looking at a boy could bring harsh retribution. Some part of her struggled to shake free of those shackles still—but not with Chaska.

He pressed his lips to her temple, her cheek, and the whorl of her ear, his hands kneading her shoulders, his kisses sending excited shivers through her.

She tilted her head to the side, gave him access to her throat.

He took what she offered, kissing her below her ear, his lips raising goose bumps on her skin, his hands sliding ever so slowly from her shoulders to cup her breasts through the irritating cotton of her bathrobe. She arched into his touch, heat pooling deep in her belly as he caught her nipples and teased them.

"I want to touch you." He whispered the words against her skin.

"*Yes.*"

He peeled the bathrobe away from her shoulders, revealing her bandage. He kissed it, then moaned when the fabric slipped leaving her naked apart from the medicine wheel, which hung between her breasts. "So beautiful."

She watched as his big hands closed over her, contact sending jolts of pleasure through her as he cupped her, circled her areolas with his thumbs, flicked her puckered nipples. The erotic sight of it made her ache.

She sank back against the hard wall of his chest, sliding her hands along his forearms to grasp his wrists, her eyes drifting shut again.

"You like that?"

"*Mmm. Yes.*"

The other men she'd been with—all two of them—would have moved on by now, but not Chaska. His erection pressed against her lower back, hard and insistent, but he didn't rush. He took his sweet time, catching her nipples with his fingers, plucking them, rolling them between his fingertips, his lips nibbling at her throat.

She'd never felt so aroused before, her body craving him. And then it all stopped, the loss of his touch leaving her hanging.

"Come here." He drew her back so that she was no longer sitting on the edge of the bed, bore her onto her back, and stretched out beside her, her bathrobe open now, leaving her naked body completely exposed.

He pulled off his shirt, his gaze raking over her. He said something in Lakota, his eyes going dark.

Panic trilled through her, mixing with her excitement, leaving her torn. As much as she wanted him, she wasn't sure she was ready for this. She didn't want to disappoint him, but she wasn't on the pill. She didn't want to get pregnant.

But whatever she'd expected from him, she'd been wrong.

He propped himself up on his elbow and looked down at her, hair spilling over his shoulders, his gaze dark. "I don't want to take this any further than you want to go, so tell me when to stop. This was supposed to be a kiss."

Her heart seemed to melt in her chest.

She decided he deserved the truth. "I'm not on the pill."

He nodded. "That's fine with me. I don't think it's good for women."

"And … I'm not a virgin."

He looked surprised—but not for the reason she imagined. "I wasn't expecting that you would be. I wasn't raised with Puritan ideas about sex."

That made her curious. "What were you taught?"

"I was taught that sex was natural and normal and healthy, but also something powerful, something sacred." He slid his hand down her bare torso, until it rested against her lower belly, his eyes looking straight into hers. "I was taught that women carry the altar of life inside them and that a man must treat a woman's body with respect."

Heat washed through her at his words, leaving her breathless, something about what he'd said deeply arousing. She managed a single word. "Oh."

"I was taught that women come from men and that men come from women. They leave their mark on one another, so neither men nor women can mistreat the other."

"What do you mean?"

He took her hand, pressed it against one of his nipples. "Men have nipples, like women, but they serve no purpose beyond sexual pleasure. I was taught that nipples are a mother's mark on her sons, a reminder to them to honor women."

Naomi thumbed the dark brown velvet of his nipple. He sucked in a quick breath, the muscles of his abdomen tensing, his nipple drawing tight.

He left her palm where it was, slid his hand down her belly again, then cupped her, one finger delving between her folds to touch her *there*.

She sucked in a breath, her hips jerking as he stroked her.

"The clitoris looks like a tiny penis." His finger explored her, stroking, flicking, the ache inside her almost unbearable. "It serves no purpose beyond sexual pleasure. It's a man's mark on his daughters, a reminder to women to honor men."

Naomi could barely breathe. "That's … not what I was taught."

His voice was deep and soft. "Forget everything they told you about your body, about sex. It was all a lie."

Then he lowered his mouth to her nipple and suckled.

Chaska drew a perfect nipple into his mouth, suckled at one breast and then the other, his hand busy between her legs. She moaned, threaded her fingers through his hair, her thighs parting to give him access. She was wet, her clit swelling and growing hard at his touch.

He focused on her response, not the ache in his groin or the drumbeat in his chest. Hell, yes, he wanted her. He wanted her so much it hurt. He wanted her more than he'd ever wanted a woman. But more than that, he wanted her to enjoy this.

Life hadn't been gentle with her, but he damned well would be.

He'd told her to forget what she'd been taught, but he knew she couldn't, not all at once, not until she'd been shown again and again and again that sex could be something free of shame, something good, something right.

Are you the man for that?

He couldn't be sure. He could only try.

He circled the tight entrance to her vagina, drew her wetness onto his fingers and rubbed it over her clit, waiting until he was certain she was ready and willing before entering her body with any part of himself.

She slid one hand into his hair, holding his head where it was, her other hand moving to grasp his wrist as if she were holding on for dear life.

And maybe she was.

Her breathing was ragged now, every exhale a moan, the knee of her left leg bent, her thighs wide apart. He circled her entrance again, her hips rising to meet him.

"Yes!" It was a frantic whisper.

He slipped two fingers deep inside her.

She moaned, her inner muscles closing around him.

He tried not to notice how tight she was, tried not to think about being inside her, thrusting into her with his fingers, stroking her inside and out, the tension inside her building, her nails digging into his wrist. This was what he wanted for her—to forget everything but the pleasure he gave her, the pleasure they gave each other.

She came with a cry, ecstasy on her sweet face, her beauty in that moment leaving him awestruck. He kept up the rhythm until her climax had passed, then held her, pressing kisses to her breasts, her cheeks, her forehead. Slowly, her breathing returned to normal, her body now limp.

She looked up at him, an expression of disbelief in her eyes. "Chaska."

He lowered his mouth to hers, kissed her soft and slow.

"I've never … I've never been able to do that." It took him a moment to realize she meant she'd never been able to climax before.

He ought to have been surprised, but he wasn't, not given her background. "Well, I guess you'll have to get used to that."

Her lips curved in a shy smile, and she reached for his fly. "I want to see you. I want to touch you. I want to do for you what you just did for me."

His heart hit his sternum, blood surging to his already hard cock. She'd get no objections from him. He rolled onto his back. "Go right ahead."

She sat up, unzipped his jeans. He wasn't wearing underwear, so his cock sprang free. She took hold of him, stroked his length. "You're not…"

"Circumcised? No way." Doctors at Indian Health Services hospitals had pushed that for a while, but many Lakota mothers had rejected it.

She explored him, curiosity on her face, drawing his foreskin back, circling the swollen head with her thumb. Then she bent down and kissed him right on the tip. It was just a kiss, not a prelude to going down on him, but it surprised him.

He sucked in a breath, the muscles of his abdomen contracting involuntarily.

She looked up at him. "Show me how to do it."

He closed his hand over hers, increased the pressure, then moved their hands together from root to tip and back again, guiding her. He had to give her credit. She was a quick learner. It wasn't long before she was on her own, and he was thrusting into her closed fist, his balls already drawing tight. He closed his eyes, willed himself to relax, to savor it, but then an image of her face as she came flashed through his mind, pushing him over the edge.

Climax washed through him in a wave of liquid bliss. He bit back a groan, breath hissing from between his clenched teeth. He lay there for a moment, floating somewhere between the sky and the earth. Then he felt her fingers tracing designs on his belly. He opened his eyes to find her playing with the pool of semen that had spilled there.

She smiled. "That was amazing."

He reached up, ran a finger over her cheek. "You're telling me."

Chapter Fourteen

Naomi lay with her head on Chaska's chest, one strong arm holding her close, her fingers moving idly over the ridges and valleys of his abdomen, his heartbeat steady beneath her cheek. They were both naked still, but he had pulled a sheet up to their hips, a cool breeze blowing through his windows. She had never felt this kind of connection with another human being. Neither of them spoke, but there seemed to be no need for words, everything they had to say communicated by touch as he held her just a little closer, brushed a strand of hair off her cheek, kissed her forehead.

After tonight, nothing would ever be the same.

She'd thought that there was something wrong with her, that she was incapable of having an orgasm. She hadn't even known what to expect or how it would feel. When Kenan, her second boyfriend, had broken up with her, he'd thrown the fact that she'd never come in her face, told her that she'd made him feel like less of a man.

She'd certainly felt like less of a woman.

But, oh, my God, she got it now—why people loved sex, talked about it, obsessed about it. Orgasm had taken over her body, the pleasure as intense and overpowering as it was fleeting. It was like getting hit with a thunderbolt of bliss.

Chaska. This was his doing. It wasn't just that he'd taken his time, that he hadn't climbed on top of her two minutes after he'd kissed her, that he hadn't watched the clock so that he could tell her how long he'd spent trying to make her come.

It was all of that together—and more.

Forget everything they told you about your body, about sex. It was all a lie.

What he'd told her about man nipples and clits was different from anything she'd heard before. The idea that sex was something natural and normal and fun and not a terrible sin—well, that was the opposite of what she'd been raised to believe. His words had silenced all the other voices inside her and set her free.

And they hadn't even had sex yet, not really.

That made her laugh.

"What's funny?" Chaska trailed a finger down her spine.

"I was just thinking that if an orgasm feels *that* good when you use your fingers, it must be incredible when..." She swallowed, refused to feel embarrassed. "It must be incredible when you're inside a woman."

He chuckled. "It does for me—and I hope for her, too. Honestly, I don't know if one kind of orgasm is different from another for a woman. I suppose you can figure that out for yourself and tell me."

He seemed to think he'd said something wrong because he quickly added, "All of that is up to you, of course—how far we go, what we do. As much as I'd love to help you find all the answers, I'm not going to push you into anything."

For the second time in a single night, her heart melted.

He kissed her hair. "Was that your first orgasm—or your first with a man?"

Heat rushed into her face when she realized what he was asking. "We… we were never allowed to touch ourselves. Ruth would have beaten us, humiliated us in front of the entire family. She did that with one of my older sisters—beat her bare bottom with a belt. She even threatened to cut off any part of our bodies down there that we touched outside of taking a bath. I just never tried."

"So that was your first orgasm ever."

"Yes." She told him how the first time she'd had sex had been incredibly painful and how the man who'd taken her virginity, a man she'd stupidly thought she might marry, had disappeared from her life not long after. She told him about Kenan, too, and what he'd said before stomping out of her apartment. "I thought it was me, that I was defective somehow, broken or not womanly enough."

Chaska rolled her onto her back, looked down at her, anger glinting in those dark eyes. "There is nothing wrong with you, angel. The problem lies with the people who raised you to fear your body—and the men who didn't respect you."

Could that be true?

"What you said tonight—I really liked it. I would love to hear more about what your people believe."

Then she remembered what Winona had told her. "Or maybe there are things you wouldn't want to tell an outsider."

"You're not an outsider—not to Win and me." He reached down between her breasts and took hold of her little medicine wheel. "This is Lakota. I'm certain of it. Despite the terrible wrong she did you, your mother must have wanted you to have it. She must have believed that someone would find you. She must have wanted you to know where you come from, who your people are."

"I used to believe that." That's why she'd taken the medicine wheel from Peter, who'd shown it to his church during a sermon on heathenism, telling them all where he'd gotten it. That's why she'd endured a beating to keep it hidden. That's why she'd taken it with her when she'd run, why she'd researched what it was and how it was made.

"And now?"

"There must be a dozen ways it could have ended up in my blanket. Maybe she stole it. Maybe she got it from a tourist shop. Maybe she—"

Chaska pressed a finger to her lips. "Maybe she was a poor Lakota girl from Pine Ridge or Rosebud who left you with the only thing she owned."

Chaska left the conference room, headed straight for the break room and his next cup of coffee. He'd stayed with Naomi until almost two in the morning, holding her, talking with her. He hadn't wanted to leave her side, but it didn't seem right to sleep with her until they'd truly become lovers. Trouble was, he hadn't slept at all, his head filled with her, his body wanting more.

He poured coffee into a mug, took a sip, an image of her face as she'd come flashing through his mind once more.

She was so damned beautiful.

No, it didn't hurt his pride to be the first man to make her come. Still, he wished for her sake that her life had been different. Peter and his wife had done their best to beat their twisted beliefs about sexuality into her, filling her with shame and fear, depriving her of the knowledge she needed to enjoy her own body. And the men she'd been with…

Chaska wanted to kick their asses. No woman deserved to be treated like that, to be made to doubt herself and her femininity because her partner was too lazy and disrespectful to please her.

He topped off his coffee mug, walked to the scanner, and drew her medicine wheel out of his jeans pocket. He'd asked her if he could borrow it for the day, and she'd let him. He scanned it, saved the image to the network in his own encrypted folder, then walked down the hallway to his office.

He logged into his computer, downloaded the scan of the medicine wheel from the folder to his desktop, then pulled out his cellphone and called Tina at Oglala Oyate College. She was both surprised and happy to hear from him. They talked for a while—the latest news from the college, what he and Win had been doing lately, what Tina's grandkids were up to these days.

"Can you do me a favor, Tina?"

"Sure thing."

"I'd like to email you an image of a medicine wheel. I was wondering if you could print it or load it onto a laptop and take it out to my grandfather." Old Man didn't have Internet or a computer or a smartphone. "It was left with a newborn baby girl who was abandoned by her mother in an alley twenty-seven years ago. I want to find out if Grandfather recognizes the work or has any ideas about who might have made it or owned it."

"Sure thing. I need to head out there anyway, see how he's doing." Tina was part of their *tiospaye*, their extended family, being his grandfather's second cousin once removed or some such. "Do you have any other information about this young woman?"

"She looks Native except for her eyes. They're blue. She has no idea who her parents might have been. She was found, close to dying, in Martin next to a dumpster."

"That's a rough way to start life."

It sure as hell was.

"This medicine wheel was tucked inside her blanket."

"I'll watch for your email, load it onto my iPad, and drive out there on Saturday."

"*Pilamayayelo*." *Thank you*. "It means a lot to me."

"I think maybe this young woman means a lot to you. How did you meet her?"

Chaska told her the whole story, including what he'd said the moment before Shota had run off. "She's staying with us for now."

"I have to agree with Winona. You were led to her. Tunkasila was watching out for this woman—and maybe for you, too."

Chaska regretted telling her as much as he had. "Don't tell Old Man that part. You know how he is."

He would get behind the wheel and drive his battered old pickup truck all the way to Scarlet just to meet Naomi.

"I'm not making any promises." Tina laughed, apparently finding this implied threat funny. "I'll give you a call or shoot you an email when I've heard what your grandfather has to say. Talk to you soon."

Chaska had just ended the call when Casper stepped into his office, coffee mug in hand, clearly pleased. "Great work, Belcourt. The NASA team was impressed with your solutions, so we're moving to the next stage."

"That's good." That's what they'd all been working toward.

"I know you've put in a lot of extra hours, working from home. Why don't you take a few days off, take a break?"

"Thanks. I'll do that."

Sheldon stepped into the room, this time wearing jeans and a button-down shirt. He saw Chaska and stopped short, his eyes going wide for a second.

Chaska decided to make it easy on him. "How are things in avionics?"

Sheldon gave a stiff nod, looking terribly self-conscious. "They're good, sir. Thanks for asking."

"Glad to hear it."

Five minutes later, Chaska was on his way back up to Scarlet—and the woman he couldn't get out of his thoughts.

Naomi sat in the little kitchen at Winona's clinic talking with Bear, who had just finished the second peanut butter sandwich Naomi had made for him. "When did your family come to Colorado?"

Across the room, Winona was on the phone talking to someone named Rose about a big snake that was living under her front steps.

"We were always here." Bear sat with his hands in his lap holding his battered Bible. "Colorado is the Centennial State."

He was a big man, well over six feet, and as shaggy as his namesake, but something had happened to him. His mind was truly that of a child.

"Do you remember your parents?" Naomi asked.

He nodded. "God took Mama and Daddy to heaven, and my sister and brother too. They're waiting for me, but God hasn't called me yet."

If anyone else had said this, Naomi would have felt uncomfortable. She'd grown up listening to Peter and Ruth talk about what God had to say. She avoided anyone who claimed to know what God wanted, but Bear was different. He was humble, sincere, not the kind to use words to bend other people to his will.

Across the room, Winona was losing her patience. "Rose, if you call an exterminator, they'll kill the snake. If you don't want to kill it, you'll need to trap it and relocate it. No, I'm not going to trap it for you. That's not what we do here."

"Why did they go to heaven? Were they sick?"

Bear shrugged. "I guess so."

"It must have been hard for you to be left alone."

"Oh, I'm not alone. Everyone in Scarlet Springs is my friend, and I have Him." He held up his Bible.

"I'm glad. I didn't know my parents." Naomi wasn't sure why she was telling Bear this. "My mother left me near a trash can in an alley after I was born. I almost died."

Bear seemed to consider this, then spoke as if trying to comfort her. "The Lord will keep you from all harm—he will watch over your life. The Lord will watch over your coming and going, both now and forevermore."

"Psalms one-twenty-one, verses seven and eight."

Bear had recited it verbatim, every word. He grinned, his smile largely hidden behind his beard. "Are you a believer, Naomi Archer?"

"I used to be." She told him a little about Peter and Ruth, how they lied to people, how they used religion to hurt and control people, to have power over them. "I ran away when I was sixteen. I quit believing in anything."

"The people who raised you—they were false prophets, Pharisees."

She'd never thought about it like that before. "I guess they were."

"No, Rose, I can't ask Chaska to do this for you. He's busy with work and the Team. He doesn't have time… Okay, I'll ask, but I doubt he'll be able to help. You'd be better off calling animal control." Winona hung up the phone and turned to Naomi, the irritation unmistakable on her face.

"Who is Rose?"

"She owns a New Age gift shop in town and does tarot readings and horoscopes—that kind of thing. She's always trying to get into my brother's pants."

That's all it took. Naomi hated Rose.

Was every woman Scarlet in love with him?

Winona went on. "She doesn't understand that he's not interested. Now she wants him to come and catch this snake for her. I'm sure she's just trying to … Hey, Chaska. Did you get fired or something?"

Naomi's head jerked around, her heart taking flight at the sight of him.

He stood in the doorway in jeans and a blue gingham sport shirt. His gaze met hers, his lips curving in a smile meant just for her. "Have a little faith, sister. The meeting with NASA went well, and I've taken the rest of the week off. Hey, Bear. Good to see you. Did my sister give you something good to eat?"

Bear pointed at Naomi with a little nod of his head. "Naomi Archer made me two peanut butter sandwiches." He lowered his voice to a near whisper. "She's awful pretty."

Chaska leaned down as if sharing a secret and gave Bear a brotherly clap on the shoulder, his eyes looking into Naomi's. "You're right. She is."

He stepped over to Naomi, kissed her on the lips. "The Team just got toned out to help a fallen climber in Eldorado Canyon State Park. I thought you might want to come and watch us in action."

"My brother wants to show off for you," Winona teased.

Naomi took hold of her crutches and stood. "I would love that."

"*Hoka hey*. Let's go."

Chaska parked behind Rescue One. "You'll need to stay here with the vehicles. You'll be able to see us. The Bastille, where we're headed, is right next to us off the road. It's going to be hot out there, so stay hydrated. There's bottled water behind the seat and some snack bars if you get hungry. Whoever is acting as Incident Command will be down here, too, so if you need anything—"

"Stop worrying about me." Naomi picked up her camera bag. "Do what you need to do. I'll be fine."

He leaned over, kissed her mouth, drawn to her. "See you soon."

"Be careful."

"You know it."

He stepped out, grabbed his pack out of the back of the truck, and walked over to Rescue One where Moretti, O'Brien, Herrera, Ahearn, and Nicole were gearing up. As the first Team members on the scene, they were Hasty Team. Dave Hatfield was there, too. He was a ranger with the City of Boulder, as well as a tenured Team member, and was on duty today and acting as IC.

Megs saw Chaska—then looked past him to Naomi. "Well, well. What a surprise. Nice to see you again, Naomi."

Nicole looked from Chaska to Naomi, hurt flashing across her face before she looked away.

Shit.

Hatfield brought them all up to date. "We've got a male, age thirty, with a probable broken knee. He was climbing Your Mother on The Bastille here when a fixed bolt broke. He took a whipper, striking his knee. He was lead climbing. His buddies have him on belay, but when they tried to lower him down, he started screaming."

O'Brien jumped in first. "I'll climb up to him, give him morphine IM, and get him as comfortable as possible while you all set up the vertical evac."

Megs nodded. "Make it happen. Nicole, you're on belay with O'Brien. Belcourt, you solve the anchor problem. Moretti, Herrera—work with

Belcourt. We've got six more members en route. They can join Ahearn as the evac team."

Chaska put on a harness, a helmet, and his climbing shoes, then grabbed a radio and a rack of climbing gear, and was off, Moretti and Herrera beside him, carrying ropes.

Herrera turned to look over his shoulder. "Looks like you got something going on with that sweet *mami.*"

"*Don't* call her that."

"Oooh." Herrera laughed. "Looks like I'm right."

"Button it, Herrera," Moretti said. "You'll have time for that kind of eighth-grade bullshit when we're done."

They reached the base of The Bastille, a huge, craggy buttress of stone, where O'Brien was already on his way up, Nicole on belay. Chaska tied into the rope, looking for the fastest route to the top of the wall. They needed to get above the victim to set up the ropes that would support the weight of the litter, the victim, O'Brien, and at least two members of the evac team—fifteen hundred pounds to be safe.

Chaska waited for Moretti and Herrera to be ready. "Are we good?"

"Let's get it done," Moretti said.

"On belay?" Chaska asked, going by the book as Megs demanded.

"Belay on," Moretti replied.

"Climbing."

"Climb on."

Chaska moved up the rock face.

Chapter Fifteen

Naomi showed Megs the photos she'd taken of the rescue, only too aware of the man who sat beside her, his hard thigh pressed against hers, this attraction between them like a living thing. Even surrounded by a pub full of people and Team members, all she could think about was Chaska.

It was a Monday evening, so Knockers wasn't as busy as it had been last time she was here, bluegrass music playing on a jukebox, the stage dark and bare. Her taco salad had been delicious, but Naomi wanted to go so that she and Chaska could be alone.

She had plans for tonight.

"These are incredible," Megs said. "You make us look like badasses."

"You *are* badasses."

Naomi was in awe of the Team. She'd watched the rescue from beginning to end, amazed by their skill and the smoothness with which they'd gotten that climber to safety. Not two hours had gone by from the time they'd gotten the call to the time the victim was loaded into an ambulance. And watching Chaska climb…

She'd be lying if she said it hadn't made her want him.

Megs looked up from the photos. "Could I persuade you or perhaps beg you to let us post these on our website? I'll happily give you credit."

Naomi was touched. "Are you kidding? I'd be thrilled to have them on your website. You all saved my life, remember? I can never repay you for that."

"You let us post the photos, and we'll call it even." Megs scrolled through the photos again. "I photograph most of our rescues, but my pictures never turn out like these."

Naomi had seen Megs' little point-and-shoot. It had a zoom feature, but that wasn't enough to get good action shots at a distance. "You need a better camera."

"Are you sure it's just the camera that needs to improve and not the photographer?" Ahearn joked from across the table.

Chaska leaned in, spoke for Naomi's ears alone. "All I want right now is to be alone with you. Let's get out of here."

Naomi's pulse skipped. "*Yes.*"

Chaska stood. "I think Naomi and I are heading out. I had an early morning meeting with a team from NASA, and I'm wiped."

Megs glanced up, looking from Naomi to Chaska. "I bet you are."

Heat rushed into Naomi's face. Did Megs know somehow?

Naomi took her camera from Megs and zipped it inside her padded camera bag. "How can I get the photos to you?"

"We can email them." Chaska held her crutches for her while she stood. "Or we can run by The Cave tomorrow so Megs can download them from the memory card."

"Good enough," Megs said.

Naomi threaded her way through the tables and chairs, Chaska beside her.

Rain waved to them as they passed. "See you Friday."

She had stopped by the Team's table earlier, and they'd chosen this coming Friday evening for the fundraiser.

"See you then," Naomi called back.

But she wasn't thinking about the fundraiser now or medical bills or the cost of getting her SUV repaired. All she could think about was Chaska.

They walked in silence to his truck. He opened the passenger side door for her and helped her in, stashing her crutches behind the seat. The moment he shut the driver's door behind him, he was there, kissing her, his mouth coming down hard on hers, one big hand sliding into her hair.

This.

This is what she'd wanted, what she'd craved, all day long. The heat of his lips on hers. The taste of him in her mouth. His body so close.

And then it was over.

"Not here." He drew back, jammed the keys into the ignition.

It seemed to take forever to drive the short distance from Knockers to the house, enough time for Naomi to work up her courage. She decided to tell him what she had in mind now—in case she chickened out later.

"I want you, Chaska." Could she actually *say* this? "I want all of you."

Well, that sounded stupid.

He slammed on the breaks, having nearly missed a stop sign.

He looked over at her, a wry grin on his face. "I don't think we should talk about this while I'm driving."

They drove the rest of the way home in silence, their fingers twined. The moment they were inside, she was in his arms, her crutches hitting the floor, her arms going behind his neck, her lips seeking his.

He took what she offered, kissing her until there was no breath left in her lungs. Then he scooped her into his arms and carried her up the stairs, the two of them sinking into his bed, hands sliding beneath fabric, eager to give pleasure. Clothing hit the floor, the wall, the sofa until they were both naked, the last golden rays of sunlight spilling through his windows, playing over their skin.

His gaze raked over her, one big hand palming her breast. "You are so beautiful."

Then he lowered his mouth to her and suckled.

Naomi gave herself over to it—the heat of his mouth, the tug of his lips, the flick of his tongue against her nipples. Her hands explored the smooth muscles of his shoulders, his hair spilling over her belly like a curtain of black silk. "*Chaska.*"

He dragged his mouth from her breasts, trailing kisses across her ribcage and belly, his lips leaving a trail of fire on her skin. One big hand slid over the curve of her hip to cup her.

"Oh, yes." She spread her thighs, already aching for him.

Skilled fingers found her clit, stroking, teasing, his teeth nipping her skin until she was going out of her mind, the tension inside her now an ache. She found herself clutching the bed covers, so lost in sensation that it took her a moment to realize what he was about to do.

Her eyes flew open to find his face between her thighs, his gaze fixed on *that* part of her. "Oh, no, you don't have to do that. I know guys don't really like—"

"*I* do." He dropped off the edge of the bed to kneel on the floor, lifting her injured leg and resting it over his shoulder before dragging her bottom to the edge of the bed. "You kissed me yesterday, remember? It's my turn."

Then his mouth was on her, the hot shock of it making her gasp. This was no simple kiss. She saw his eyes drift shut, heard him moan, his tongue taking over for his fingers, his lips doing to her clit what they'd done to her nipples, suckling, tugging.

It felt so … *incredibly* … good.

She buried her fingers in his hair, her hips lifting of their own accord, the breath leaving her lungs in little moans, the ache inside her bordering on torment. Then he thrust his fingers inside her, penetrating her, stroking that ache, taking her to the brink.

And then it all stopped.

She moaned in frustration and opened her eyes to see Chaska standing between her legs, his cock full and thick. Her mouth went dry.

He crawled up the bed until he loomed over her, his gaze fixed on hers, a little smile on his wet lips. He balanced his weight on his knees and one arm, reaching with the other to pull something out of his nightstand.

A condom.

Naomi watched as he tore open the packet with his teeth, helping him to roll it down his length.

He kissed her, her taste and scent all over him. "Are you sure?"

"Yes. *Hurry.*"

Rather than lying down on top of her as she'd expected him to do, he sat back on his heels and drew her hips into his lap, draping her injured leg over his shoulder once more and wrapping the other around his waist. Then he nudged himself into her, slowly burying himself to the hilt, breath hissing between his clenched teeth. "You are *so* tight."

His eyes drifted shut, and his head fell back.

She'd never found it all that pleasurable to have a man inside her, but this felt incredible, his cock stroking that inner ache, stretching her, gliding in and out of her. She fisted her hands in the bedcovers again, fought not to close her eyes, made breathless by the sight of him, his hips curling as he thrust himself slowly into her, his muscles tensing, dark hair spilling over his shoulders.

The tension inside her began to build again.

He brought his head up, opened his eyes, looked to where their bodies joined, then met her gaze, hunger for her naked in his eyes. He reached down to tease her clit again, the combined sensations almost too good to be true.

"Chask—*aah*." She tried to say his name, but the last part turned into a moan.

But she was beyond words now, out of control, every exhale a moan, her eyes squeezed shut as he drove into her, her body needing more… wanting more… aching for more. God, yes, deeper. So perfect. It was so perfect. *He* was perfect.

She cried out, arched off the bed, climax blazing through her in a flash fire of bliss, white hot and radiant. Her inner muscles contracted around him, the sensation both erotic and satisfying, one thought passing through her mind.

This is how it was supposed to be.

Chaska kept up the rhythm until the tremors inside her had slowed, then he stretched himself out above her and kissed her, his chest slick with sweat, his body tense. He whispered her name, the sound of it reverent. "Naomi."

She reached up to cup his face, tears blurring her vision.

"Are you okay?" He kissed a tear from her cheek.

She nodded, smiled up at him. "I didn't think it could ever be like this for me."

"Aw, Naomi." He kissed her lips, her cheeks, her forehead—and began to move inside her once more. The rhythm was different this time, and it hit her that he'd been holding back, reining himself in, focusing only on her pleasure.

No man had done that for her before.

She wrapped her arms around him, held him, sliding her hands over the sweat-slick muscles of his back. Harder and faster he went, until he was pounding himself into her, his thrusts slamming the bed into the wall. Then his breath caught, and he groaned into her hair, his body shaking apart in her arms as he let himself go at last.

Chaska held Naomi against his chest, kissed her, stroked her hair. His heart was still pounding, her sweet, musky scent still filling his head, his body floating. He'd had his share of great sex, but he'd never experienced anything like this. It had been more than physical. Something about it—something about *her*—had broken him wide open.

You're falling in love with her.

The thought sent his heart soaring—and made his stomach knot. He sure as hell hadn't seen this coming. He'd only known her for a week after all. He had no idea how she felt about any of this, beyond enjoying what he did to her body. Though he couldn't imagine why she'd want to go back to the loveless, friendless life she had in Rapid City, there was still a chance that she wouldn't want to stay in Colorado.

You were led to her.

Win's words came back to him, reassuring him. If he truly had been led to Naomi, this would all work out and he had no reason to worry.

He let it go, savored the post-orgasmic lethargy that had taken over his body and the sweet feel of the woman in his arms. Outside, the sun had set, a breeze wicking the sweat from his skin.

"Are you cold?" He kissed her hair, unable to get enough of her.

She snuggled deeper into his chest, her voice soft and sleepy. "A little."

He pulled up the sheet, covering them both, his fingers tracing the graceful line of her spine. A golden silence stretched between them, the minutes passing, long and languid. Whatever they'd had to say had been communicated through touch, through kisses, through the union of their bodies. What were words compared to that?

After some time, she spoke. "What are those wreaths?"

He followed the direction of her gaze. "They're not wreaths. They're Sun Dance rings or crowns. I made them myself to wear during the ceremony."

"You wear them on your head?" She narrowed her eyes if trying to imagine this.

"I'll show you." As reluctant as he was to leave her side even for a moment, he climbed out of bed, crossed the room, and took down one of the crowns. He placed it on his head so that the ribbons trailed down his back, then did a slow turn so that she could see how it looked. When he faced her again, he found her sitting up in bed, her bare breasts exposed, her gaze moving over his naked body, stopping at his penis. "Of course, I wasn't naked."

She laughed. "What did you wear—besides the crown?"

"Most dancers also wear smaller sage rings around their ankles and wrists. Men wear a kind of long loin cloth, almost a skirt, that covers their lower body to the ground." He removed the crown, set it back on its nail, and got back in bed, settling down once again with Naomi in his arms.

"Winona told me that's how you got these." Naomi ran her fingers over the piercing scars on his chest, her touch cool. "Don't be angry with her. She told me only because I asked."

"I'm not angry with her." He tucked a strand of hair behind Naomi's ear. "Yeah, these are my piercing scars from my three Sun Dances."

She kissed one and then another. "It must have been painful."

Oh, yes—more painful than he'd imagined it would be.

"The pain is the point—or part of it. Women bleed every month for the good of their people and suffer when they give birth. That's how new life comes into the world. Sun Dance gives men a chance to bleed and suffer for their people, too." That's how it had been explained to him. "Warriors make an offering of their flesh so that *Wakan Tanka* will watch over their families and communities."

The frown on her face told him she was struggling with that idea. "Can't you just pray or fast or something?"

He tried to explain, simplifying things, struggling to translate both words and the concepts behind the Sun Dance into English. "Sun Dance is one of seven sacred Lakota rites. Nowadays, it's part of the Red Road, the spiritual way of life, for many Native peoples, not just plains nations. Mostly men, but also women, give up food and water for four days and nights and dance in the sun. Warriors—"

"Are you a *warrior*?" She looked up at him, amusement on her face.

He chuckled, caressed her shoulder. "The word means something different to us. A warrior isn't someone who fights wars. He—or she—protects those who are weaker than he is, takes care of the vulnerable people in the community, takes responsibility for the things that need to be done. Sometimes that means fighting. Most of the time it's simple stuff like shoveling snow off an elder's sidewalk or defending a kid against bullies or speaking out at a meeting against a bad tribal government policy."

"Or rescuing people?"

"That, too." He went back to the Sun Dance. "Warriors who choose to self-sacrifice are pierced with sharpened pegs. The protruding ends of the pegs are attached to leather thongs that hang from the tree that stands at the center of the Sun Dance area. The idea is to dance while looking into the sun and pulling back until the pegs tear through your skin."

She winced, her fingers explored his scars again. "How can you survive four days in the heat and sun without water? Do people ever get sun stroke and die?"

"One of the duties of a Sun Dance chief is to watch out for people. Those who look like they're in trouble get sage tea. But Sun Dance is a way of life, a discipline. Sun Dancers spend a year preparing through prayer, sweatlodges, and *hanbleceya*—vision quest—which also requires you to go four days without food or water. By the time a man reaches the Sun Dance grounds, he ought to be ready."

"Did you do all of that—sweatlodge, vision quest?"

Chaska nodded. "My grandfather put me on top of a mountain and kept watch that entire time to make sure I was safe."

"Did you have a vision? That's what it's about, right?"

"Yes, but it's also about getting clear in your mind, understanding the path you're meant to take. That's where I decided to go to college to study engineering."

"You've done three Sun Dances then."

"I was supposed to do four. Every cycle includes four Sun Dances, so once you've committed to it, you repeat that entire year-long process four years in a row. But I walked away from it."

He told her how proud he'd been to step into the arbor with his father and grandfather, how proud he'd felt to be part of a tradition that passed from father to son for countless generations. "Old Man wanted me to start learning the ropes, to take my place in the arbor, even though my heart was set on engineering school. For a while, I thought I could do both."

"What changed?"

"On the night after the third day of my third ceremony, I heard laughter coming from just outside the arbor. People are supposed to be respectful of the dancers, so I went to ask them to be quiet. I found my father and one of the holy men smoking weed, eating junk food, and drinking. They were supposed to be fasting. Drugs and alcohol aren't allowed on the Sun Dance grounds, but there was my father, bringing dishonor to the entire ceremony, disrespecting the sacrifices of the dancers."

"What did you do?"

He'd been angry, upset. "I woke Old Man, told him what I'd seen. He went and got my father, and they had words in private. Afterward, he wanted to ban my father and that holy man from the ceremony, but people thought he was being too harsh. He stepped down from running the Sun Dance after that year, and I refuse to be a part of it with my father in charge."

"I'm so sorry." There was true empathy in her eyes, and he knew she understood. "You must have felt so let down. It hurts to find out that people you love aren't what you thought they were."

"Yeah. I haven't spoken to him since." But Chaska didn't want to spend the night talking about his father or Sun Dance or the Red Road. "Come here."

He made love to Naomi again, this time slowly, the beauty on her face as she came like an arrow through his chest. They held each other afterward, falling asleep in each other's arms.

Chapter Sixteen

Naomi woke to the sound of Chaska speaking quietly in Lakota. She rolled over, saw him standing near an open window, still naked. He lit a bundle of sage, blew out the flame, then set the bundle in its abalone shell and wafted its smoke over his head with an eagle feather.

So that's why he always smelled of sage.

She sat up, not wanting to interrupt, but curious. "What are you doing?"

"Smudging. Praying." He finished his prayer in silence, then set the abalone shell on the table. He lay the eagle feather in its long wooden box, carried the box to his chest of drawers, and put it on top.

"Do you always wake up so early?"

"Most of the time." He crossed the room and bent down to kiss her. "Did you get enough sleep?"

She couldn't hold back the smile. "Couldn't have slept better."

He picked up his boxer briefs off the floor. "Want to join me in the shower?"

The invitation was irresistible.

Naomi put on her bathrobe and followed him across the hall. He stopped, pressed a finger to his lips, and gave a nod toward Winona's room.

Her door was still shut. She was still sleeping.

So much for making her shower sex fantasy come true.

She shut the door behind them, took off her robe and hung it from a hook on the door while he stripped off his briefs and started the water. He stepped under the spray, held out his hand for her. "I won't let you fall."

They didn't have a lot of room, so they stood close together, soapy hands sliding over wet skin as they took turns shampooing their hair and washing each other. His hands conjured up the most delicious sensations as they moved over her arms, her breasts, her belly. She returned the favor, enticed by the hard feel of him, her hands moving from his pecs to his belly.

He grew hard in front of her, his cock straining for her.

She couldn't help herself. She took hold of him, stroked him from base to tip, soap making him slippery. He bit back a moan, splayed one big hand against the tile wall, the other at her waist holding her steady. She tried to remember how he liked it, letting him set the pace as he thrust into her hand.

He held his breath as he came, his eyes squeezed shut, semen shooting over her breasts and his belly. When he opened his eyes again, they held a predatory glint, his lips curving in a slow, sexy smile. "Your turn."

He took down the handheld shower head, turned her so that she stood with her back to him. He washed the proof of his climax from her skin, taking time to palm her nipples, teasing them until they were hard and puckered. Then both hands moved down her belly—the one that had been tormenting her breasts and the one that held the shower head. "Just lean back against me."

She did as he asked, gasping as the spray hit her *there*. She'd never imagined having an orgasm like this. There's no way it would be enough to…

Oh, but it was.

He angled the spray just right, his free hand pressing circles against her, moving slowly around and around just above her clit. The pulsing bursts of warm water. Pressure. The hard feel of him behind her.

She came hard and fast, muffling her cry with her hands as pleasure washed through her in a liquid rush. She sagged against him, breathless. "*Wow.*"

She was living in a new world, one where her fantasies came true.

He chuckled, bent down to kiss her cheek. "Hungry?"

"Starving."

They finished washing and helped each other dry off.

He wrapped his towel around his waist, waited for her to slip into her bathrobe, then opened the door and stepped out.

"It's about time." Winona walked through the door—and froze. "Oh. Sorry!"

Naomi's face burned. "That's okay. I'm … uh… done."

Naomi left the bathroom and made her way across the hall, the bathroom door closing behind Winona.

Chaska stood there in his towel, chuckling to himself, a big grin on his face.

"I'm so embarrassed."

"Why?" He ran a finger over her cheek. "We aren't doing anything wrong."

From across the hallway came a shout. "You used all the hot water!"

Chaska was the first one downstairs. He made coffee and then started on breakfast burritos, first putting sausage in a pan to cook and then peeling a few potatoes, his mind on Naomi and how she'd come apart in his arms just now. He didn't realize he was smiling until he saw his reflection in the aluminum surface of the refrigerator.

Damn, kola. *You've got it bad.*

He did, and he was okay with that. Somewhere in the night, he'd reached a kind of peace about all of this. If it were meant to be, nothing would keep him and Naomi apart. If it wasn't… Well, he would never forget her.

She came into the kitchen wearing a turquoise skirt and a white tank top that had his gaze going straight to her breasts. He willed himself to look up. "Coffee?"

"Please, yes! Can I help?"

"Want to dice these?" He set her up with a knife, a cutting board, and the potatoes he'd peeled, then went to the fridge for the eggs and half-and-half.

They talked about small things while they got breakfast on the table—Naomi's appointment Thursday to get her stitches out, their promise to go by The Cave so that Megs could have Naomi's photos, the tour Chaska had promised Naomi of his workshop.

"There's not much to see, really."

Then Chaska remembered.

He walked over to his work backpack, unzipped the front pocket, and took out Naomi's little medicine wheel. He carried it to her, slipped it over her head. "Thanks for trusting me with this."

"What did you do with it?"

"I scanned it and sent the images to one of my relatives at Oglala Oyate College. She's going to make sure my grandfather sees them. I thought he might know something about who made it."

Naomi froze, knife hovering above the cutting board. "Do you think there's a chance that he might?"

"It's a long shot, but I wanted to try."

She went back to chopping. "I'm not sure I'd want to meet my mother even if someone found her. She left me alone by the garbage to die."

Chaska moved up behind her, wrapped an arm around her shoulders, kissed her hair. "I don't blame you for feeling that way. I'd feel the same way. You don't have to meet anyone you don't want to meet."

Winona flew into the kitchen, dressed in scrubs, her hair damp. "Did the two of you sleep well last night?"

Naomi's face flamed, her gaze shooting to Chaska's. He would have found it adorable if he didn't know where it came from. She was freer sexually than she'd been before, but the shame those people had beaten into her still lurked inside her.

He handed Winona a mug of coffee. "We did. Thanks. You?"

"I stayed out way too late. I went to Knockers thinking I'd find you there, but you had already gone. I ended up staying until closing talking with Nicole, who is fine, by the way. I think it made her feel better to know that you were together with Naomi."

Naomi looked up at Chaska, doubt in her eyes.

Are we together?

He could almost hear her thoughts. He held her gaze. "But Nicole understands now, right? She and I are not going to happen. I'm with Naomi."

The doubt vanished from Naomi's eyes, a soft smile lighting up her face.

That didn't mean she wanted to stay with him, but for now, it was enough.

"Nicole does understand, and she's not mad at you, either. I think she's embarrassed about what she said when she was drunk."

Chaska had forgotten about that.

"Oh, I forgot to tell you that Rose wants you to come by and catch a king snake that's living under her front steps and scaring away customers."

"You're kidding me." He set plates on the table, held out Naomi's chair, then took her crutches, while Winona told him about Rose's call yesterday.

"I'm afraid if you don't move it, she'll call an exterminator."

Chaska sat, picked up his fork. "Well, I guess I've got a snake to catch."

"Are you afraid of snakes?" Chaska drove through the roundabout, where Bear stood in the hot sun, preaching his gospel.

Naomi waved to him, saw him wave back. "I grew up on a farm. We had snakes all over the place. I got used to them."

"You seem unhappy."

"I'm not unhappy. I'm … jealous." There. That was honest.

"Jealous—of *Rose*?" He seemed to find this funny, laughing harder than she'd seen him laugh before. "You have nothing to worry about where Rose is concerned."

"Win said Rose just wants to get inside your pants."

Chaska grinned. "In that case, it's a good thing you're coming with me. You can show her that my pants are already occupied."

How Naomi was supposed to accomplish this, she didn't know. "I'm not going to say anything to her."

"Oh, angel, you won't have to."

He turned a corner, drove past a beautiful yellow Victorian inn where a woman with short tousled hair was watering a bed of bright daylilies in flip flops and a pink floral kimono that stopped mid-thigh. Chaska pulled over in front of a smaller Victorian house, this one painted white with a pink sign hanging over the porch.

Rose's New Age Emporium

The front door opened, and a woman with long silver hair stepped out. She was wearing a black broomstick skirt and a lacy white peasant top.

Naomi felt silly. "You didn't tell me Rose was old enough to be your mother."

Chuckling, Chaska climbed out. "Hey, Rose."

He made his way around the front of the truck to Naomi's door, helping her to the ground, then ducking down to press a kiss to her mouth. "See? Nothing to worry about."

He walked with her over to the front step, where a large black snake with yellow markings was sunning itself on the concrete. "Hello there, little guy."

The moment Chaska's shadow fell over it, it disappeared back into its hole.

"Rose, this is Naomi. Naomi, this is Rose."

Naomi caught the disappointment that flashed across Rose's face, but it was gone in an instant, the smile that took its place seeming genuine.

Rose reached out, touched Naomi's cheek. "I read about what you went through, dear. My goodness, you're brave—and beautiful. Are you Native American, too?"

Chaska didn't give Naomi time to answer—his attempt to prevent her from having to answer uncomfortable questions. "Tell me what's going on with this snake."

Rose launched into a long story about how it had moved in this spring and how she couldn't get it to leave. "I've smudged it. I've dropped garlic in its hole. I put that plastic hawk up on my porch railing. I got some coyote urine from the hardware store, but that didn't work either."

Chaska looked like he was fighting not to laugh. "Well, it sounds like you've tried everything."

"I respect the snake's energy. I really do. They're a symbol of the Goddess, a symbol of rebirth, but most of my customers aren't as evolved as I am. It scares them. I don't want to call an exterminator, but it's hurting my bottom line."

The snake stuck its head out again, and Rose jumped, proving that it scared her, too. So much for being evolved.

"You here about that damned snake?"

Naomi turned toward the sound of the voice and saw that the woman in the pink kimono wasn't a woman, but an older man, his face unshaven, the robe open at the top to expose a wedge of gray chest hair.

"Hey, Bob." Chaska didn't seem surprised at all, as if Bob and his pink kimono were the norm here in Scarlet. "This is Naomi Archer. Naomi, this is Bob Jewell, owner of the Forest Creek Inn across the street. He's Lexi's dad."

"And grandpa to the cutest baby girl on earth. Nice to meet you." Bob wiped his palm on his kimono and held his hand out for her. "Glad you're okay, and glad they got those bastards."

"I've met Emily, and she *is* cute. And thank you."

The two men went back to talking about the snake. They decided to run water down the hole with Rose's hose. Chaska would catch the snake when it surfaced and stick it in the canvas bag he'd brought. Then he would release it at an old quarry above town.

"If the snake doesn't come up quickly, we'll stop, and I'll go buy a trap. I don't want to drown it. Agreed?"

Chaska went to get the bag out of the back of his truck, while Bob, whose white underwear showed when he bent over, went after Rose's garden hose.

Rose turned to Naomi. "How long are you planning to stay in town?"

"I'm not sure. I was going to be here for a week, but things have changed."

Rose lowered her voice, leaned closer. "I've always thought Chaska would be amazing in bed—all that intense Scorpio energy. I'll bet he's well hung, too."

Naomi gaped at Rose, her cheeks burning. "I … I can't talk about him like that."

"I've shocked you. Sorry, dear." She gave Naomi a motherly pat on the arm. "I would have thought a Native girl would be more open about sexuality."

Naomi fought to keep the rage from her voice. "Open or not, I would never turn something as beautiful and sacred as my sex life with Chaska into a topic of cheap gossip. I respect him too much for that."

She said it loud enough that she was afraid Chaska had heard her.

Although she'd just told Rose off, Rose seemed delighted. "So, you *are* lovers."

"What?" Hadn't Rose known that already?

No, she'd been fishing, and Naomi had just told her what she'd wanted to know. How was she going to explain this to Chaska?

He glanced over at the two of them, then went back to what he was doing. He got into position off to the side of the snake's hole where he wouldn't make a shadow, his hand inside the bag, which he had turned inside out. "Ready."

Bob turned on the water, a slow stream running down into the hole.

The seconds ticked by, and nothing happened. Naomi was sure that Chaska was going to call it off when the snake's head popped up.

In a blink, Chaska had grabbed it just behind its head, drawing its body out of the hole and turning the bag right side out, trapping it. The snake fought to escape, its tail curling this way and that.

"Oh, God!" Rose looked repulsed. "I don't know how you can touch that thing."

Naomi reached over, grabbed its tail, and pushed it into the bag.

"Thanks." Chaska flashed her a smile, then spoke soothingly to the snake. "There you go, buddy. You're okay. No one's trying to hurt you."

Bob walked over to the house to turn off the water, chuckling to himself. "What happened to all that bullshit about respecting the snake's energy?"

Rose spluttered. "Well, I…"

"What the hell are you doing over there in my bathrobe?" A woman stood across the street at the inn, hands on her hips.

"You told me not to come out in my underwear, woman!" Bob shouted back.

"Put on some damned pants!"

Naomi had to fight not to laugh.

"Rose, you're going to want to plug that hole before something else moves in."

"Right. Thanks so much, Chaska. Stop by for a free tarot reading anytime. You, too, Naomi. I would love to see what's in your cards."

That was *never* going to happen.

Chaska tied off the bag, looked over at Naomi. "Ready to go for a ride?"

Chaska drove up the winding dirt road to the site of the old quarry, where much of the stone for Scarlet's earliest buildings had come from. He could tell something was bothering Naomi, though she hid it well, laughing about Bob and his kimono.

"I've got to say it—Scarlet Springs is a little weird."

"Only a little? We must be slacking." Chaska chuckled. "I like it that way. Kendra—the woman you saw yelling at Bob—is Lexi's stepmom. Lexi's mom died in a car accident when Lexi and her sister Britta were very little."

"That's awful. It must have been so hard for them."

"Yeah." Chaska knew first hand how that felt.

Naomi had never asked about his family, but then she'd probably learned early in life not to ask others unless she wanted to answer questions herself.

He decided to come right out and tell her. "My mother died when I was twelve and Win was ten. She got drunk and wandered outside in a snow storm when we were with our dad. They found her frozen to death ten feet from our front door."

Naomi reached over, rested a hand on his thigh. "I didn't know. I'm so sorry."

"For a long time, I blamed myself for not being home that night, for not being there to save her."

"You were a child. It *wasn't* your fault."

"I know that now, but then…" Chaska changed the subject. "So, what were you and Rose talking about?"

She looked guiltily down at her hands. "She … She tricked me into admitting that you and I are lovers."

So that's what was troubling her.

Naomi told him the whole story—what Rose had said to her, what she'd said to Rose. "Then she said, 'So you *are* lovers.' I gave her exactly what she wanted. I'm sorry. I shouldn't have—"

"You have no reason to apologize." Chaska kept the grin off his face, touched that Naomi would stand up for his dignity the way she had. "Rose is Scarlet's biggest gossip. She's been tricking people into telling her things since before we were born. But just so you know—the entire town is going to know about us before sunset."

"You're not angry?"

"No. I'm touched by what you said. 'Beautiful and sacred.' I like it. I think poor Rose is the one who's jealous now. Did she really say she thinks I'm hung?"

Naomi gave a laugh. "You are."

He pulled over to the side of the road when they reached the base of the quarry, the mountainside cut away to reveal the limestone beneath. He left Naomi in the truck, got the bag out of the back, and released the snake several feet off to the side of the road. It slithered away in a blink, taking refuge beneath some nearby scrub. There were lots of rodents here for it to eat and plenty of warm stone for it to sun itself on.

He tossed the empty bag into the back of the truck and climbed inside. "One snake successfully relocated."

Naomi looked over at him, her eyes narrowed. "Your decision to help Rose—that was you being a warrior, wasn't it?"

He liked that she understood. "Old Man taught me to take responsibility. The more people willing to step up, the happier and safer the community. Now what? I suppose we should head to The Cave. Maybe we can grab some lunch afterward, and then I can give you a tour of my workshop."

They found Megs in the ops room listening to traffic on the radio. She smiled when she saw them. "Hey, you two. Lost hiker. Taylor and the other park rangers are in touch with her by cell phone and going to get her, so there's no need for us to get involved. Did you bring those photos?"

Chapter Seventeen

"Do you like tacos?"

Naomi stared over at Chaska. "Who doesn't like tacos?"

"Good answer." He drove them into town and parked on the street near a taco truck with the words *Tacos Sabrosos* painted in bright red on the side. "The name means Tasty Tacos. Juana makes the best street tacos in Scarlet. They're also the only street tacos in Scarlet."

This made her laugh.

He helped her out of the truck then walked beside her, his hand resting against her lower back. "When you get rid of those crutches, I'll finally be able to hold your hand."

His words filled her with hope. "That will be five weeks from now. Are you sure you're going to want me around that long?"

"Oh, yes."

His answer, and the warmth in his eyes, chased her doubts away—for a while.

They ordered and paid, Chaska speaking Spanish to the woman at the window, presumably Juana. The sun beat down from a clear sky, and they were lucky to find a table in the shade, the street crowded with tourists. Chaska went back to get their order, returning with drinks, napkins, wet wipes, and two plates of tacos.

"These are delicious." The chicken in Naomi's tacos was tender, the sauce spicy enough to leave a nice burn on her tongue.

"Told you so."

After lunch, they strolled down what served as Scarlet's main street, passing small shops that sold everything from old fashioned hard candy to tourist stuff to handmade soap and candles. There was more than one empty storefront, big glass windows beneath false fronts with Victorian trim.

She found herself standing in front of the prettiest one. It was desperately in need of paint, but she looked past that to the delicate scrolling on the trim, the wooden floor inside, the interior brick walls.

Chaska nuzzled her ear, his hand coming to rest on her back again. "You know, if someone opened a jewelry store in this town, I bet it would do well."

She looked up at him, surprised that he'd known what she was thinking. "You really think so?"

He nodded. "There's nothing like that here, and your work is so good… You would become one of the reasons people come to Scarlet."

He believed in her.

Chaska believed in her.

The entire world seemed brighter.

They went for ice cream after that. Naomi got a cone with butter pecan and strawberry, while Chaska got rocky road. She was licking drips off the sides of the cone, when she noticed that Chaska was watching her tongue.

Okay, she could have fun with this.

She licked her way up the mound of ice cream, swirling her tongue around the tip.

Chaska's brows drew together, his eyes going dark.

She did it again and again, flicking the top of the ice cream now.

"I see what you're doing. I'm onto you now."

"Yeah?" She didn't stop, consuming the rest of her ice cream the way she might consume him, both amused and titillated by the effect she had on him.

By the time she had finished, he was more than ready to go home.

"What's the hurry?" she asked sweetly.

"You're going to find out."

He was on her the moment they were inside, crushing her against him, kissing her hard, one hand sliding inside her shirt to caress her breast. He swung her into his arms, stomped up the stairs, then set her on the bed and started taking off his clothes.

She did the same, as eager for him as he was for her. The moment his cock sprang free, she reached for it, taking the hard length of him into her hand—and then into her mouth. She stroked him with her hand and mouth in tandem, teasing the head with her tongue just as she had the ice cream cone.

"Stop. Stop! Oh, shit!"

She drew back, saw pain on Chaska's face. "Wh-what did I do?"

"Jalapeños. I didn't think about that. Damn!" He took off at a run, hand cupped over his penis. "Son of a bitch!"

She tried to follow, but her crutches were downstairs. "Should I call 911?"

"No!" he shouted back. "God, no!"

She hopped out of his room to the stairs, then clutched the rail, hopping down one stair at a time, moans coming from the kitchen, cupboards opening and closing. She picked up her crutches and hurried into the kitchen.

Chaska leaned against the refrigerator, stark naked, eyes squeezed shut, holding a bowl of milk to his crotch, his penis submerged.

"Are you sure I shouldn't call for help?"

"I do *not* want Hawke over here administering first aid to my dick." He moaned again. "Milk will neutralize it. It's not as bad as it was when I came down."

"I'm so, so sorry. I didn't think—"

"It's not your fault. I should have thought of it." He gave a tight little laugh, the lines of pain on his face starting to ease. "It's kind of funny, really."

Naomi didn't think so.

"I'm *really* glad Win isn't home." He laughed again—and kept laughing.

Naomi thought about how this must look, the two of them naked, his penis in a bowl of milk, and she laughed, too.

Chaska spent a good hour soaking his dick in milk and then washing himself with soap and cool water. He knew Naomi felt terrible about what had happened, but it really wasn't her fault. With his dick out of commission for the moment, they'd ended up in his bed again, snuggling together and talking.

"What do you normally do when you're on vacation?" she asked him.

"I sleep more, and I climb a lot. Sometimes I head up into the mountains for some alpine climbing. Mostly, I spend a lot of time in Eldo—Eldorado Canyon State Park, where we rescued that guy from The Bastille."

"You're not getting to do much of that with me here."

He kissed her temple. "I'm not complaining."

They talked for hours, a lazy breeze tousling the curtains, the scent of Winona's roses drifting through the windows. He told her about growing up on Oglala. Swimming in the creek in the summer. The long walks and fishing trips with his grandfather. The teacher who'd recognized that he was gifted and had fought to get him tested. Going on the powwow trail with his grandparents. Learning to ride a horse. Sitting around the fire and listening to his grandfather's stories about the Iktomi, the spider-trickster spirit.

She listened, laughed, but something was bothering her. The more he shared about his life, the more wistful the expression on her face became, those beautiful blue eyes filling with shadows.

"Hey, you're not still blaming yourself for my case of jalapenis, are you?"

She shook her head. "I was just thinking how normal you and Winona are, what a normal, happy life you've had."

He let out a laugh. "Yeah, normal. I'm thirty-three. I work on rockets and climb rocks, though I'm supposed to be a Sun Dance chief. Also, I live with my sister and her wolf. That's as normal as it gets."

She smiled, but the smile didn't reach her eyes.

He kissed the top of her head, gave her a squeeze. "You know you can tell me anything, right?"

Her gaze was fixed on some faraway place. "I keep expecting to wake up and find that this is all a dream—that you and Win aren't real. Or for you to tell me that you don't really want me and that I have to go."

He turned with her in his arms, rolling her onto her back so that he could look straight into her eyes. "That is *not* going to happen. That's just a worry in your mind, the voice of your past talking about things that happened before you met me."

Tears pooled in those blue eyes. "I just don't know what a man like you, who could have any woman in Scarlet, who's smart and sexy and successful—did I say good looking yet?—sees in a woman like me. I came from nowhere. I was raised by crazy people. I didn't go to college. I'm not intelligent like you and—"

"Stop." It put a physical ache in his chest to hear her talk about herself like that. "You want to know what I see in you? I'll tell you. I see kindness. The way you treat Bear, the way you are with animals—I could never be with a woman who didn't have love and kindness in her heart."

"Yeah?"

"That's at the top of my list." He wiped the tears from her cheeks with his thumbs. "You're plenty smart. I know lots of people with college educations, some with doctorates, who are anything but intelligent."

She sniffed, smiled. "Really?"

"Really. Come to work with me sometime, and I'll show you educated people with no brains." He slid his fingers into her hair, lifted it away from her face. "You're honest. I know it took a lot of courage to tell me this. You were honest about being jealous of Rose, too."

He went on, wanting so very much to reach her. "You're talented. You're a true artist, Naomi. I could never do what you do."

He got a genuine smile for that.

He ducked down, brushed his lips over hers. "And, damn, woman, you're beautiful. *Everything* about you turns me on."

But then it hit him. This wasn't about facts. It was about emotions. It was about the people who'd abandoned her, who'd abused her, who'd tried to beat their sickness into her, who'd made her believe there was something wrong with her.

He pulled away. "I know you've been disappointed by people before, but did you ever think that maybe you and I were meant to meet, that I was supposed to find you?"

Tell her, kola. *Tell her the whole of it.*

It was on the tip of his tongue, but when he opened his mouth, other words came out. "Maybe the Great Mystery behind this world sees all you've endured, knows how brave you've been and how alone, and wants you to be happy."

Her blue eyes glittered with tears. "Do you really believe that?"

He knew it had been a long time since she'd believed in anything, so he would have to claim this for both of them. "Yes, I do. With everything I am, I do."

"Hey, I'm home!" From downstairs came Winona's voice. "Are you *still* in bed?"

Winona had worked all day, so Chaska stepped up to make dinner. While he grilled buffalo burgers, Naomi chopped vegetables for a garden salad, his words running through her mind.

Did you ever think that maybe you and I were meant to meet, that I was supposed to find you?

It was a pretty thought, but Naomi had been around the block a few too many times to believe that some benevolent force was watching over her.

And yet…

Chaska understood her the way no man—or woman, for that matter—ever had. He saw inside her so clearly, saw her as she wished to be, not as the frightened, lost person she was. He respected her work. He listened to her. He was an incredible lover—yes, Rose had been right about that. Most of all, he cared about her. He'd made that clear in so many ways today.

The intimacy she had with him was more than she'd believed she'd ever have with a man. It was everything she'd wanted. *He* was everything she wanted.

Then why couldn't she shake this feeling that it was all going to fall apart?

That's just a worry in your mind, the voice of your past talking about things that happened before you met me.

Could it be that simple? Could she just let go—and be happy?

She stopped chopping a tomato, closed her eyes for a moment, inhaled the scent of grilling meat. She heard Winona's cheerful voice as she told Chaska about the antics of the mountain lion cubs today, heard his deep chuckle.

This life, this place, these people—Naomi could come to love this.

You're in love with him already.

After just one week? She had to be crazy.

The back door opened, jerking Naomi from her thoughts.

She went back to chopping the tomato, felt Chaska come up behind her, his arms going around her waist, his lips pressing a kiss to her neck.

Okay, maybe not so crazy.

"I'm almost finished here. How are the steaks?"

"They're done. I need to grab a plate so I can bring them in." He reached past her, took an oval-shaped platter out of one cupboard and disappeared outside again.

Winona came back in, started setting the table. She lowered her voice. "My brother really likes you."

Naomi dropped the chopped tomato into the salad and handed the bowl to Winona to carry to the table. "That's what he told me today."

Winona beamed. "You like him, too, right?"

"Yes, I care about him so much that—"

But then Chaska stepped back inside, three grilled steaks and three potatoes wrapped in aluminum foil on the platter.

Winona hid her smile and went to the refrigerator for salad dressing. She stared in disbelief. "Where's the milk? I just bought a new carton yesterday. How can it be gone?"

Chaska's gaze met Naomi's. "Sorry, yeah, I drank it all. I'll run to the store."

It was everything Naomi could do not to burst out laughing.

The food was delicious, the company even better. Naomi told Winona about Rose tricking her and Bob and his pink kimono. She helped with the spirit plate, too, adding a little piece of potato and some of her salad, earning an appreciative glance from Chaska.

They had finished with the meal but were still talking when Chaska's cell phone rang. He drew it out of his pocket. "It's Tina. I'd better take this."

He answered in Lakota and then stepped out the back door.

Winona leaned forward. "What were you going to say before he stepped inside? You like him so much that…"

"I like him so much that it scares me. I think I'm in love with him."

For some reason, Winona didn't look surprised. "Don't be afraid. He feels the same. I'm sure of it, though he'd kill me if he knew I'd told you. He…"

Her words trailed off, her head turning toward the backyard, as if she were listening to Chaska's conversation. A look of surprise came over her face, her gaze jerking to Naomi. "He's speaking with our grandfather."

Naomi's pulse spiked. "What are they saying?"

"I'm not sure. It's about your medicine wheel." Winona looked confused. "What would my grandfather know about that?"

Naomi drew it out, held it, her heart pounding now. "Chaska sent scans of it to him, hoping he might know who made it."

"Oh. Wow. It sounds like he does."

Chaska ended the call and walked back inside, wondering how Naomi was going to feel about this news. She watched him, a hint of wariness on her face. Winona must have overheard and shared at least some of what he'd said with her.

He sat, took Naomi's hand, came right out with it. "My grandfather is certain he knows who made that medicine wheel—Maggie Otter Tail."

"I remember her," Winona said. "She was old even when we were little."

Chaska nodded. "She made the journey to the spirit world a long time ago."

"Did she have any daughters?" Naomi asked.

"No. She had one son, but he's gone now, too. He had two sons who are still alive. Maggie also had many nieces and great nieces through her two sisters. Old Man says she made these for the people she loved, the people in her family. He said you can tell it's her work by the two black X marks on the back at the bottom."

Naomi drew the leather cord over her head, turned the medicine wheel over, and examined. "They're right here."

She handed it to Chaska, pointed. "I never noticed them before."

To be fair, they were tiny and disappeared into the overall pattern—until you knew what you were trying to find.

"He and Tina are going to talk with Maggie's grandsons tomorrow to see what they have to say, whether they know who this one might have belonged to."

"You know what this means?" Win looked like she was about to explode from excitement.

"It means I've come a step closer to knowing the name of the woman who gave birth to me and then left me in that alley to die." Naomi lifted the leather thong over her head, let the medicine wheel drop back inside her shirt.

"It also means that you're probably Oglala Lakota just like us. Wouldn't it be fun to find out we're long-lost cousins?"

Chaska glared at his sister, who seemed to realize what she was saying.

She grimaced. "No, that wouldn't be good at all."

"Why not?" Naomi asked.

Winona busied herself with clearing the table, leaving Chaska to answer. "Well, because you and I have… uh…."

Naomi's eyes went wide. "Oh. Do you think there's any chance—"

"No. Maggie Otter Tail wasn't related to anyone in our family." Now came the hard part. "Grandfather wants me to send a photo of you to Tina's phone. I told him—"

"A photo of me? Why?" Confusion and anger flashed in her eyes. "I don't want a photo of me going to the woman who abandoned me."

"I told him you wouldn't be comfortable with that. He says it might help him find your mother, but I think he just wants to see you for himself. He knows that you mean a lot to me."

"You told him?" This seemed to surprise her, but in a good way.

"Of course, I told him. He's important to me—and so are you."

This seemed to spur Naomi into action. "Well, if you have to send a photo to your grandfather, I can't look like this. Win, you have to help me."

What was she talking about?

"You look fine." Chaska raised his cell phone to snap a photo.

Naomi blocked him with her hands. "Please, not yet."

She stood and made her way upstairs with Winona beside her. "I need to do something with my hair and my face."

Chaska shouted after them. "He wants a photo of you, not makeup!"

Twenty minutes later, Naomi sat on the sofa in different clothes, her hair brushed to a shine and pulled into a barrette, mascara on her lashes, gloss on her lips. She looked lovely—and nervous as hell. "What do you think?"

"I think you're beautiful." Chaska held up his cell phone, saw the tension on her face. "Don't look at the camera. Look at me."

She lifted her gaze to his, some of the tension easing from her face.

He clicked. "Perfect."

"Wait! Can I see?"

He turned his phone. "See? You look amazing."

"That's good!" Winona said.

Naomi smiled. "Okay. Thanks."

Chaska sent the image in a text message to Tina. "Now I guess we wait to find out what the two of them learn tomorrow."

He hoped that, whatever the news, it would bring Naomi peace.

Chapter Eighteen

Naomi woke to the delicious feel of Chaska's lips against her nape.

He whispered against her skin. "*Hihanni waste*. Good morning."

She tried to repeat what he'd said. "Hi-hanni wash-tay."

He chuckled. "*Lila waste*—very good."

"Are you giving me a language lesson?"

"Hmm. Not a bad idea. Pay close attention. There will be a test afterward."

They lay spooned together on their sides with him behind her, his erection pressing against her bottom, one big hand resting on the curve of her hip.

He slid his hand back and forth over that curve. "*Nite*. Hip."

"Nee-tay," she repeated.

His hand moved higher, tickled her ribs, making her wiggle. "*Tucuhu*. Ribs."

"Tu-chu-hu."

His hand moved higher still, cupping and shaping her breast. "*Aze*. Breast."

"A-zay." She pressed her breast deeper into his hand, his touch kindling that now familiar ache between her thighs.

His fingers found her already puckered nipple, rolling it, flicking it. "*Azepikpe*. Breast tip."

She didn't repeat the word this time, too caught up in what he was doing to her, his lips on her throat, fingers that were strong enough to support his body weight teasing her nipples with such finesse.

His hand left her breast behind, slid down her belly to cup her. Then he slid a finger inside her. "*San*—vagina."

"*Shan.*" She opened her thighs, gave him more room.

He withdrew his finger, spread her wetness over her clit, stroking her just right, until she was going out of her mind.

"I want you inside me."

"Mmm." He stopped what he was doing long enough to put on a condom, leaving Naomi hanging.

She moaned in protest.

"Patience." He caught her right leg, brought it carefully over his thigh, opening her to him. Then he ran his cock between her labia, nudged her clit with the tip, circled the entrance to her vagina with the head. "*Ce*—penis."

"*Che.*" Her left hand was clenched in the sheets now, her hips tilted to ease his entry, her body aching for penetration, the anticipation all but unbearable.

He slid inside her with a single, slow thrust, burying himself until she could feel his testicles against her. "You are … *perfect.*"

Oh, God, it felt good.

Naomi closed her eyes, gave herself over to the sensation of him moving inside her, one slow, deep thrust after the other, his cock stretching her, filling her.

He nuzzled her ear, nipped her earlobe, his free hand returning to caress her breasts, palming their sensitive tips, every flick of a nipple sending shivers of pleasure all the way to her womb. "*Cante skuye. Lila wiyan waste. Tecíhila yelo.*"

She had no idea what he was saying, the words whispered against her skin, his big body seeming to enfold hers, the scents of sex and sage surrounding her, his rhythm slow and relentless. "*Chaska, please!*"

She wanted his hand between her thighs, knew he could push her over the brink and extinguish the fire inside her if only he would do to her clit what he was doing to her nipples. But his hand stayed where it was, and so she lay there on her side, feeling deliciously helpless, with him thrusting into her from behind … so … slowly.

In. *Oh, yes.* Out. *More.* In. *God, yes.* Out.

Oh, she couldn't take this.

Climax took her by surprise, a slow tidal wave that surged through her, rising higher and higher, drowning her in pleasure, before leaving her, breathless and panting, in Chaska's arms.

Her climax seemed to push him over the edge, his body tensing as he finished with a few deep, hard thrusts.

For a time—Naomi couldn't say how long—they lay as they were, Chaska's heart pounding against Naomi's shoulder, their breathing returning to normal.

Then he chuckled, nuzzled her hair. "Are you ready for your test?"

Chaska unlocked the door to his workshop, flipped on the light, and stood back while Naomi made her way inside. She was doing her best to be cheerful, to act like today was just another day, but Chaska knew where her mind was. She was thinking about the medicine wheel and the news she might get from Pine Ridge.

"Wow! This is nice." She sounded genuinely surprised.

"What were you expecting?"

"I don't know—cobwebs, spiders, empty potato chip bags."

"It's an engineer's workshop, not a slob's man cave."

"Oh! You have your own lathe." She moved over to look at the machine, which sat on the main work table against the back wall.

"It's actually a combination lathe, mill, and drill."

"Cool! That must have been expensive."

"That's why I drive a crappy, old pickup. I spend all my money on climbing gear and tools to make climbing gear." There were tens of thousands of dollars in tools locked in chests and cupboards and hanging from hooks on the walls.

She gave a little laugh. "I know the feeling. Other women drool over clothes, shoes, and handbags, but I daydream about tools and storage space. I don't want Manolo Blahniks. I want a fancy, new stone-setting kit or a set of wire-shaping pliers."

"I knew there was a reason I liked you."

She made her way over to the smaller workbench and picked up a bit of twisted steel. "What's this?"

"That is my latest attempt to create a better wheel-locking mechanism for our rescue litters like the one you rode in." He told her how attaching an ATV wheel to the bottom of the litters, which had been an innovation on its own, wasn't easy, especially if the victim didn't hold still or if it was very cold. "Your fingers freeze against that metal while you're trying to get the wheel locked into place. When every minute counts, it sucks to waste four or five minutes under the litter, fighting with the lock."

"You want to make it easier and faster."

"Yes, but without compromising safety." That was always the trick.

He showed her some of the other innovations he'd made, explaining what was different and how they worked—a self-belaying device that might help arrest a fall, a brake plate that accommodated several ropes, enabling one person to belay an entire vertical evac team, the original wheel lock mechanism for the rescue litters.

"You really are a genius." She set the wheel lock down. "Have you ever thought of leaving your job and just making climbing gear?"

"I have thought about that." He'd thought about it a lot. "I'm not sure I could make a living at it, and I'm afraid that turning something I enjoy into a job would take all the fun out of it. This is where I come to relax—when I'm not climbing."

"Have you patented any of your designs?"

He shook his head. "I want other rescue teams to be able to use these and to improve on them. Remember when I said that part of life is finding out what your gift is and sharing it? This and the Team is how I share it. No patents."

She reached up, put her palm against his chest. "You have a big heart, Chaska Belcourt."

He bent down to kiss her, when his pager went off, making her jump. He drew it out of his back jeans pocket, scrolled through the message.

Man set to jump off 1st Flatiron. Has a firearm.

Shit.

"A rescue?" Naomi asked.

"Yeah. Looks like some poor person has lost it."

Naomi followed him out of the workshop. "I'll come with you."

"Not this time." He locked the door, explained. "The guy is threatening to jump off the First Flatiron—and he has a firearm."

"What are you supposed to do—climb up to him and get shot?"

"I have no idea." Chaska hurried toward the house, Naomi following as fast as she could on crutches. "We've never been toned out on something like this before. Usually, we get called about suicides after the fact. Body recovery."

"How terrible."

He opened the back door for her. "You can stay in the ops room at The Cave and listen on the radio. Or maybe you'd be happier staying home or spending the afternoon with Win at the clinic. Regardless, you need to decide now."

"He's standing on the edge with a pistol in his mouth now."

Naomi sat in the ops room beside Megs, barely able to breathe, listening to a tactical channel on the radio as a man's life fell completely apart, the drama punctuated by bursts of static and long stretches of silence.

"Flatiron Command, have we made contact?"

"Negative. We're still waiting for that bullhorn. I'm not putting anyone in the line of fire here."

Megs had explained to Naomi what was going on. Naomi wouldn't have been able to understand most of it otherwise. Right now, Chaska and the other Team members were in a staging area, out of range of the man's pistol, wearing their gear plus body armor, and waiting for the green light to move in and bring the man down. But first, the man had to put down his weapon and agree to be saved.

"What happens if he jumps?"

Megs pulled up an image of the First Flatiron on her computer screen. It was a massive slab of red rock that jutted out of the mountainside. "If he jumps, we'll pick up the pieces. It's a thousand feet down, and he'd be bouncing on rock the entire way."

The thought made Naomi's stomach knot.

Long minutes ticked by, until, finally, the bullhorn arrived.

"Flatiron Command, he says his name is Lucas Graham. He says he'll shoot anyone who comes near him."

Naomi's stomach knotted. She knew that Chaska and the other Team members had been issued body armor, but that didn't cover their entire bodies, did it?

Then the radio fell silent while the hostage negotiator began speaking with the man. Every once in a while, someone gave an update over the radio, keeping everyone in the staging area informed.

"I've spent my life around men, especially young men—climbers, like Chaska. I've watched dozens upon dozens, maybe hundreds, of guys try to hook up with women, go from one girlfriend to the next. I've watched all the mating ritual bullshit. You name it, I've seen it, been the target of it. But I've never seen Belcourt with any woman—until you. He's one of the good ones. Hold onto him."

Naomi stared at her, touched that Megs, who seemed so flippant most of the time, had shared this with her. "I'll do my best."

A burst of static. "Flatiron Command, we ran that name, break."

"Go ahead."

"The suspect is a thirty-nine-year-old male. He's a combat veteran. He was recently arrested for disorderly conduct at the Denver VA. Charges were dropped."

The information was conveyed to the hostage negotiator, while the sheriff's department went back to digging, trying to find the pieces of this man's identity, the broken fragments of his soul, so that the negotiator could reach him.

Naomi waited for a break in the radio traffic to ask Megs another question. "If he puts down the gun and agrees to come down, will the Team go up at that point and bring him down?"

Megs shook her head. "If he puts the gun down, he can always pick it up. I don't want my people going in until that weapon is beyond his reach."

"Flatiron Command, we have more information for you. Break."

"Go ahead."

"The suspect's wife recently filed for divorce. He has three kids—two boys and a girl—all under age ten. His wife told us he has PTSD and was at the VA trying to get treatment when he was arrested. Apparently, he was waitlisted. The wife's name is Kaylee. The children's names are Pike, Flynn, and Harper."

Naomi's heart broke for him.

The deputy went on to spell the children's names phonetically and give them their ages, trying to arm the hostage negotiator, a woman, with information she could use.

Five minutes. Ten. Fifteen.

Another burst of static. "He's sitting down now. He is sitting down, and he has dropped the weapon."

"Flatiron Command, is that confirmed?"

"Affirmative. He has dropped the weapon over the back. Sixteen-ninety-four has retrieved it."

Naomi let out a relieved breath.

"That's Moretti." Megs got to her feet. "You hungry?"

Naomi shook her head. She couldn't eat now.

Megs disappeared into the kitchen.

"Sixteen-ninety-four. I'd like to leave my position to speak with the negotiator."

"Sixteen-ninety-four, go ahead."

"I'm a combat veteran. I've walked in his shoes. I think I can help."

Megs reappeared with a granola bar and an apple. "I hope Moretti knows what he's doing."

For the next hour, Moretti talked with the man, first via bullhorn, and then via cell phone after the man gave Moretti his number.

"Flatiron Command, he says he'll let us bring him down if we guarantee that he gets to see a doctor."

It struck Naomi as tragic that a man with PTSD, a man who'd served his country, had to threaten to kill himself and others to get immediate attention. Now, all of these people—sheriff's deputies, rangers, and the Team—were scrambling to try to save him.

Megs picked up the mike. "Flatiron Command, this is Team Ops."

"Team Ops, go ahead."

"No member of the Team is to approach the suspect without first being on belay. They should set up the anchor before anyone goes near him." Megs set down the mic, turned to Naomi. "I don't want him changing his mind and dragging one of my people over the edge with him."

Dear God! Neither did Naomi.

"Team Ops, copy that."

Time dragged by.

"Flatiron Command, the Team is in position. The anchor is ready."

"That would be Belcourt," Megs said. "That's his specialty."

Another burst of static. "Sixteen-ninety-four has reached the suspect. He's getting the climbing harness on him now."

Finally, the news they'd all been waiting for.

"They're bringing him down. They're on the way down the back rappel now. Sixteen-ninety-four has him with Sixteen-seventy-two on belay."

"That's Moretti and Chaska."

"Oh, thank goodness!" Naomi took a deep breath.

It was over.

When Chaska backed Rescue One into its bay, Naomi was waiting for him. By the time he'd opened the door and stepped out, she was there, a beautiful smile on her face. He drew her into his arms, kissed her. "Were you able to listen in?"

"I listened to the whole thing. I was so scared for all of you—and for him, too. But you all got him down."

Hawke walked up behind them. "Moretti got him down. Where is that bastard?"

Chaska glanced toward the parking lot. "He's just pulling in."

They welcomed him with cheers and high fives.

"Way to go, Moretti."

"It's a good thing you did, man."

"That took guts, bro."

Moretti wasn't having it. "Okay, all right. Everyone shut up."

Then Megs stepped out of the ops room, walked over to him, and gave him a hug. "I don't know whether to kick your ass or buy you a drink. Way to go."

She stepped back. "Let's do a sort and reload on the gear and do a quick debriefing. Moretti, I think I will buy you a drink."

Moretti shook his head. "I promised him I would look in on his wife and kids, explain to his wife what had happened, ask her maybe to wait on the divorce."

Megs gave him a motherly pat on the arm. "You are a brave man."

Chaska helped unload the rope bags and carry them to the large sinks where they'd be washed by hand and then sat through a quick debriefing with the others who had participated in this rescue. The idea was to talk about what they'd done right and what they ought to have done better. Everyone agreed that their part of this operation had gone off without a hitch.

"I've got a suggestion," Chaska said.

Megs looked up from the clipboard where she was making notes. "Out with it."

"We ought to buy two bullhorns, one for each rescue vehicle."

Moretti nodded. "Great idea."

"Yeah. Right on."

Chaska explained. "The county brought its hostage negotiating team, but they didn't have a bullhorn. We waited for more than an hour with this guy threatening to jump or shoot himself or shoot us while they had some deputy drive a bullhorn from halfway across the county. If we'd been able to get in contact with the victim sooner, things might not have escalated to the degree that they did. Who's to say we won't be in need of one ourselves one day?"

Megs nodded. "If the rest of you agree, I'll look into it."

There was general assent, and so the meeting was over.

Chaska took Naomi's hand. "Everyone's heading to Knockers. Would you like to go with them, or would you rather—"

His cell phone buzzed.

He drew it out of his pocket, saw that it was Tina. "This is Belcourt."

"Are you someplace where you can talk?"

"Hang on a second." He turned to Naomi. "I need to take this. It won't be long."

There was wariness in her eyes. "Is it your grandfather?"

"It's Tina." He walked out of the ops room and out the bay doors. "Go ahead."

"I'm standing here with Maggie Otter Tail's youngest grandson, Doug, and he has a few questions for you about the medicine wheel and this woman who wears it."

"Okay. Put him on."

As it turned out, Doug had more than a few questions, and Chaska did his best to answer them. No, he didn't know Naomi's date of birth. He only knew that she was twenty-seven. Yes, she'd been found in Martin, close to dying, with the medicine wheel tucked in her blanket. No, police had never found her mother. No, she hadn't been raised among the Lakota. Would she agree to a paternity test?

Chaska had no idea how Naomi would feel about taking a paternity test, and he wasn't about to ask her without knowing what was going on first. "Why do you ask? What is this about?"

"That medicine wheel used to belong to me."

Chapter Nineteen

The moment Chaska stepped into the ops room again, Naomi could see that something had happened. There were lines of tension on his face, his brow bent. His gaze warmed when he saw her. "Let's go home. I'll make dinner."

"Aren't we going to Knockers with the others?"

"Not tonight. That was Tina calling with news. We need to talk."

Naomi's heart beat against her breastbone, voices drowned out by the thrum of her own pulse. "Did they find her?"

"No." Chaska walked with her to his truck. "But they might have found *him*."

Him? Her *father*?

"You mean my father?"

He opened the door for her. "Let's talk at home."

He climbed into the truck, sent a text message to someone, and then drove the short distance to the house, the wait grating on Naomi's nerves.

She managed to contain herself until they were inside the front door. "What did Tina say? Who is he? How do they know he's my father?"

"No one knows anything for sure at this point." Chaska walked with her back to the kitchen, poured them each a glass of lemonade, and sat beside her at the table. "I don't have all the details, but Maggie's younger grandson, Doug Otter Tail, told my grandfather and Tina that the medicine wheel belonged to him. Tina said he recognized it right away and wanted to know how she'd gotten a photo of it."

Naomi had to know. "Did he leave me in that alley?"

She'd always thought it must have been her mother, given that she'd been a newborn, her umbilical cord uncut and still attached to the placenta.

Chaska shook his head. "I don't think so. Doug says he gave the medicine wheel to a *wasicu* girl he met twenty-eight years ago at a summer youth camp. He said they had sex a couple of times. He lost touch with her after that. He was fifteen. She was sixteen."

"How do we know he's telling the truth?"

He gave Naomi's hand a squeeze. "I guess we don't, but Tina says he's a good man. She says the people think well of him. Also, he wants to pay for a paternity test."

A paternity test?

Winona stepped through the back door. "I came as soon as I could. What's going on? Naomi, what is it?"

While Chaska told Winona about Tina's phone call, Naomi's mind reeled. A man in South Dakota whose name was Doug Otter Tail said that her medicine wheel had once belonged to him and that he'd given it to a teenage girl he'd hooked up with twenty-eight years ago at a summer youth camp.

Summer.

Naomi did a little quick math. "I was conceived in June."

Chaska and Winona stopped talking and looked over at her.

She explained. "They found me on March 12, and they say I was just a few hours old, so I've always thought that must be my birthday, though Peter never let us celebrate birthdays because that's a pagan tradition. If I was born in early March, I must have been conceived in June. That doesn't prove or disprove anything, but it fits his story."

You're babbling.

Winona got herself a glass of lemonade and joined them at the table. "Do we know what Doug looks like? Does he look like Naomi?"

Chaska drew out his cell phone, tapped it a few times, turned it so Naomi could see. "What do you think?"

Blood rushed into Naomi's head. She found herself looking at the face of a handsome man in his early forties, a man whose nose and lips and cheeks were familiar because she saw them every day in the mirror. No, she had to be imagining it.

She looked up at Chaska and Winona. "Do you think we look alike?"

Chaska handed the phone to Winona, who glanced down, then stared at Naomi through wide eyes. "You *do* look like him."

"There's more." Chaska took Naomi's hand again. "He and Old Man are on their way here. They're staying with some of Grandfather's powwow buddies in Cheyenne tonight, but they'll be here tomorrow. Tina found a lab in Denver that does legal paternity tests with a twenty-four-hour turnaround, and Doug wants to get the tests done there."

This was all happening too fast. Ten minutes ago, she'd learned for the first time that she might have found her real father, and now he was coming to meet her?

She shook her head. "I don't know about this. What if he's lying? What if he's not my father? What if…"

Okay, so she'd run out of questions for the moment.

Chaska pressed her fingers to his lips. "I know this must be overwhelming, Naomi, but there's only one way to find the answers."

Chaska couldn't imagine being in Naomi's shoes right now, wondering whether a man who was a total stranger would turn out to be her biological father. He'd told Old Man that he'd thought it was a bad idea for the two of them to drive down now, that they should do the paternity test first and wait for the results, but Doug had been dead set on meeting Naomi as soon as possible, certain that she was his daughter.

Chaska made lasagna, the fanciest meal in his limited arsenal, he and Winona doing their best to support Naomi through a difficult evening. She barely ate, all of their attempts to distract her failing until Chaska began telling her about the massacre at Wounded Knee and the later occupation of that same site. This led to a conversation about famous Oglala people.

"Crazy Horse was Oglala."

"He was?"

His quick biography of Crazy Horse led to Winona giving Naomi a history lesson about Pine Ridge and the Oglala Lakota people. "We've had two women presidents, which I think is pretty cool."

"That *is* cool." Naomi got a faraway look on her face. "Wouldn't it be strange if this is *my* history, too?"

Winona reached over and took Naomi's hand. "I think it would be wonderful."

Naomi helped Chaska with the spirit plate and then the dishes, while Winona went out to feed Shota and give him some attention. Then the three of them settled in front of the television to watch a movie.

Chaska pointed to the DVDs. "You get to pick, Naomi."

"I didn't watch movies growing up," Naomi said. "Do you know how amazing it was the first time I went to a movie theater?"

He'd grown up with it, so of course he couldn't imagine. "What did you see?"

She handed a DVD to Chaska—*Harry Potter and the Order of the Phoenix*. "I saw this. I hadn't read the books, so I had no idea what was happening. I loved it anyway. It seemed incredible to me."

"I bet it did." He bent down, loaded the DVD into the machine, trying to imagine all the things that had been new to her after she'd run away—not just movies or technology, but paying bills, holding a job, dealing with paperwork, getting a bank account, finding her way around a big city. She'd had to adjust to an entirely new way of life, and she'd done it by herself at the age of sixteen.

"I read all the Harry Potter books after that. I identified with Harry."

"Why?" Chaska wasn't the biggest Harry Potter fan, but he'd have sat there watching paint dry if it had made Naomi feel better. He clicked Play and went to sit down beside her.

She gave him a heartbreaking little smile. "He is the Boy Who Lived. I figured I was the Girl Who Lived."

That hit Chaska right in the solar plexus.

"Thank goodness for that!" Winona called from the kitchen, where she was popping corn. "And, hey, popcorn is Oglala, too."

"It is?"

Chaska chuckled. "She's joking—I think."

Naomi snuggled against him while they watched the movie, her gaze on the screen. But his gaze was on her, watching the subtle shifts in her expression as she reacted to what was happening to Harry and his friends.

You were led to her.

How could he have gotten so lucky?

Afterward, Winona dragged herself up to bed, Naomi and Chaska giving her time in the bathroom before heading upstairs themselves.

It felt right to go through the normal bedtime rituals together, sharing toothpaste, Chaska brushing her hair, the two of them undressing in the bedroom, throwing their clothes onto his sofa. Oh, yeah, he could get used to this—sharing life's most mundane moments with her. But then nothing felt mundane with Naomi.

They lay together in silence, skin against skin, her head on his chest.

"I'm afraid," she said. "I don't know why, but I am. I can't shake the feeling that everything is going to crash in on me."

"You've been through a lot, Naomi. Finding your father—that's a big deal. It's only normal that you're nervous."

"I don't know what I should hope for—that the test shows he is my father or that it shows that he isn't."

"Then why don't you just leave it to fate? Nothing you can do will change the outcome of that test."

But she couldn't let it go, not yet. "I guess if he isn't my father, I'm no worse off than I was before, right?"

"True."

"And if he is my father…"

He trailed his fingers down her spine. "If he is your father, then a whole new world opens up for you—a new family, a new community, a new way of life."

"That's part of what scares me."

He could understand that. "You're a survivor, Naomi. You survived Peter and Ruth. You ran away and survived life in a world that was completely unfamiliar to you. You fought back and survived those bastards up in the mountains. You did all of that on your own. You can handle this. I will be right there beside you—Winona, too. You're not alone. Oglala is our world."

Some of the tension left her body as he spoke. Then her hand slid down his chest and belly to stroke his cock. "How about you take my mind off all of this by giving me something else to think about?"

"Angel, I think you're onto something."

Naomi woke with a start, dreams giving way to reality in a rush of adrenaline. She sat upright, saw that it was early still, the sun not yet high enough to spill its light onto the backyard.

Chaska sat naked on the sofa, lighter in hand, about to do his morning prayer, the eagle feather sitting in its box before him. "Come."

She got out of bed and went in search of her bathrobe, not quite as free with nudity as he was.

He waited for her, made room for her to sit beside him. When she had settled, he lit the sage bundle, letting it burn for a moment before blowing out the flame, a column of white smoke filling the air with the sharp scent of burning sage. Next, he took his eagle feather out of its box, passed it over the column of smoke four times. Then he smudged himself, fanning the smoke over his head and onto his body with the feather.

She expected him to speak a few words in Lakota and then put everything away, as she'd seen him do before. Instead, he picked up the abalone shell with the sage bundle in it, turned toward her, and wafted the smoke over her.

"*Tunkasila*, Creator, I ask that you be with Naomi today, giving her strength, guiding her to the right path. She has not had an easy journey, but she is strong and courageous. Help her to know that she is not alone, and help her to find the answers she seeks. All my relations. *Mitakuye Oyasin.*"

Tears trickled down Naomi's cheeks. Not knowing what to say, she went with what she knew. "Amen."

It was the first time she'd said anything to God in ages.

Chaska put the eagle feather back in its box, kissed her, took her hand. "It's going to be okay. No matter what happens, it will be okay."

"I hope you're right. What if he doesn't like me? What if …?" There were so many "what ifs."

Chaska was quiet for a moment, his brow bent. "Some of our ceremonies can become difficult at times—Sun Dance, *hanbleceya*, *inipi*. Before my first Sun Dance, my grandfather said to me, 'When you're afraid or weary, pray for strength for the man next to you.' On the third day, the day I was supposed to pierce, I was nervous. I started praying for all of the other dancers—not for myself, but for them. When it was my time to pierce, I walked up to that tree, feeling strong, my fear gone."

She wasn't sure why he was telling her this.

He went on. "I know you're nervous, angel, but I'll bet Doug Otter Tail is nervous, too. What if you don't like *him*? What if you're angry at him? How is he going to explain all of this to his wife and children? When you feel afraid, think good thoughts for him."

Chaska's words came together for her, putting a lump in her throat.

"I hadn't thought about that." Somehow, knowing that this man would be nervous, too, made her feel less afraid. "Your grandfather must be a very special man. God, what if he doesn't like me?"

This made Chaska laugh. "He's going to love you."

They dressed and went downstairs for breakfast, where Winona was getting the guest bedroom ready. "You're sleeping together, right? Old Man can stay in here?"

Naomi's face burned.

Chaska chuckled. "Yes."

After breakfast, Winona headed off to the clinic, while Chaska drove Naomi to her appointment, where they took X-rays of her ankle, removed her stitches, and told her that everything looked fine. Dr. Renshaw examined her, gave her a boot to wear for stability, and warned her not to put weight on that leg for another month.

They made a quick trip to Food Mart after that to grab things that Chaska knew his grandfather liked to eat—Spam, Cup Noodles, and lots of Coca-Cola—and drove home again. There were no cars in the driveway, no one waiting for them.

"When do you think they'll get here?" Butterflies danced in Naomi's stomach.

"That depends on how much time Old Man spends talking with his buddies. It's only a two-hour drive from Cheyenne to Scarlet."

Naomi did her best to keep busy. She helped Chaska clean Winona's hummingbird feeders one by one and then cooked a batch of hummingbird food based on a recipe of Win's. When it had cooled, Chaska carried the pitcher of liquid out to the porch for her and gave her a plastic measuring cup to use to refill them.

But Naomi wasn't fast on her crutches, and the hummingbirds discovered the food in the measuring cup before she could pour the mixture into a feeder. They flocked to her, sipping straight from the cup. One even landed on her hand, perched there for just a moment. "Chaska, come see!"

"They like you."

"They like the sugar water."

Like bright jewels, they hovered only a foot from her face, dipping their beaks into the sugary concoction, drinking it up.

That's how Chaska's grandfather found her—standing on the porch with her crutches, holding a measuring cup, hummingbirds flitting around her.

Elderly and bent with a face that resembled a weathered, old pumpkin, he chuckled when he saw her. "*Hihanni waste.* Good morning."

Behind him walked another man—tall, with short dark hair, his face now familiar.

Doug Otter Tail.

Naomi's pulse spiked, her heart taking off.

When you feel afraid, think good thoughts for him.

Then she looked into his eyes and saw that he was nervous, too.

Chaska helped Naomi finish with the hummingbirds, taking a moment to be alone with her before joining Old Man and Doug in the kitchen. He took her hands, kissed her fingertips. "No matter what happens, I'm here. It's going to be okay."

He texted Winona, who turned the clinic over to volunteers and came home. She gave Old Man a big hug then got everyone settled with something cold to drink. They talked for a while about the drive, how hot it was in South Dakota, Grandfather's powwow friends in Cheyenne.

"How did they get so old?" Grandfather chuckled at his own joke.

Then he set his medicine bundle on the table, took out his sage and his eagle feather, a feather that had belonged to his grandfather. "We're talking about some important things today, so it's right for us to pray first."

That's how life was when your grandfather was a spiritual leader. No one did anything important without getting right with the spirit world first.

When the feather had been stowed away, Old Man looked over at Naomi. "My grandson has told me about your recent difficulty with these men in the mountains. He told me how you escaped from them. You are very courageous to have come through that as you did. I am glad to see that you are healing."

"Aho," Doug and Chaska said almost in unison.

"Thank you," Naomi said.

"Now, we would like to hear about the medicine wheel you wear."

Chaska reached under the table to hold her hand.

Naomi told them the whole story—how she'd been found by the dumpster with the medicine wheel tucked inside her blanket, how she'd been adopted by Peter and Ruth, how she hadn't known about the medicine wheel until Peter had shown it to his congregation during a sermon about the evils of heathenism, how she'd wanted nothing more than to hold it with her own hands.

Chaska could tell she was nervous by the tight grip she had on his fingers, but she spoke clearly and without hesitation or bitterness or tears.

"I found it in his room, and I took it. It was the only connection I had to the person who had given birth to me. It seemed important that I should have it, and yet I hadn't known it existed until that day. When no one was looking, I hid it beneath a floorboard in my room."

She told them how Peter suspected her of taking it and how he'd tried to beat the truth out of her with his belt. She told them how she'd taken it with her when she'd run away and how learning about it—what it meant, how it was made—had instilled in her an interest in making jewelry. "I bought a leather cord for it, and I've worn it every moment since—except for when Chaska took it to work and sent a photo of it to you."

The two men nodded, both of them considering what she'd told him.

Then Old Man turned to Doug. "You, too, have ties to this medicine wheel."

Doug nodded. "May I see it?"

Naomi lifted the cord over her head and handed it across the table to him.

He held it between his finger and thumb, running the pad of his thumb over the quillwork. "Granny Otter Tail gave this to me at my naming ceremony. She made these for all of her grandchildren, always with the two little Xs on the back, right here."

Doug told them how he'd gotten a scholarship to a summer youth camp and how he'd met a girl there, a *wasicu* girl, who caught his eye. "We became friends. She had blond hair and bright blue eyes. I'd never met anyone like her before. We became close. She was my first, and I was hers. I wanted to keep in touch with her. She said she wanted to stay in touch, too. We traded phone numbers, and I gave her this."

He told them how he'd tried to get in touch with her in the weeks that followed, only to have her mother call him and tell him to leave her daughter alone. "She told me that no daughter of hers was going to date an Indian boy."

He handed the medicine wheel back to Naomi. "That's the last I saw of that medicine wheel until Tina showed me the photo on her cell phone. If I got that girl pregnant, no one told me. If I had known, if she had only told me …" Doug's voice broke. He swallowed, took a breath. "I would never have left any child of mine in an alley to die, not even when I was fifteen."

Chapter Twenty

They talked for the rest of the morning. Naomi answered Doug's questions about her life as best she could, while Winona put lunch together.

"Ruth taught us all at home. As a girl, I was taught sewing, canning, cooking, and some basic math for recipes. She also taught us to read because we needed to be able to read the Bible. I didn't graduate from high school. I had to get my GED later."

It was mortifying to admit all of this when the man she loved, the man who sat beside her holding her hand, was a rocket scientist and a genius.

Chaska gave her hand another squeeze, as if sensing her embarrassment.

"Degrees don't make a person intelligent." Grandpa hadn't said much until now. "A degree is a piece of paper. I don't have any degrees, but people still call me wise."

"She taught you some good skills," Doug said, "but they're not enough in today's world. These are the people the state thought fit to raise you? It's cruel to withhold education from a child."

Naomi didn't know what to say. "From the outside, they look like the perfect, loving family—eight kids of their own, a preacher and his stay-at-home wife, a beautiful farm. I don't think anyone looked beyond that."

Winona put lunch on the table—egg salad sandwiches and apple slices—and they ate, Grandpa Belcourt making a spirit plate. Over the meal, they agreed that Naomi and Doug should get the paternity test. It was the only way to answer the biggest question: Was Doug Naomi's father?

After lunch, they climbed into Doug's SUV and drove down to Denver to a lab that did DNA tests, including legal paternity tests. The whole thing felt surreal to Naomi, like she was in a movie or living someone else's life. She'd left South Dakota ten days ago wanting to relax, and now she was hobbling along on crutches with her lover on one side and a guy who might be her father on the other.

Chaska held the door for Naomi, staying close to her, as he'd promised he'd do.

Doug asked a lot of questions of the people at the front desk. "Are the results admissible in court? Can they be used as a basis for tribal enrollment?"

"He's an attorney," Chaska whispered in Naomi's ear.

She hadn't known that. "Tribal enrollment?"

"If he's your father, you're legally Oglala Lakota and able to enroll."

"Oh. I hadn't thought about that." Naomi couldn't think that far ahead, especially now that she'd met Doug.

There was so much she didn't know about him, this man who might be her father, but she liked him. More than that, she believed what he'd told her—that the medicine wheel had once been his and that he would never have left her in that alley. If it turned out now that he wasn't her father…

After the young woman at the desk had reassured them that the results would be legal for tribal enrollment, they were brought back to fill out paperwork.

Mother: Unknown.

Child: Naomi Archer

Alleged Father: Doug Otter Tail

A tech, a young man, came and read through the paperwork.

"You don't know your mother. That's a first. How does that happen?"

Naomi found the question tactless but answered, if for no other reason than to show him how rude he'd been. "I was abandoned as a newborn in an alley and almost died. I was adopted. They never found my mother."

The tech looked shocked and then embarrassed. "Oh. Sorry."

His gaze darted to Doug, and he looked like he was going to ask another question, but he didn't. He opened two sterile kits and swabbed the insides of their cheeks with what looked like little mascara brushes, explaining that the results would be available in about twenty-four hours and would be emailed to them.

"If you're not her father, the result will say that you're excluded and show a zero percent probability of paternity. If you are her father, it will say that you cannot be excluded as her father and that there is a 99.99 percent probability of paternity."

"Why not a hundred percent?" Doug asked.

The lab tech gave an explanation, which Winona translated for her grandfather, but Naomi was too tense to care.

Twenty minutes later, they were back in the car.

"So now we wait," Doug's gaze sought Naomi's.

It was going to be a long twenty-four hours for him, too.

When they got back to Scarlet, Winona took Grandfather and Doug back to say hello to Shota, then shown them around her clinic. Old Man had seen it all before, but he held a great deal of respect in his heart for the four-legged and winged ones. Chaska knew that Winona's work was a source of great pride for him.

Chaska had just a little while alone with Naomi, who seemed to be holding up well. They sat together on the front porch, watching the hummingbirds flit from feeder to feeder. "What do you think?"

"I adore your grandfather. He wants me to call him Grandfather, too."

"That's how it is back home," Chaska told her. "Young people often call elders Grandmother and Grandfather or Uncle and Auntie, even when they're not related."

"Oh." She looked disappointed. "I thought he was saying … Never mind."

"What? Tell me."

"I thought he was saying he thought of me as family."

Chaska smiled at her confusion. "That *is* what he means. Our family is more than our parents and brothers and sisters. It's our cousins—*so* many cousins—and our aunties and uncles and the elders in our community. It's our heroes and teachers. It's all the people who make our lives good and strong. He's bringing you into that circle. Think of it as him taking you under his wing."

She smiled. "I like that."

"What about Doug?"

"He seems like a good person. He's been very kind to me. As for the rest—I can't get my hopes up. If he's not my father…"

He drew her closer, kissed her hair. "If he's not your father, then we'll keep searching for answers, starting with the woman he gifted with that medicine wheel."

When Winona got home with Old Man and Doug, it was time to make dinner. Chaska put himself in charge of grilling the meat and left figuring out the rest of it to his sister. He fired up the grill and put on the steaks, his gaze on Naomi, who sat on the porch next to Doug, showing him her photographs and sketches.

"Your Naomi is quite the artist," said Old Man in Lakota, coming up from behind him. "I saw that owl she drew. It looks just like the real one. Have you seen those pictures she took of hummingbirds? It's like she froze them in the air. I did not know they had so many colors. They move too fast for me to see with these old eyes."

"I have seen those photos." Chaska brushed marinade over the steaks then set ears of corn Winona had given him to roast in the back. "I was with her when she took them."

"I want to hear from you what happened that morning when you met her. Is what your sister tells me true? Did you dare Creator to bring a woman to you?"

Thanks, Winona.

He would get back at her one day.

"Not exactly." Chaska told him how they'd been out for a hike with Shota and how Winona had been bugging him about getting together with someone. "I told her I would wait until the right woman came along."

Old Man nodded. "Sensible."

Yeah, well he wasn't going to like this next part.

"Then I said that Creator could bring her into my life at any time."

"How is that respectful—to ask something of Creator when you and I know you were just running your mouth?"

Chaska ignored that. "A moment later, Shota took off running through the forest. When we found him, he was sitting beside Naomi, who was badly hurt."

Old Man gave a nod. "That's what Winona told me. She believes Creator answered your foolish jest and led you to Naomi."

"I didn't believe that at first—or I didn't want to believe it. I haven't believed much of anything for a long time. But now, with all that has happened, I can't see it any other way. She doesn't know any of this. I haven't told her yet."

Naomi laughed at something Doug said, the two of them sitting in lawn chairs on the patio. The resemblance between them strongest when they were both smiling. Could they see it?

"So, when is the wedding? Will it be a Lakota ceremony? I hope so. That would make this old man happy."

Chaska rolled his eyes. "You're worse than Winona. We haven't talked about getting married yet. She and I haven't even known each other for two weeks. She's had so much going on, so many things to cope with. Ten days ago, she was in the hospital. If she and I are meant to be together, everything will work out in time."

Grandfather looked at him through eyes that seemed ancient, his wrinkled face splitting in a big grin. "Maybe you're not so foolish after all."

Old Man walked away chuckling to himself. "Hey, you got horseshoes? Let's play some horseshoes."

"This is Star Tall Grass, my wife. We met in law school and got married the next year. She is Miniconjou Lakota from the Cheyenne River Reservation."

Naomi looked at the photograph of a smiling woman on Doug's laptop screen. She had a pretty face and shoulder-length dark hair, her gaze soft as she looked toward the camera. "She's lovely."

"I guess it's true that opposites attract because she was much more traditional than I was. I didn't care about all the Indian stuff. I just wanted to be like everyone else. But she turned me around, showed me how special it was just to be Lakota."

And then Naomi had to ask. "Did you tell her—about me, I mean?"

"Oh, yes. It was a shock for both of us. But don't worry—she's not angry with me for something that happened a decade before she met me. She certainly won't hold it against you. She was upset to hear that you'd been abandoned."

The house was quiet. Winona and Grandpa had gone to bed, while Chaska had gone to his office to work, giving Naomi and Doug time alone together. Naomi had already showed him her website and told him about her plans one day for a jewelry store. He had seemed impressed and had ordered a pair of earrings for his wife, insisting that he pay for them. Now, he was sharing his family with her.

"This is my oldest son, Mato, who is thirteen. His name means 'bear.'"

The boy in the image wore a football jersey and held a football as if he were about to throw a pass.

"Star and I have our Indian names, but our given names—the names on our birth certificates—aren't Lakota. She insisted on giving our kids Lakota names."

"Mato is big like a bear. I take it he likes football?"

"Oh, yes." Doug chuckled. "This is my oldest daughter, Chumani. That means 'dewdrop.' She's eleven and has started to learn about beadwork. She wants to be a singer when she grows up."

"She looks just like her mother."

"Chayton is eight. His name means 'falcon.'"

"He's adorable."

"Yeah? Well, his mother spoils him. This is our youngest, Kimímila. She's five. Her name means 'butterfly.'"

Naomi stared at the little girl. "She looks like…"

"She looks like *you*." Doug looked at the image for a moment, then met Naomi's gaze. "That's what Star said when she saw that picture of you. 'She looks just like Kimímila—apart from her eyes.'"

Naomi had to ask. "How could I have blue eyes? Brown eyes are dominant. Even if my mother had blue eyes, I should have brown eyes."

Doug chuckled. "We Otter Tails have done a fair amount of mixing it up, if you know what I mean. My grandfather—old Maggie's husband—was supposedly mixed, and my mother was half Irish. There are some interesting recessive genes in this pool."

Naomi found hope in his answer, but the very act of hoping brought her worry to the surface again. "If it turns out that you're not… that you're not my father, I just want you to know how grateful I am that you took the time to come up here. It means more than you could ever know that you took this seriously, that you care."

"How could I not care? A young woman with unknown parents comes forward with the medicine wheel my grandma made for me—there are a lot of questions there that demand answers. We're going to find them, Naomi. If I'm not your father, we're going to keep searching—together—until we have the answers you need to find peace. I'm not going to disappear from your life. That medicine wheel you wear—that's an unshakable bond between us, no matter what our DNA says."

Naomi drew the medicine wheel out. "I suppose this belongs to you."

"No!" He held up his hands, palms facing her in a gesture of refusal. "It's yours. It's your birthright. I gave up any claim I had twenty-eight years ago when I gifted it to a young woman I thought I loved."

She dropped it back inside her shirt again. "Thank you."

They spoke late into the night, until after Chaska, too, had gone to bed, Shota's plaintive howls drifting in through the open kitchen windows.

"Time for me to get to bed." Doug stood. "Can you make it upstairs on those crutches alone?"

"I'll be fine. Thanks for a good evening."

"Thank you, Naomi."

She climbed the stairs, undressed, and slipped into bed beside Chaska, who woke and took her into his arms. "I feel like the whole world is holding its breath."

He kissed her. "Sleep, angel."

Eventually, she did.

Chaska stayed in bed, watching Naomi sleep, not wanting to wake her. Today was going to be a long day for her, and the longer she slept, the better. It was almost eight when she finally stirred.

He kissed her forehead. "Hey."

She stretched, smiled—then sat bolt upright. "What time is it?"

"Relax. It's almost eight."

"We left the lab yesterday at about two, so that means the results ought to arrive in my email at around two this afternoon."

Yes, it was going to be a long day.

She joined him for his morning prayer, learning to say *Mitakuye Oyasin* instead of *Amen.* Not that he objected to her saying the latter, but she'd asked.

"It means 'All my relations' or 'All my relatives.' Maybe a better translation would be 'We are all related.' It reminds us that we are related to all life on this planet, from the birds to the animals to blades of grass."

Okay, so his grandfather could probably explain that better than he had, but she seemed to understand.

She showered while he went down to find Winona on her way out the door to work and Old Man sitting with Doug at the table, arguing good-naturedly about tribal politics over scrambled eggs, bacon, and strong coffee. They looked up when he entered. "Good morning."

He poured himself a cup of coffee. "Did you two sleep well?"

"Can't complain," Doug said.

"I got this arthritis in my knees," Grandfather said. "It keeps me awake."

This led to a discussion of the travails of growing older, which thankfully came to an end when Naomi appeared. She wore the sundress she'd worn the first day she'd come to stay with them, her dark hair damp.

"*Hihanni waste*," she said.

Old Man chuckled, clearly pleased. "We'll make a real Lakota of you yet."

Chaska set a plate of food on the table for her, poured her a cup of coffee. "The locals are holding a fundraiser for Naomi tonight at Knockers, the local brew pub."

"A fundraiser?" Doug asked.

Chaska explained how the attack by the two escaped cons had left Naomi with medical bills, car repair bills, and other problems. "The state of Colorado will cover most of her medical bills out of a victim's compensation fund, and Frank, the guy who owns the local garage, is donating his time to repair her car, while some of us pay for parts. But there will still be expenses. No one in Scarlet wants to see Naomi pay a dime for what happened to her."

Old Man nodded. "These are good people in this town."

Doug had a torn expression on his face, as if he wanted to say something he knew he probably shouldn't. "I'm happy to hear it. I hope we're invited."

Naomi looked up from her smartphone, where she'd been checking her email. "Of course, you can come. I would love to have you there."

After breakfast, she asked Chaska to help her set up her tools and her PMC stuff, including the little kiln, or silver pot. "I have something I want to make for your grandfather and Doug."

He thought this was a great idea, in no small part because it would take her mind off the test results. Soon she was busy cutting and sculpting something from sheets of PMC, while Old Man and Doug watched and asked an annoying number of questions.

Chaska decided to get a jump on the weekend by mowing the lawn. By the time he'd finished, Naomi's work had begun to take recognizable shape.

She held out the pieces in her palm to show him—two small eagle feathers and two small medicine wheels, each with a little hole in it and each featuring tiny details carved into the surface. "Now I fire them."

Chaska helped her light the silver pot and spotted the third aspen leaf she'd made that night when she'd made Winona's earrings. He handed it to his grandfather. "Naomi made this."

"That looks like someone took an aspen leaf and turned it into silver."

"In a way, that's what I did." She explained how she'd made it using PMC paste and a real aspen leaf.

When the pieces were done firing, she asked Chaska to help her remove them from the silver pot. He carried them inside for her and set them on the table, getting her a bowl of water. He'd missed watching her work that night. He'd been in his office trying to avoid her, as if being in another room could stop him from falling in love with her.

Old Man was right. He *was* foolish.

She took a little brush and scrubbed each piece, the glint of silver emerging. She held out the first finished feather. "See?"

"That's fantastic. How did you get that detail?" Doug asked.

"Now I seen everything," Old Man said.

She scrubbed the other pieces, then put what she called jump rings through the holes at the center of the medicine wheels to attach the feathers. When she was done, she handed one to Old Man, who chuckled, and one to Doug. "You gave me a medicine wheel. I'm giving you one back."

Doug nodded. "Thank you, Naomi. Good trade."

Chaska saw her reach for her cell phone again. It wasn't yet noon, so there was no chance that—

Her head jerked up, her eyes wide. "The results. They're here."

Chapter Twenty-One

Naomi looked up at Chaska and then Doug.

Doug gave her a nod. "Go head. Open the email."

Hands shaking, Naomi tapped her screen. The email itself said nothing, but there was an attachment. She clicked on the attachment, which took a moment to download. The text was small, so she had to enlarge the document, her pulse racing as she read it, her gaze moving over the page, searching for the relevant part. Then she found it—the news she'd been waiting for.

Oh, God!

Her eyes filled with tears, relief and joy rushing through her with such force that her world seemed to tilt on its axis.

Chaska was there, holding her, trying to comfort her. "It's okay, Naomi. We'll keep looking."

But he didn't understand.

She drew back, laughing through her tears. "Look."

She handed him her cell phone, then sought Doug's gaze. It was right that he be the first to know. "You're my father."

Doug's eyes shut, and his head fell back. He muttered something in Lakota. "*Pilamayayelo*."

Chaska read through the email, then thrust one fist into the air and let out a whoop, the excitement on his face bringing tears to Naomi's eyes again. He sent off a quick text message—probably to Win.

Yes, she should be here, too.

Then Chaska read the document aloud. "The alleged father, Doug Otter Tail, *cannot* be excluded as the father of Naomi Archer. Based on the genetic testing results, the probability of paternity is 99.99 percent!"

He drew her into his embrace again.

Naomi came completely apart this time, sobbing against his shoulder, the fear and grief and loneliness and pain of the past twenty-seven years spilling out of her.

She had a father. She had a *father.* And he *wanted* her.

She could hear Grandpa Belcourt singing in Lakota somewhere nearby, smelled burning sage, and knew that he was praying.

Then the back door flew open with such force that it hit the wall, and Winona rushed in, wearing green scrubs. "You got the results?"

Naomi fought to get the words out, her throat tight. "He's my dad."

Chaska made way for his sister, who hugged Naomi tight, tears spilling down her cheeks, too, a smile on her face. "I am so happy for all of us. It's like finding out you and I are sisters or something."

Chaska handed Naomi and Winona tissues.

Naomi wiped her eyes, tried to pull herself together. "I want to dance and sing and run down the street, screaming, 'I have a dad!'"

"You've got more than a dad." Doug made his way around the table. "You've got a family. You've got a stepmom and two little brothers and two little sisters. You've got … I don't know how many cousins. You've got aunties and uncles. You have a *people* now. You are part of the Oglala Lakota nation."

He let out a whoop at this, and so did Chaska.

Chaska made room for Doug, who knelt down in front of Naomi where she sat, opening his arms to her, giving her a choice. "Welcome to the family, daughter."

She sank into him, his arms enfolding her. How strange and wonderful it was—this first embrace from her father. Her *father.*

Would she ever get used to that?

He pulled away, wiped the tears from her cheeks—and his own. "I am so, so sorry. Forgive me. If I had known… You will never be out in the cold again."

Grandpa Belcourt was still singing.

Then Doug got to his feet, cleared his throat. "If you all will excuse me, I need to call my wife. Star has been waiting, too."

Winona decided they should go for ice cream to celebrate, and there was really no changing his sister's mind once she got an idea in her head.

Chaska pinned her with his gaze. "You just want ice cream."

"Naomi wants ice cream, too, don't you, Naomi? Tell my brother you want ice cream, too."

Naomi looked from Winona to Chaska, laughing. "I could go for ice cream."

"Okay, fine."

And so, they were off.

Chaska locked the door behind Doug, who was the last one out—and who didn't look as happy as he had a while ago. "Is everything okay?"

"Oh, yes. Star was relieved to hear the news. We're going to wait to tell the kids until I get home. This will be as good a time as any to give the older two some lessons about birds and bees and what might happen if you're not careful."

Chaska walked with Doug to his SUV, where the others were waiting. He sensed something was wrong, but he didn't want to pry.

Doug switched to Lakota. "I keep thinking about how Naomi was found—a little baby alone, freezing to death. That is partly *my* fault. I left that girl alone with the consequences of what we'd done. I believed I loved her, but I left her to face having a baby without me. I'm not making excuses for her. What she did was terrible and wrong. But if I had ignored her mother and stayed in her life somehow, maybe it would have been different. I hate to think of what Naomi has been through. I might have been able to prevent all of that. I missed twenty-seven years of her life."

There was no disputing what Doug said. Every word was the truth.

"For what it's worth, I don't think Naomi holds any of that against you."

"Since I'm her father, I guess it's high time I asked what your intentions are toward her."

Chaska stammered, taken by surprise. "Well, I—"

Doug chuckled. "Got you."

Chaska glared at him. "Nice."

They piled into the SUV, passing Bear in the roundabout and parking down the street from the ice cream shop. Chaska found a table for them and left Naomi there so she wouldn't have to stand in line. He thought Old Man might rather sit, too, given his knees, but he insisted on going with Chaska.

"I got to see what flavors they have."

Chaska got double chocolate chip for himself and butter pecan for Naomi.

Old Man ordered three scoops—all different flavors—and seemed as excited as a five-year-old. "I haven't had mint chocolate chip since that last powwow in California."

Doug insisted on paying for everyone. "You saved Naomi's life. Without you…"

He didn't finish. Everyone understood.

If Shota hadn't led them to her, she most likely would have died, and Doug would never have known he'd had another daughter.

They sat together in the shade enjoying their cones, Doug and Winona going back and forth, talking about Naomi's future.

"You can enroll as an Oglala now," Doug said. "My wife can't wait to meet you. "I'm sure the kids will be excited, too, once we explain."

"There are lots of places on Oglala where you can study the Lakota language," Winona added.

Doug nodded. "You can use your GED to enroll at Oglala Oyate College. I think they offer a fine arts degree."

Tribal enrollment. A new family. Language classes. An arts degree.

Chaska had a few ideas about Naomi's future, too, specifically his prominent place in it, but he saw the bemused expression on her face. "This must be overwhelming."

"A little—but in a good way." She looked up at Chaska through those sweet blue eyes. "Two weeks ago, I didn't know any of you. Now, we're enjoying ice cream and talking about a future I never thought I could have."

"That's a lot to process." Doug wiped his fingers on his napkin, his cone devoured. "I don't you to feel pressured."

Then Old Man piped up, ice cream on the tip of his nose. "No person can tell another what to do. Whatever you decide, Tanagila, we will be right beside you."

Naomi stared at him. "Did you just call me 'hummingbird'?"

"You remember." Chaska was impressed. He nudged her leg with his knee under the table. "I should test your vocabulary later."

Naomi's smile told him that this was one idea for her future that she liked.

Naomi stood in front of the bathroom mirror, brushing her hair. She still wore the sundress Ellie and the other nurses had given her, but she'd put on mascara, lip gloss, and a touch of bronzer. "Should I change into something else? I don't think I have anything dressier than this."

Chaska walked into the bathroom, rested his hands on her hips. "You look fine. This is Scarlet. You're going to a fundraiser at Knockers. Really, you're beautiful in anything, so just wear what makes you comfortable. You can go nude if you want. I like you that way, too."

"Right." She met his gaze in the mirror. "Are they going to expect me to say anything, give a speech?"

He shook his head. "No, I don't think so. Joe might say a few words, but he's not going to expect that from you. If you want to say something or thank everyone, I'm sure he'd be good with that, too."

"I hadn't thought about that." She'd never talked in front of a crowd before, and the idea filled her stomach with butterflies.

Chaska ducked down, kissed the side of her throat. "You don't have to do or say anything tonight. Just be yourself."

Winona appeared outside the bathroom door, wearing a cotton Aztec print skirt with a red tank top. "Can I squeeze in?"

Chaska stepped out to make room for her. "I wanted to let you know that I told Joe and Rain what happened today. They knew the basics of your story, and I wanted to fill them in so that they would understand why you suddenly have a father."

That made sense to Naomi. "Thanks."

Winona looked her brother up and down. "Is *that* what you're wearing?"

He looked down at his T-shirt and climbing pants. "What? We're just going to Knockers. The wait staff doesn't even dress up."

"Yeah, but it's Naomi's fundraiser."

Naomi and Chaska left Winona in the bathroom and made their way downstairs to find both Grandpa Belcourt and Doug—her *father*—waiting for them. Doug had changed from jeans and a shirt to black slacks and a blue dress shirt with a bolo tie that had a silver buffalo skull on it. Grandpa Belcourt was wearing new jeans and a polo shirt, a small medicine wheel with an eagle feather tied into his hair in back.

"Don't you both look nice?"

"This is the first time I'm going out in public with my new daughter. I don't want to disappoint her," Doug said.

Naomi's heart melted at those words.

Grandpa looked at Chaska, frowned. "You look like we're goin' to the drive-through pizzeria in White River."

Naomi didn't know exactly what this meant, but clearly, Grandpa wasn't happy.

"What? This is Scarlet." Chaska put his hands on his hips, looked from his Grandfather to Winona, who was bouncing down the stairs. "Okay, fine. I'll change."

He turned and took the stairs two at a time.

They waited for him on the front porch, watching the hummingbirds, Naomi naming those she could identify. "That's a broad-tailed hummingbird. That's a rufous female, I think. The females aren't brightly colored like the males. That's a …"

Chaska stepped outside again, and Naomi's mouth went dry.

He had changed into a black dress shirt and gray slacks, a black belt around his narrow waist. His dark hair hung freely down his back, a medicine wheel with a small feather tied near his temple. "Is this better?"

"Look at Naomi's face," Win said, laughing.

Aware that she was staring, Naomi snapped her mouth shut. "You look ... Wow."

Once again, they piled into Doug's SUV with Chaska driving since he knew the way. They arrived at Knockers a few minutes later to find the parking lot full to overflowing. Chaska dropped Naomi and the others off near the front door and drove off in search of a parking spot.

"I haven't seen so many cars here since the fundraiser for the victims of the school bus crash." Winona said.

People crowded the entryway, waiting for tables, their voices competing with music from the stage, making it difficult to hear. Naomi did her best to get through, her crutches once again making it awkward.

"What kind of music is that?" Doug shouted.

"That's mountain zydeco," Winona shouted back. "That's the Timberline Mudbugs. They're pretty popular around here."

Rain found them and gave Naomi a gentle hug. "Here's the guest of honor. Chaska told us your wonderful news. I am so happy for you, Naomi. Congratulations." She turned to Doug. "You must be the proud father."

"Yes." Doug's gaze rested gently on Naomi. "Yes, I am."

"I'm Rain, the general manager. I saved a spot for you near the Team's table. Follow me."

Chaska found Naomi and the others in the back next to the Team. Pretty much everyone was there, except for Conrad, of course. Even Gabe Rossiter was there with his Navajo wife, Kat. He was sitting with … Zach McBride? McBride had also brought a woman.

"Aren't you pretty?" Herrera teased.

Hawke piled on. "You *do* clean up awful nice, Belcourt."

"Oh, my gentle Jesus." Meg stared at him. "Ahearn, I lied when I said you were the most handsome man I'd ever met."

Ahearn grinned. "You never said that."

"That must be because it isn't true."

Laughter.

Chaska had had enough. "Okay. All right. Can you all just give it a rest?"

He introduced his grandfather and Doug to his fellow Team members, then told them that Doug was Naomi's father. That caused some confusion for Hawke and Taylor. He'd told both of them on the day of Naomi's rescue that she didn't have a family. Well, he'd have time to explain later.

"These are the people who helped save Naomi's life?" Doug went around to each person and shook his or her hand, thanking them.

Chaska had to give Doug credit. Fate had dropped one hell of a surprise on his doorstep two short days ago, and he'd met the challenge with honesty, decency, and courage. If that wasn't a test of a man's character, Chaska didn't know what was.

Their server came and took their orders, and then the fun began.

Sasha was the first to hit the wall, the expression on Old Man's face as he watched her climb priceless. "She's like a spider. Can you do this, Chaska?"

"You bet I can."

Naomi leaned close, whispered in his ear. "Go show off for him and for me. You know I love to watch you climb."

Chaska traded his shoes for an extra pair of climbing shoes that Herrera had brought with him and then worked himself into the rotation, Team members taking turns, egging each other on, going for speed, practicing riskier moves, cheering and jeering for one another. Rossiter and McBride joined in the action, too. Chaska managed to get in a few laps on a 5.11c route before their food arrived.

Out of breath, he walked back to the table to find Old Man watching him and chuckling to himself, pride unmistakable on his face. "Now I know why you have such big muscles."

"Such big muscles," Naomi whispered. She took a quick sip of her soda through her straw to hide her smile, but there was no mistaking the heat in her eyes.

They'd just started to eat when Rain walked up and bent down beside Naomi. "Joe is about to say a few words, and he wanted to know if there was anything you'd like to say. Don't feel obligated. It's entirely up to you."

Chaska saw indecision and nervousness in Naomi's eyes, but when she answered Rain, there was nothing but determination on her face.

"I would like to say something. Thank you."

"I'll let Joe know." Rain hurried away.

Chaska helped Naomi get to her feet. "I'll walk up with you."

Naomi couldn't believe she was going to do this. She'd never spoken in front of people before. But if they could take their time and their money to help her, then she could find the courage to thank them.

She made her way toward the stage, Chaska beside her, weaving through the tables. They passed Bear, who was most of his way through a small deep-dish pizza, and then Chief Deputy US Marshal McBride, who was on his way back from the dance floor with a woman he introduced as his wife, Natalie.

"Just call me Zach," he said when Naomi stumbled over his full title.

The dance floor was teeming with couples, their bodies moving to a distinctly Creole sound.

Chaska spoke into her ear so she could hear. "When you're able to walk again, you and I have a dancing date."

"Okay," she said, not really able to think about that now.

Joe was waiting for her, still in his bartender apron, his long hair in a bun. "Hey, Naomi. I hope you're having a good time."

"I am." She tried not to act like she was terrified. "Thank you—and thank you for this. It's amazing to me that so many people want to help."

The song came to an end, applause cutting off whatever Joe had been about to say in response. He had to wait for it to die down to continue. "I'll go up and say a few words, and then you can join me."

"Okay." Naomi drew a deep breath, her heartbeat picking up.

Chaska gave her hand a squeeze. "You're the woman who beats up bad guys, remember? I don't know anyone braver than you. You can do this."

When he put it like that…

She'd done a lot of riskier things in her life. She could do this.

Joe walked up onto the stage, said hello to the guys in the band, then stepped up to the microphone. The pub fell quiet—apart from a shout from the back corner.

"Oh, Moretti! You nailed it, man." That was Herrera.

"Hey, guys, button it." That was Megs.

Laughter.

"I want to thank everyone for being here tonight. It's been almost two weeks since a young woman who was camping in the mountains near here was attacked by a couple of escaped cons. Naomi Archer came to Colorado for a vacation and instead had to fight for her life. It's not right that a victim of violence should have to pay medical bills that are the result of that violence. That's what tonight is all about. A portion of this evening's proceeds is going to help Naomi get on her feet again—no pun intended. There's also a big jar on the bar for anyone who wants to drop in a few extra bucks. Any leftover funds will go to benefit the Team, and we all know what a worthy cause that is. And now I think Naomi would like to say a few words."

People cheered.

Naomi's throat grew tight.

You can't cry.

Chaska gave her hand another squeeze, helped her up the stairs. "You'll do great. We're all with you—me, Win, your father.

Your father.

Oh, great! If any two words in the world were capable of making her cry, it was those two. Still, some of her fear lifted, a sense of calm settling in its place. She made her way over to Joe, who angled the microphone down for her. She took a deep breath, looked over at Chaska one last time, then spoke.

"My vacation here in Colorado didn't go the way I thought it would, but thanks to the people of Scarlet Springs, it hasn't been a disaster, either. From the Team members who carried me out of that ravine, to the doctors and nurses who treated me and gave me clothes to wear, to someone named Frank who I don't even know who is fixing my car, everyone has been incredibly kind. I've never been anyplace quite like Scarlet."

This brought laughter, which made Naomi laugh, too.

"All I really wanted to say was thank you. Thank you, Joe and Rain. Thanks to Megs and the Team. Thanks to Dr. O'Brien, Dr. Thorne, Dr. Renshaw, and Ellie Meeks and the other nurses. Thanks to Zach McBride and all the law enforcement officers who helped catch the bad guys. Thanks to Frank, whoever you are."

A thin man with a receding hairline and a wispy gray ponytail stood and waved at her, still wearing his work coveralls. "That's me, honey, and you're welcome! I'll have your Honda ready to go by Monday."

More laughter.

Then Naomi's gaze met Chaska's, her throat growing tight again. "Most of all, I want to thank Chaska and Winona Belcourt for finding me and saving my life and giving me a place to recover. There's nothing I can do to repay you—any of you."

People cheered and applauded.

Naomi stepped back from the microphone and made her way back to Chaska, who helped her down the stairs. "How did I do?"

"You were fantastic." He pressed a kiss to her temple. "I think you made Frank's day—heck, his entire year."

The band started playing again, making it impossible to talk. They'd just passed the dance floor when someone stepped into their path.

It took Naomi a moment to recognize him, her heart giving a hard knock when she did. "Peter."

Chapter Twenty-Two

Peter's hair was mostly gray now, his face thinner, sharper, crueler than Naomi remembered. He looked her up and down, self-righteous disgust on his face, his attire plain. It was all for show—the black pants, the white shirt, the black suspenders. "Hello, Tabitha."

The sight of him and the sound of his voice awoke the terrified child inside her, ice taking over her body. She raised her chin, determined to stand up for herself, fear clotting her throat. "That's not … That's not my name."

He ignored her. "I am sorry to find you in a place like this."

"Who the hell are you?" Chaska took a step toward him, standing at an angle, clearly ready to step between her and this man who had once terrified her.

"My name is Peter Emmanuel. I'm Tabitha's adoptive father. I will thank you to keep your coarse language to yourself."

"If you don't like how I talk, maybe you should get out of here. Keep this up, *kola*, and I'm bound to say other things you don't like." The warning note in Chaska's voice was unmistakable.

Ruth appeared beside Peter, bitterness lining her round face, her graying hair pulled back to hang down to her hips. "God, in his mercy, has led us to you. One of our parishioners saw your face on the news, Tabitha, and told us what happened. We came to bring you back into the fold, saw posters for this event, and here you are. You shamed us, running away like you did. This attack on you was God's judgment, but you still have time to repent."

Chaska glared at them. "Naomi, you don't have to listen to this. These people have no authority over you."

"I come with the authority of God." Peter was using his sermon voice now. "I speak in His holy name."

All at once, it seemed so absurd and sickening—this little man with his threats and self-righteousness.

Fear became rage. "You are so full of shit. Was it holy when you married underage girls to old men? Was it holy when you beat me with a belt for dropping eggs or asking questions or for no reason at all? Is it holy when you control every element of people's lives?"

She realized she was shouting, but she didn't care. "There is nothing holy about you, and there never was!"

Peter held up his Bible. "If any man has a stubborn and rebellious son who will not obey his father or his mother, and when they chastise him, he will not even listen to them, then his father and mother shall seize him—"

"Get away from my daughter!" Doug stood there now, Win beside him. "We ought to file charges—for parental neglect, child abuse…"

"How about disturbing the peace and harassment?" McBride said, his marshal's badge showing on his jacket.

Ruth looked uncertainly up at her husband, clearly afraid now.

Naomi met Peter's gaze straight on. "Get out, and don't come near me again."

"The eye that mocks a father and scorns to obey a mother will be picked out by the ravens of the valley and eaten by the vultures." Peter was quoting Scripture again. He opened his mouth to continue, but was cut off.

"Beware of false prophets, who come to you in sheep's clothing but inwardly are ravenous wolves!" Bear's booming voice filled the pub. He towered over Peter, glaring down at him. "By their fruits you will know them!"

Peter took a step backward, fear on his face.

Up on stage, the band stopped playing.

And then Rain was there. "What's going on? Who are you people?"

Peter and Ruth looked at her, saw her dreadlocks and tattoos, the expressions on their faces turning to contempt.

"This is a den of harlots, a home for the servants of evil," Ruth said.

Naomi laughed. "There is more true Christian kindness among these people than you've ever shown anyone."

Ruth drew her hand back to strike.

Chaska caught it, held it, his voice laced with menace. "Don't you dare, bitch."

Ruth looked up at Chaska, eyes wide with shock.

"Get your hand off my wife, or I'll—"

"You want to take me on, preacher man?" Chaska held fast to Ruth's wrist for a moment, then gave her a little shove and released her, moving to stand between her and Naomi. "I'm game. Go ahead and hit me—or have you never hit anyone who wasn't a woman or a little child? You're a stinking hypocrite."

Team members had gathered around them now, Eric and Austin pushing their way to the front.

"Need some help, Belcourt?" Austin asked.

"Hey, Joe," Eric called. "Looks like it's time to take out the trash."

Joe came up beside them. "I don't know who you are, but this is my house, and these are my guests. Get off my property before I have you arrested—and before these men kick your ass."

"One last chance, Tabitha," Peter said.

"That's enough." Chaska grabbed Peter by the collar, dragged him toward the door, which Moretti opened for him. "Don't come near my woman again."

He shoved Peter out the door.

Ruth ran after her husband, the doors shutting behind her.

"Rico, make sure they leave the property," Joe said to a big man who wore a hairnet on his beard. "I don't want them hanging around out there."

Naomi turned to Rain and Joe. "I'm so sorry. I didn't know—"

Rain hugged her. "It's not your fault, sweetie. Some people are just nuts."

Joe rested a hand on her shoulder. "Are you okay?"

"I'm fine." She was fine—if she ignored the shaky feeling inside.

"I hope you'll stay and enjoy the rest of the evening with us." Then Joe turned toward his patrons. "Sorry for the interruption, folks. It's over. Enjoy the evening."

The band started playing again.

And then Chaska was there, drawing Naomi into his arms. "They're gone. I watched them climb into their car and drive away."

Naomi let out a relieved breath. "Thank you."

A muscle clenched in his jaw, anger still on his face. "I should have punched him. I *wanted* to punch him."

That made Naomi laugh.

"What was that ruckus?" Old Man asked when they returned to the table.

Chaska answered in Lakota for Naomi's sake, Doug adding his perspective.

Grandpa listened, nodding and eating his fries. "I'm proud of you, grandson. You were a warrior for your woman. That's how it should be."

Chaska sat next to Naomi. "Do you want to go home?"

She shook her head. "I won't let them ruin this evening."

Doug reached across the table, pressed his hand over hers. "They won't bother you again. We'll make certain of that. There are legal remedies we can pursue, but we'll talk about that some other time."

They stayed for another hour until Old Man had gotten his turn on the dance floor with Winona and Doug had taken a shot at the climbing wall, making it to the top on the easiest route with Sasha coaching him and Naomi cheering him on.

"This is a fun place," Old Man said, waving goodbye to the Team and getting a kiss on the cheek from Sasha. "Friendly people."

Naomi stopped on the way out to give Bear a hug. "Thank you. You were my hero tonight."

The small part of Bear's face that was visible—that band from his upper cheeks to his forehead—turned bright red. "Those people were no good. I don't like them."

Neither did Chaska. They'd been even worse than he'd imagined, the fear he'd seen on Naomi's face the moment she'd recognized Peter making Chaska want to take the bastard apart—or at least give him a taste of his own belt.

Chaska watched for them and their vehicle on the short drive home, some part of him worried that Peter might be crazy enough to try to take Naomi against her will, but was relieved to see no sign of them.

It wasn't yet nine o'clock when they got home—too early for Chaska to head to bed with Naomi, which is what he wanted to do. They'd had little time alone this past couple of days. While Winona went out to feed Shota and make sure he was safe for the night, Chaska did what Old Man told him to do and got out the games.

"You seriously want to play Chinese checkers?"

"What's wrong with that? We can sit and amuse ourselves and talk."

Okay, fine—whatever it took to get through the next hour.

They played without Doug, who disappeared into Chaska's office to call his wife again. Winona went first and took the green marbles. Chaska was black, while Old Man was red and Naomi was yellow. By the time Doug returned ten minutes later, the game was almost over, Old Man on the brink of winning—as usual.

Doug sat across from Naomi. "I'll be driving home in the morning."

Naomi's head came up, disappointment in her eyes. "So soon?"

"Star and I want some time to talk about what to say to the kids. We'll tell them on Sunday. I have to be back at the office in Pine Ridge on Monday." Doug clearly had something else he wanted to say, his gaze fixed on Naomi. "I can come back down next weekend, drive you and your SUV up to our house. You're free to stay with us while you recover. It would give you time to get to know us. We can get you enrolled, introduce you to the rest of the family."

His words hit Chaska in the chest.

What did you expect, kola?

He'd known she had to leave Scarlet eventually. She had an apartment in Rapid City, an online business to run, jewelry to make. She couldn't stay here forever.

"I… I really hadn't decided what I want to do next. I had thought I might stay here until I'm able to drive myself home." Her gaze met his, questioning.

Chaska didn't want her to go, not now, not ever. But it would be selfish of him to try to keep her here when she had a new family and a new world to discover.

He willed himself not to show emotion. "You're welcome to stay here as long as you like, but I'm sure your family is going to want to meet you sooner rather than later. You have a lot of catching up to do."

There. He'd said the right thing.

Idiot.

"We've got a nice house," Doug said. "You would have your own room. There's running water and electricity, too, and Internet."

"Doesn't everyone have water and electricity?" Naomi jumped one of her marbles over a string of Winona's.

Chaska realized that life on the reservation was going to come as a shock to her. "There are lots of people who don't have either. Old Man only got electricity out at his place—what, eight years ago?"

"That's right, but I'm outta light bulbs. Got to get some light bulbs." Old Man jumped one of his marbles over four of Chaska's, landing his last piece in Chaska's corner. He chuckled. "Good game."

Chaska glanced at the clock. It was almost ten.

He pushed to his feet. "I'm heading to bed."

"So early?" Grandpa teased. He looked over at Doug and Winona. "You two want to stay up and have another game?"

Doug nodded. "Sure, but you'll have to teach me the rules."

Naomi stood too, reaching for her crutches. "Thank you all. I'll never forget this day or how kind you all have been."

Doug stood. "Sleep well, daughter."

She kissed him on the cheek. "Goodnight, Dad."

Chaska followed Naomi up the stairs, arguing with himself. Part of him wanted to tell her what he'd said before they'd found her, explain that he'd been led to her, tell her that he loved her. She ought to know before she decided anything that he wanted to spend his life with her. But the other part of him was afraid that this might influence her decisions, turn her away from the path she was meant to walk. Besides, if they were truly meant to be together, she would find her way back to him on her own.

He shut his bedroom door behind them, leaned her crutches against the sofa, and sat on the bed beside her. "Alone at last."

She leaned against him. "What a day."

There was one way he could tell her how he felt about her, a way to tell her he loved her without words, a way to show her how much she meant to him.

He turned her in his arms and kissed her.

Naomi gave herself over to Chaska's kiss, her emotions frayed after all that had happened today. She didn't want to think about the future—where she would go and what she would do. She just wanted *him*.

He kissed her out of her dress and bra and panties, lowering her to the bed, his lips magic against her mouth, her throat, her breasts. She opened her eyes to find herself naked, Chaska looking up at her through brown eyes gone black as his mouth blazed a trail over her skin. Lower he went and lower, her need for him building, anticipation making her ache.

He took her injured leg, parted her thighs, and knelt between them. "Show me. Reach down, and show me how beautiful you are."

It took her a moment to realize what he was asking.

Her pulse skipped.

She did what would have been unthinkable until she'd met him, reaching down with her fingers to part herself and expose her most private flesh to his view.

His gaze scorched her. "Mmm. Perfect."

Just watching the effect she had on him, and knowing that he was aroused by what he saw, turned her on. But she knew it wouldn't end here. Before she could draw another breath, he lowered his mouth to her.

It was a sensual onslaught, one sensation colliding with the next as he sucked her inner lips into the heat of his mouth, teased her with his clever tongue, tugged on her clit with his lips. Her fingers dug into his hair, and she fought to hold on. Oh, but he knew her now, knew just what pleased her. Two fingers slid deep inside her to stroke her, and soon she was on the edge of an orgasm.

He lifted his mouth from her, turned to kiss her inner thigh, his fingers still moving inside her. "The climax is more intense when you wait."

This was *deliberate*?

"That's not fair." The tension inside her eased a bit, but the need didn't.

He chuckled. "I'll make it worth your while. I promise."

He lowered his mouth to her and began again, lips and tongue and fingers and even his teeth driving her crazy.

Four times he brought her to the very edge of orgasm, and four times he stopped, leaving her panting and aching and frantic. It was torture. It was ecstasy. It was driving her crazy. "You're killing me."

His lips were wet, and there was little smile on his face, his fingers still inside her, stroking, stretching. "I hope not."

And then his mouth was on her again.

This time he didn't stop, climax sweeping her away in a wild rush, the intensity of the pleasure leaving her stunned and breathless.

She lay there, boneless, floating somewhere between heaven and earth.

The sound of a zipper brought her eyes open.

He stood there, shirtless, his erection springing free as he pushed down his slacks and boxers. She sat, scooted up the bed, then lay down against her pillow and reached for him. He lay down beside her and took her into his arms, and for a time he just held her, his erection hot against her hip. "You mean so much to me, Naomi. You will always have a home here with me. Do you hear that?"

It wasn't "I love you," but it was close.

"I don't want to leave you."

He closed his eyes, pressed his forehead to hers. "You need to meet your family and sort through all of this."

Then he reached between her thighs and began to stroke her.

Naomi gasped, her hips jerking, her clit almost too sensitive to touch.

He seemed to know that. He took it slow, touching, stroking, teasing, until the fire he'd just put out began to blaze again. He reached for a condom, sheathed himself and settled between her thighs, nudging them farther apart with muscular legs. And then he was inside her.

He held himself off her, his gazed locked with hers, the intimacy of looking into his eyes while he moved in and out of her like nothing she'd ever known. Then he sank into her, his mouth taking hers in a rough kiss, big body enfolding her.

"*Naomi.*" He quit kissing her long enough to whisper her name, his eyes still open, still looking into hers. "*Cante skuye*. Sweetheart."

His rhythm began to build, his breathing rapid now.

Then he held himself still inside her, moving the root of his cock against her clit again and again in slow circles, back and forth until she was out of breath, too.

She reached down, grasped the shifting muscles of his ass with her hands, her nails digging into his skin. "*Yes.*"

She'd never believed in multiple orgasms, but it hit her suddenly that she was well on her way to her first, the ache inside her already blossoming into bliss.

He ground himself into her, giving her everything she needed.

"*Chaska!*" She cried out his name as she came, heaven raining down around her, drowning her in pleasure.

He reached down to cup her bottom, driving into her hard and fast now, every muscle in his body tense as he focused on his own climax. At last, he came, finishing with deep, powerful strokes, his body shaking apart in her arms.

Afterward, he held her, stroked her cheek, kissed her, showing her such tenderness that it made her heart ache.

Long after he'd fallen asleep, she lay awake in the dark, thinking.

Chapter Twenty-Three

Chaska awoke to find Naomi sitting up in bed. She looked like she hadn't slept, circles beneath her eyes. He sat up, tucked a dark strand of hair behind her ear. "Hey, what's wrong?"

"I've decided to go to Pine Ridge with Doug next week."

So, she'd made up her mind.

He ignored the way those words cut through him. "That will make your father happy. It's good for you to spend time together, to get to know each other, to meet the rest of your family."

She leaned against Chaska's chest. "Will you visit me?"

It was a five- or six-hour drive to Pine Ridge, something he could only pull off on weekends when he didn't have extra work. "As often as I can."

It wouldn't be often enough, not nearly often enough.

You were led to her.

The thought was no comfort as they took turns in the shower and went down to breakfast. He had a week left with her at most. After that, who knew where life would lead her?

They joined the others downstairs for a big Saturday breakfast of pancakes, eggs, and bacon with lots of coffee. Doug was delighted by Naomi's decision, his happiness making Chaska feel selfish. The man had lost twenty-seven years of his daughter's life and wanted to make that up to her. Naomi had a family she'd never met, a heritage she had yet to discover.

How could Chaska stand in the way of that?

While he sat there, drinking his coffee and trying to pretend that he didn't have a hole in his heart, the two of them started making real plans. They decided Doug would fly back next Friday night and that they would leave Saturday morning, Doug driving Naomi's Honda to Rapid City. They'd stay overnight there, pack up some of her things, and then head out on the land in the morning.

"We'd like to have a big reunion, bring the *tiospaye* together to meet her, and we would love it if the three of you could be there, too. You are the reason Naomi is alive. You're the reason I found her."

Naomi looked hopefully over at him.

He took her hand. "Of course, we'll be there."

Old Man got to his feet. "Chaska, come take an old man for a walk."

Chaska knew this was his grandfather's way of saying he wanted time alone to talk before he left for the drive home. He tossed back the rest of his coffee. "Let me get my shoes."

The sun was high above the horizon as they made their way out the front door, down the steps, and out to the sidewalk, turning right and going downhill.

Old Man spoke first. "It's a good thing you've done—saving this woman's life, helping her to find her father. I see goodness in her. You love her."

There was no denying that. "With everything I am."

"It will be hard for you to be away from her."

"I want to tell her what happened, how I was led to her. I want to tell her I love her. But I don't want to interfere with her life. It is right for her to go home, to meet her family, to meet her people."

"You must come up and visit her—and me."

"I will."

"What about your own father?"

Aiii.

Chaska ought to have known there was a trap in here somewhere.

"You know how I feel about him."

"He dishonored the Sun Dance. I agreed with you. I agree with you still. But for you not to see him and not to speak with him—is what he did so terrible that you would treat him as if he no longer exists?"

Chaska had no answer for this.

"One never knows how many journeys around the sun anyone will get. My son isn't as young as he once was. He knows what he did was wrong. He misses you."

"Is he still drinking and smoking weed at Sun Dance?"

"I do not know, but if you were to dance next month, you could find out."

"Next month?" Chaska laughed. "I don't think I can get a month off right now, even if I wanted to be part of his Sun Dance."

Sun Dance lasted twenty-eight days from start to finish, with the actual dance being four days. Chaska hadn't done any of the preparation.

"You made a four-year commitment, and you need to complete it."

It was the first time Old Man had spoken so bluntly to him about this.

"I'd have finished my commitment if you hadn't stepped down. I don't want to be part of a ceremony run by a hypocrite."

"Whether your father is a hypocrite is on him. Whether you finish the commitment you made to *Wakan Tanka* is on you."

Chaska fought back his temper. He would never speak harshly to his grandfather—not now, not ever. "I hear what you say. I will think on it."

"That's all a grandfather can ask." Old Man turned around. "Let's go back inside. It's hot out here."

"Grandpa, you live near the Badlands. How can you think this is hot?"

Old Man just chuckled.

Naomi sat on the porch, watching while Doug loaded up his vehicle. A few days ago, she'd never heard of him. Now it was hard to watch him leave.

The front door opened and Grandpa Belcourt stepped outside.

He sat beside her. "The hummingbirds are busy today."

"Even though they're small, they have to eat a lot to keep up their energy."

"How do you make those pictures? It looks like the birds are frozen in place."

"It's all about the settings on the camera. They need to be fast enough to catch the light for just that split second when the wings are open."

He nodded as if this made sense to him. "I am glad I was able to meet you."

"I'm glad I got to meet you, too."

"My grandson cares for you. I am happy for him because you have a good heart, and I am happy for you because Chaska is a good man, a true warrior. I saw how he protected you last night. If he had to, he would sacrifice flesh and blood for you."

"I love him." Why was it easier to tell Chaska's grandfather this truth than it was to tell Chaska himself?

Grandpa Belcourt nodded. "I know my grandson. He loves you, too."

Naomi closed her eyes, hoped this was true. She had no right to ask him to wait for her. They'd made no commitment to each other.

"Soon, you'll be out on the land, the land of your people. Some might find the idea of going to a new place and meeting new people to be scary."

Naomi didn't think she could fool Grandpa Belcourt. "I *am* scared. I don't know what to expect. My life is changing in so many good ways, but it is all so sudden."

He reached over, put a weathered, wrinkled hand on hers. "You lived through much difficulty, even as a newborn baby, and you survived. That is the story of the Lakota people, too. I do not think the difficulty that lies ahead of you will be more than a woman of your strength can handle. When times get tough, remember that medicine wheel you wear. It has already gotten you through many dark days. Remember always that you are the great-granddaughter of Maggie Otter Tail."

Naomi's eyes filled with tears, her fingers finding the medicine wheel. "I'd never thought about that. I'm her great-granddaughter."

"That's right. That old woman didn't take crap from anyone."

Naomi laughed, understanding why Chaska and Winona loved this old man so much. "*Pilamayaye, tunkasila.*" *Thank you, Grandfather.*

She had looked that up online and spent five minutes memorizing it so that she could thank Grandpa Belcourt. He'd been the one to recognize the medicine wheel and track down her father, after all.

He chuckled, patted her hand. "That is good. *Waste.*"

Doug jogged up the front steps. "We're all loaded up. You ready to go?"

Naomi followed Grandpa Belcourt down the stairs, joining Winona and Chaska to say goodbye, the two of them speaking in Lakota to their grandfather.

"There's no word in Lakota for goodbye," Grandpa Belcourt told her. "Just say, 'I'll see you soon.'"

She gave him a hug. "Thank you for everything. I'll see you soon."

Doug stood there, looking uncertain about what to do or say. "A week ago, I had no idea you existed. Now, you feel like a part of me. I can't wait for Star to meet you. I know I haven't been there for you, but I'm going to do my best to make up for that if you'll let me."

"Thank you for coming all this way. Thank you for caring, for insisting on the paternity test. There are probably a lot of men who would have turned away."

"It's easy to care about you, Tanagila."

"See you next week." He gave her a kiss on the cheek and then walked around the vehicle and climbed in.

"Where's that CD of sick powwow tunes?" Grandpa Belcourt asked.

"We are *not* listening to powwow songs all the way home."

Doug started the engine, whatever Grandpa said next lost when they rolled up the windows. And then they were gone.

"Your grandfather is a real character."

Chaska put his arm around her shoulders. "A real character—and sometimes a pain in the ass."

Chaska drove Naomi to Estes Park and got a room at the historic Stanley Hotel. He wanted some time alone with her before he went back to work on Monday. They checked into their room and then went for a drive along Trail Ridge Road, Naomi getting out of the car time and again to take photos.

He knew it was frustrating for her to be stuck viewing the mountains from the front seat of his truck rather than from the trails, but there was nothing to be done about it. "Next time you're in Colorado, we'll come back. You'll be able to walk then."

He drove her over the top of the Continental Divide and back again, then found his way to Bear Lake in the shadow of Hallett Peak, dropping her off near the trailhead, then going to park his truck. He reached in the back, grabbed his jacket, knowing the temp would start to drop as soon as the sun was behind the mountains.

He found her sitting on a bench, waiting. "Bear Lake isn't far. If you don't feel like you can make it on your crutches, I can carry you as I did on Sugarloaf."

But the trail was wide and not too steep, and she made it with no problem.

He found a bench on the edge of the lake, one that gave them the best view of Hallett Peak—and the sunset. They sat there for more than an hour, talking, Naomi leaning back against him and taking the occasional photo as the sun dipped behind the mountains. Sitting there with his arm around her, Chaska could feel the minutes slipping away along with the daylight, each second precious and so quickly gone.

"This is incredibly beautiful. Thank you, Chaska. Thanks for all of this."

He kissed her hair. "You wanted to see mountains, right?"

He drove them back to the hotel after that, promising they'd come back to the park tomorrow morning. They ate dinner at one of the hotel's restaurants, then went up to their room, where they made love until they were both replete and ready for sleep.

The next morning, they had a quick breakfast, then made the short drive back to Rocky Mountain National Park, where he hoped she'd be able to see the bighorn sheep that often came down from the steep slopes at dawn and dusk to eat the mineral-rich grass and drink at Sheep Lakes.

"Where are these alleged sheep of yours?" she asked, looking down at the lakes, which sat slightly downhill and just off the road.

"There they are." He pointed with a jerk of his head toward the slope opposite the lakes.

As if on cue, a herd of dozens of bighorn ewes and lambs ambled down the mountainside and into the road.

"Oh, my God! Look! There's so many of them!"

The sheep made their way nonchalantly across the road and down the embankment to the lakes, where they grazed and drank.

Park rangers did their best to keep tourists from encroaching on the sheep, cars piling up along the roadside in no-parking zones.

Naomi leaned out the window, her camera buzzing. “Where do they spend the rest of the day?”

“They live higher up, where it’s cool and rocky. I’ve seen herds of a dozen or more males with the big horns up above timberline.”

After the sheep had cleared the road, Chaska drove her to a few of the more remote overlooks. They stopped a couple from Germany and asked them to take a photograph of the two of them with the mountains behind them. And then their mini-vacation was over, and it was time to head back to Scarlet.

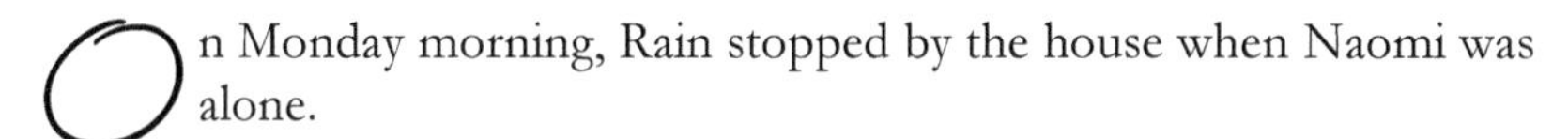

On Monday morning, Rain stopped by the house when Naomi was alone.

“This is for you.” Rain held out an envelope.

The fundraiser.

Naomi had completely forgotten about it.

She opened the envelope—and the blood rushed to her head.

Inside was a check for twenty-three thousand dollars.

“Oh, my God!” Tears blurred her vision. “I can’t believe this.”

“People were really touched by what happened to you. They wanted to help. Hopefully, that will cover everything. If there’s any left, you can donate it to the Team or the hospital—whatever you choose.”

“I don’t know how to thank you all.”

“There’s no need, Naomi. People here take care of each other.”

They talked for a while, Naomi answering Rain’s questions about how she was found, about Peter and Ruth, about the medicine wheel that had led to Grandpa Belcourt finding her father.

“Sorry to ask so many questions. It’s just … I feel like I have a personal connection to what happened to you.”

Naomi waited for Rain to explain.

"I had a baby when I was sixteen, too. I gave birth alone in an old VW van while my musician boyfriend, the baby's father, performed a set and then got drunk, dropped acid, and screwed around with other women. I never once considered abandoning my baby girl. I cannot bear to think of you or any other baby being left to die like that."

Then Rain showed Naomi photos of Lark, her daughter, a lovely young woman with a bright smile. "She's twenty now. It's hard to believe."

"She's beautiful. She looks just like you."

"Thanks."

Rain asked about Naomi's jewelry making, which led to Rain wanting to see Naomi's website—which gave Naomi an inspiration.

"Rain, can I ask a favor of you?"

The next five days seemed to fly by. Naomi spent most of each day with Winona at the clinic, taking photos, sketching, or helping with the animals when she was physically able. Her nights were spent with Chaska, cocooning in his room. They discovered new ways to please each other, his body her own personal paradise.

But all too soon it was Friday.

Chaska picked up Doug from DIA after work.

He swept Naomi up in a hug. "Star and the kids can't wait to meet you. They're helping to decorate your bedroom as we speak to have it all ready for you."

"That's so sweet."

As good as it was to see Doug again, Naomi couldn't shake the deep sadness she felt about leaving Chaska.

She lay in bed with him that night, her body sated, her heart heavy. "I don't want to be away from you. I'm afraid …"

"You're afraid of what?"

She had nothing to lose at this point by telling him the truth. "I'm afraid that the next time I see you, you'll be with someone else—Nicole or Rose or any one of the women from Scarlet who adore you."

For some reason, this made him chuckle.

"I know we haven't made each other any promises, but…"

"But what?"

Her heart gave a hard knock at what she was about to say. "I love you, Chaska. I don't want to go away and wind up losing you."

She looked up to see him smiling. "What?"

"How about I tell you why I know that won't happen."

"Okay."

"That day when we found you out there, Win and I were out taking Shota for a run. She was bugging me to ask out Nicole, telling me it was time for me to meet a woman. I told her didn't want to go out with Nicole. Win said something like, 'Don't you want to be with a woman?' I told her I did, but that I would wait till the right one came along. Then I said, 'Creator can feel free to put her in my path at any time.' It was at that moment that Shota took off running. When we found him, we found you."

Naomi sat up, gaped at him. "You didn't tell me this before."

"I wasn't sure how you'd react if I'd said, 'Hey, Naomi, I was led to you by Creator, so we're meant to be together.'"

Okay, she could see his point there. "That does sound a little crazy."

Chaska nodded. "Win didn't offer you a place to stay only because you needed one. She felt in her heart that I had been led to you. I was happy to have you stay with us, but I didn't buy the whole idea that the Creator had anything to do with it. It's been a long time since I believed. But even before you and I made love for the first time, I decided Win was right. I *was* led to you."

"Why are you telling me this now?"

He sat up, brought his face close to hers. "I don't want you to be afraid. If you and I are meant to be together, nothing can pull us apart. Creator led me to you and saved your life, and I believe we'll be together again one day. But you need to go now and meet your family and find out what it means to be Lakota, to have roots. That's something you've never had before. I'll be right here when you're ready to come home."

Home.

"Is this my home?"

"It is if you want it to be." He tucked a finger beneath her chin, raised her gaze to meet his. "I love you, Naomi. That's not going to change. When you leave tomorrow, leave with your head high, knowing that nothing can keep the two of us apart."

Chapter Twenty-Four

Chaska and Naomi smudged together the next morning, holding hands, smoke swirling between them as Chaska prayed. "Watch over Naomi, *Tunkasila*, and guide her on this new path. Help her to find her way as a Lakota, and help her to know that I love her. Bring us together again in a good way. *Mitakuye Oyasin.*"

Tears rolled down Naomi's cheeks. "*Mitakuye Oyasin.*"

Ignoring the lead weight in his chest, Chaska worked together with Winona to get a good breakfast on the table. The four of them made pleasant conversation, as if no one's heart was breaking.

Snap out of it, kola. *You wanted this for her. You helped make this happen.*

Yes, he had, and he was happy for her. He was a little less happy for himself.

After breakfast, he stood to clear the dishes away.

Naomi caught his arm. "Please, Chaska, sit. I have something for you and Win."

He took his seat once more, waiting while Doug stood and went to get something from the guest room. He returned and handed two small packages to Naomi.

"This is for you, Win."

"For me? Exciting!" Winona opened it—and held a hand over her mouth, tears filling her eyes. She gaped at Naomi. "Are you sure?"

Chaska watched as Win took the bracelet with the raven flying in front of the setting sun out of the box and put it on her wrist. She had loved that bracelet when she'd seen it on Naomi's website, and Naomi had remembered.

Naomi reached over, adjusted the band to make it fit Winona's slender wrist. "There. It's perfect for you."

"It's more beautiful in real life than it was online. Thank you, Naomi." Win came around the table and gave her a hug.

"Can I see it?" Doug leaned forward, examined it. "That is amazing artistry."

"Thank you." Naomi handed the second box to Chaska. "I know you don't really wear jewelry, but I hope you'll like it."

"I'm sure I will." Chaska opened the box and found himself smiling.

Inside, was a silver and turquoise pendant at the center of which was a bear of inlaid onyx. The bear had one paw raised, as if it were walking.

Chaska drew out the cord, held the pendant in his hand, and looked up to find Naomi watching him, her eyes bright. "Is this to remember the day we saw the bears?"

Not that he would ever forget that regardless.

She nodded, smiled.

"*Pilamayayelo.* I love it." He put the cord over his head, settled the pendant against his shirt, and turned so that Doug and Winona could see it.

"The manager of my apartment complex picked them up from my place and shipped them to Knockers. Rain dropped by yesterday and hid them in the guest room for me. You've both done so much for me. I wanted to do something for you."

Chaska rested his hand over the pendant. "I am proud to wear this."

They cleaned up the dishes, and Chaska helped Doug load Naomi's things into his SUV. "Are you heading straight to Pine Ridge?"

Doug shook his head. "We need to run by her apartment. She's been gone longer than she intended and has bills and things to manage. We'll spend Sunday there, pack up her stuff, and then leave for Pine Ridge Monday after she makes a trip to the bank. That's the plan at any rate."

And then it was time.

Naomi insisted on saying goodbye to Shota, who whined and wagged his tail when he saw her, licking her fingers through the enclosure fence.

"*Pilamayaye,* Shota. Thank you for having such a good nose and finding me. You saved my life."

Then they walked together back through the house and out the front door to Doug's waiting vehicle.

Doug shook Chaska's hand and then Winona's. "Thank you both for everything. I will never have the words to tell you how grateful I am. I'll see you around."

He climbed into the vehicle, giving Naomi some privacy.

She hugged Winona, the two of them in tears. "A month ago, I didn't know you, and now you're my best friend. We *are* sisters."

"Yes, we are." Winona kissed her cheek. "I'll see you again soon."

Chaska took Naomi into his arms, savored the precious feel of her, not wanting to let go and yet knowing he must. "Promise me you'll give this all you've got. Throw yourself into it."

She buried her face against his chest. "I promise."

He stroked her hair. "I'll visit. When you can drive again, you can visit us. *Tecíhila.* I love you."

"I love you, too." She drew away, smiling up at him through her tears. "We'll see each other again soon."

"Yes, we will." He kissed her soft and slow, then helped her into the vehicle, waving to her as Doug drove away.

Naomi watched Scarlet Springs disappear behind them.

"You don't have to call me 'father' or 'dad' unless you want to," Doug said. "You can call me Doug."

"I like calling you 'dad.'"

"Tell me about it—tell me about how you grew up."

So, Naomi told him everything she could remember, sparing him no detail.

He listened, and she could see that her words distressed him. He reached over at one point to hold her hand. "That is no way to treat a child. In the old days, when the Lakota people were strong in their traditional ways, it was unheard of for a parent to strike a child. I'm so sorry, Naomi."

"You don't need to apologize."

"It sounds like some kind of crazy cult, not a church."

"That's what Chaska said."

"If you want, I'll file a request with the state to annul your adoption."

She stared at him. "Is that even possible?"

"I'd have to check case law, but because you're Native and no attempts were made to place you with a Native family, we might stand a chance."

"Wow." Could she truly erase Peter and Ruth from her life? "I would like that."

"If it's okay with you, I'd like to get my name added to your birth certificate. I'm not sure what's involved there, but that's why I wanted the paternity test to be admissible in court."

He'd really thought ahead.

"Of course, it's okay with me." It was beyond anything she'd hoped for.

Naomi's heart began to lift, she and Doug singing along to the Beatles, Doug sharing his stories of growing up and telling her about Star and the kids.

Seven hours after leaving Scarlet, they reached Rapid City and pulled into the parking lot of Naomi's apartment complex.

Doug helped her up two flights of stairs, then carried her stuff up. "Nice place."

It felt strange to be home. Everything was so familiar and yet part of a different life. The Naomi who had lived here and worked here and dreamed here had left three weeks ago hoping to relax—and she'd returned a new person, living a different life.

Doug got himself settled, called Star, and then logged into Naomi's wireless, while she sorted through her mail, balanced her checking account, and paid bills. There was already an invoice from the hospital in Scarlet for almost forty thousand dollars. There was also a letter from the State of Colorado Victims of Violent Crimes Compensation Fund, telling her that she had gotten approval for assistance and explaining how to file a claim. She needed to file a claim with her health insurance, too—and get the check from Knockers to the bank.

So much to do.

Doug came up behind her, rested his hands on her shoulders. "I would be happy to help with all of that."

Maybe it was the fact that he was an attorney, but Doug seemed to have a special knack for making paperwork easy, helping her to finish much more quickly than she had imagined and with none of the stress. After that, he helped her package online jewelry orders, including the earrings he'd bought for Star, and get them ready to mail on Monday, examining each piece before he boxed it.

"I know some people—artists—who are going to be very excited to meet you and see your work."

He packed the boxes up and set them in a plastic mail tote by her door, then came to stand by her. "What's next?"

And it hit Naomi.

This is what it was to have a father.

ENTERING

PINE RIDGE INDIAN RESERVATION

LAND OF THE OGLALA SIOUX

CHIEFS

RED CLOUD * BLACK ELK * CRAZY HORSE

NO HUNTING

WITHOUT TRIBAL PERMITS

The wooden sign stood off on the shoulder of the road, Naomi's throat growing tight when she saw it.

"Let's get a photo." Doug pulled over, helped her out of his vehicle, then took a few shots. "I'll send one to your Chaska, let him know we're here."

Doug took the long way home, wanting her to get a feel for the land. "This is the land of your ancestors, of Maggie Otter Tail, your great-grandmother whose mother ran from the Seventh Cavalry through the snow to Stronghold and survived the massacre."

"You mean Wounded Knee?"

Doug nodded. "This is our land, but it comes with the memory of much loss. There is pain here, the genetic trauma of terror and violence, but there's hope, too."

The landscape was beautiful, but the way people lived…

Naomi wasn't sure what she'd expected, but she was astonished by the poverty as they passed dilapidated trailers and ramshackle houses that didn't look fit for human habitation, children playing in the dirt.

"Out on this end of the rez, there's no running water or electricity. People use car batteries or generators when they can."

"This is like …" She stopped herself, not wanting to offend.

"It's like a third-world country?" Doug nodded. "You're not the first person to say that. This is the poorest county in the United States. Our median annual income here is four thousand dollars."

Naomi stared at Doug, shocked. "How do people survive?"

"Charities. Government commodities. Relatives. Odd jobs."

Outside her window, teenagers sat in the bed of a broken-down pickup truck with no tires, its paint long since bleached away by the sun.

"People who visit see the poverty. They see the crumbling houses and the rusted-out vehicles. They read about the alcoholism and the high dropout rate and suicides. But they miss the real story—the economic growth, the rising number of kids finishing college, the strength of our elders, the sense of community, the resurgence of our language and culture. The story of the Lakota is a story of survival against all the odds—and that's your story, too, Tanagila."

"That's what Grandpa Belcourt said."

Doug grinned. "Elders like him are important to us. They know the old ways, and those ways will make us strong again."

They reached the town of Pine Ridge an hour later. They passed a Subway, a Catholic church, a Pizza Hut, then Doug turned down one of the streets and pulled into the driveway of a blue, two-story house.

"Look what the kids did for you."

A hand-made banner hung over the garage. Covered with smiley faces and handprints, it read, "Welcome home, Naomi!"

She swallowed the lump in her throat. "How sweet."

Doug helped her out of the vehicle. “You go on in. I’ll get your things.”

The door opened, and a woman Naomi recognized as Star stepped out.

She was petite and prettier than her photograph, a bright smile on her face as she hurried over to Naomi and drew her into her arms. “What a long road it’s been for you, Naomi, but now you’re home. Welcome.”

Three weeks after Naomi came to Pine Ridge, her tribal enrollment was approved. Her story had been big news around the reservation since she’d turned in her application, word of her ordeal spreading. The local newspaper, radio station, and TV station dredged up the old articles and news footage from when she’d been found as a baby, sharing clips and quotes. Naomi had never heard or seen any of this before, and reading and listening to it wasn’t easy, especially when the TV news ran a photograph of her taken at the hospital the night she’d been found.

“Why did your mama throw you away?” Kimímila crawled into Naomi’s lap, her gaze on the TV screen. “You were a pretty little baby.”

Naomi swallowed hard. “I don’t know.”

She would probably never know.

Star stepped in. “Naomi’s mother, whoever she was, must have had some kind of sickness in her mind. We should pray for her.”

“I’m glad they found you,” Chayton said.

“So am I.”

Star and Chumani had baked a cake to celebrate Naomi’s enrollment, her nickname written in squiggly scrawl in white icing—*Tanagila*.

“Now that you’re official, I think it’s time to get everyone together and introduce you. It would be a good time for a naming ceremony.”

“A naming ceremony?”

“I hear you’re officially one of us.” Chaska lay back on his bed, the sound of Naomi’s voice taking the edge off a rough day.

"Yes. It's been all over the news here. They showed a photo that police took of me the night I was found. Mato called it my baby mugshot."

That made Chaska laugh. "Is there any way to get a copy of it?"

Chaska wanted it, even if Naomi didn't.

"I think Star already has it. Oh, I started Lakota classes last week."

"Yeah? Let's hear it. Say something."

"*Toníktuha he.*" *How are you?*

He replied. "*Waste.*" *I'm well.*

Yes, he was fine, but, damn, he missed her. It had taken only a day for him to realize how colorless and empty his life was without her. She'd been gone three weeks now. Though they texted and emailed every day and tried to talk at least once a week, it seemed like she'd been gone forever.

"I'm not sure I'll ever be fluent like you and Win."

"That's okay. Just keep at it."

"The kids have been helping, especially the two little ones. Chay and Kimi run around touching things and naming them. It's impossible to remember everything."

She told him how her father had filled out the paperwork to have himself added to her birth certificate and how he'd hired an attorney to annul her adoption. "Peter and Ruth sent a letter, agreeing to the annulment on the condition that he pay them more than a million dollars to compensate them for the expense of raising me."

"What? That's outrageous." They were lucky they weren't in prison.

"My dad told me not to worry about it, that it was just them making noise. He's pretty sure we're going to win."

Chaska found himself smiling at the easy way she called Doug *dad.* Things were going so well for her, and that's what he needed to remember.

"I asked my father if he was ever going to tell me my mother's name. He said he'd tell me one day, but not yet."

Chaska wondered what Doug's reasons were for keeping the woman's name secret. "How long before you find out about the annulment?"

"It could be months."

She changed the subject then, telling him how Doug had set up space for her to work in the garage and how he'd introduced her to some artists at the college. "I asked about taking classes, but after they saw my work, they wanted to know whether I'd like to teach next term."

He didn't like the idea of her staying so long, but he didn't say that. "That doesn't surprise me at all."

"I told them I couldn't do that, of course, because I wasn't staying here that long. As much as I love it here and feel at home, I want to be with you."

Chaska tried not to let his relief show. "I'm sure they understand."

"Star is taking me to an orthopedic surgeon in Rapid tomorrow to see if I've healed enough to walk again. I can't wait to get this boot off and get rid of these crutches. I want to be able to drive again at the very least."

Chaska's bedroom door was open, so, naturally, Winona popped her head inside. "Are you talking to Naomi? Tell her about the owl."

"Win wants you to know that they released the little burrowing owl back into the wild a few days ago."

"Really? Wonderful! How is Win?"

"Ask her yourself—in Lakota." He handed the phone to Win, listening as the two women caught up, talking for what felt like a very long time.

"I'd better give you back to my brother. He misses you a lot." Win handed him the phone again and left him in peace.

"Did you know your grandpa is doing my naming ceremony?"

"Yes. We'll be there." Chaska wouldn't miss it.

"How is everything with you? You sound down."

He did? "We're moving ahead with the system design for this NASA project, and I've been putting in a lot of extra hours. We got toned out today for a fatality."

"Oh, no. What happened?"

He hadn't planned on telling her, but some part of him needed to talk about it, especially with the woman who held his heart. "A teenage kid was goofing around with some of his friends, slipped on some loose rock, and fell more than a hundred feet. His mother was waiting by the ambulance when we got down. It was … a rough scene."

"Oh, God, Chaska. I'm so sorry—for her, for that kid, for all of you."

"Thanks."

She listened while he shared his grief, his sense of helplessness, her understanding helping to smooth away his roughest edges.

"I know you think you did nothing, but you brought him down, you returned him to his family. There was nothing more anyone could do."

They talked until Naomi's cell phone battery was almost gone.

"I miss you so much. See you in two weeks," she said. "I love you."

"*Tecíhila*. I love you, too."

Megs sat at the front of the ops room, clipboard in hand. She'd called a budget meeting and had some equipment concerns to discuss with them. That was all fine and good, but it was making Chaska miss his phone time with Naomi.

"Mitch Ahearn. Chaska Belcourt … is brooding."

Chaska's temper flashed. "I am *not* brooding."

"Correction. Chaska Belcourt is brooding *and* cantankerous."

Laughter.

Chaska forced his teeth together. No one here deserved his anger.

Hawke leaned in, put a big hand on his shoulder. "You miss her."

That was an understatement. "Yeah."

"When are you going to see her again?"

"Two weeks. Her folks are holding a naming ceremony for her, and my grandfather will be running the show."

Hawke gave him a sympathetic nod. "Those two months when Vicki was back in Chicago—damn, I just about fell apart. I wound up drinking at Knockers with Hank, of all people, trying to give me relationship advice."

Okay, that was pretty bad. "Advice from *Hank*?"

Hank was famous locally for blowing up his own house while trying to extract hash oil from marijuana using butane.

At least Chaska hadn't fallen that far.

Megs' voice intruded. "Eric Hawke … is trying to cheer up Belcourt. Aw, that's sweet."

Megs could be such a pain in the ass.

When roll call was done, they got down to business.

Megs held up a check. "I received this today—a check for twelve thousand dollars from Naomi Archer, who is an angel for being true to her word."

Whoops, whistles, and applause greeted this news.

Oh, yeah. Chaska had forgotten to tell Megs to expect that.

"This wasn't figured into our budget, so I'd like to use it for new gear, including those bullhorns."

"We need Camalots and some Big Bros, man," Herrera blurted.

And then it was on.

"We need to replace some ropes and slings."

"What about ice tools?"

"What we really need is an overhaul on Rescue One's engine."

Sasha bounced up and down in her seat. "This is like Christmas!"

Hawke ignored them. "You'll see her again soon, man, and when you do… Let me just say that reunion sex—it is *insane*."

Chaska looked over at his friend. "Thanks, Hawke."

That had given Chaska something new to think about.

Chapter Twenty-Five

Star looked out the window. "He's here."

Naomi jumped to her feet, looked outside, felt her heart melt at the sight of him. Chaska stepped out of his truck, wearing jeans and a white T-shirt, long hair pulled back in a ponytail, the bear pendant she'd given him hanging from its cord around his neck.

She stepped into her flip flops, opened the front door, and ran to him. Okay, so it was kind of a limping run, but it took her straight into his arms.

He crushed her against him, kissed her deep and hard, his familiar scent enfolding her. God, it felt good to touch him again, to feel his strong arms around her, the long weeks of missing him finally over—for now.

"I want a boyfriend to kiss me," she heard Chumani say from the doorway.

"You can kiss boys when you're twenty-seven like Naomi," Dad said.

Then the front door closed, and Naomi and Chaska were alone—or as alone as they were likely to be this weekend.

"I'm glad you got here early." Her naming ceremony was the day after tomorrow, and tomorrow more than a hundred relatives were expected to arrive, people she hadn't met before. "At least I get some time with you."

"This is the first time since I've known you that you've been walking," Chaska said, a grin on his face. "How does it feel?"

"My calf muscle is weak from not being used, and my ankle is stiff and sore, but it's so nice not to have crutches."

"I bet it is."

They walked around the yard, talking, their fingers laced together, until Naomi remembered her manners. "Star and my brothers and sisters want to meet you."

Inside, Naomi introduced Chaska to Star and then to the children. Chumani was shy like a girl who'd been hit with her first crush, barely able to say a word, a little smile on her face. Kimímila rushed up and gave him a hug.

Mato shook Chaska's hand, very much the young man. "Thank you for saving my sister's life."

"I was happy to do it," Chaska replied, his gaze meeting Naomi's.

Chayton shook Chaska's hand, too. "Is it true you have a pet wolf?"

"I'm not sure he makes a very good pet because he's still pretty wild, but, yes, we live with a wolf in our backyard. His name is Shota."

Chay seemed fascinated by this. "Can you bring Shota next time?"

"Probably not. He wouldn't be happy leaving his home." Chaska held out his hand to Doug. "Good to see you again."

"You, too. Naomi has missed you."

Star invited them to sit down at the kitchen table and enjoy some iced coffee. She asked Chaska questions about his work and the Team. "My husband saw you climb and said you have true skill. He said it was like watching a real, live Iktomi."

Then they talked about the ceremony.

"Naomi has been busy making gifts for all the relatives who come," Star told Chaska. "Chumani and Kimi love to watch her work."

It was a custom after a naming ceremony for the family of the person who'd been given a new name to host a giveaway for those who attended.

"You made jewelry for everyone?" Chaska's brows rose in surprise.

Naomi nodded. "I made silver and turquoise earrings for the women and girls and silver dream catcher pendants for the men and boys."

"Good." Chaska looked like he was fighting not to smile.

"So, Doug and I were thinking… We're going to need some extra tables for the barbecue. We found a rental place that has some available, but it's in Rapid City. Would you two be willing to head into the city for us?"

Naomi's dad reached into his pocket and pulled out a credit card. "We'll pay for the tables, of course, but if you could pick them up, that would be great. It's kind of late in the day, so you might have to stay overnight at Naomi's apartment—that is, if you don't mind."

Naomi looked from her father to Chaska as it dawned on her what Star and her father were doing. They were giving her a way to be alone overnight with the man she loved. "We don't mind, do we?"

Chaska shot to his feet. "We'd be happy to … uh … help."

Chaska hurried with Naomi up two floors to the door of her apartment and stood there, his blood burning, while she fumbled with her keys. "Let me."

He took over for her, sliding the key into place and turning the deadbolt. Then he pushed the door open and followed her inside.

The moment the door closed behind him, she dropped her handbag and jumped into his arms, kissing him, tugging his shirt from his jeans, fumbling with his zipper.

He backed her up against the wall, yanked down his fly, freed his cock, then lifted her skirt to cup her, sliding his fingers inside her panties, moaning when he found she was wet.

"*Please*, Chaska."

He had just enough presence of mind to put on the condom he'd tucked in his jeans pocket before lifting her off her feet, pinning her against the wall, and burying his cock in her heat.

They moaned in unison, her legs wrapping around his hips, drawing him closer, holding him in place. He'd forgotten how damned good it felt to be inside her. She was so tight, wet. *Perfect.*

He tried to fall into an easy rhythm, but it had been so long, too long for both of them. In a heartbeat, he was thrusting hard, driving himself into her, his hips a piston, his fingers digging into her buttocks.

A framed photograph fell off the wall, glass shattering.

Neither of them so much as looked.

All he could think about was Naomi, beautiful sweet Naomi. He lusted for her, loved her, was close to losing his mind over her.

Her head was tilted back now, her nails digging into his shoulders through the cloth of his T-shirt, her lips parted as she moaned out her pleasure in time to his thrusts. "*Chask-aa-aa-aaah.*"

He loved the way she said his name when she was about to come, loved the look of sexual bliss on her face as she unraveled, loved the musky scent of her arousal, the way her soft body yielded to him again and again and again.

He pounded himself into her, needing her, wanting only her, only Naomi.

She cried out, arching against the wall as she came.

He was right behind her, climax swamping him with pleasure.

For a moment he stood there, his body holding hers against the wall, his cock still inside her, her legs wrapped around his waist. Then he grabbed the condom and withdrew, lowering her slowly to her feet.

She gave him a contented kitten sort of smile. "God, I've missed you."

He managed one word. "Yeah."

She laughed. "We knocked a photo off the wall."

While he cleaned himself up and disposed of the condom, she swept up the glass and set the photograph on the coffee table.

Her cell phone buzzed. She hurried to her handbag, which she'd dropped on the floor just inside the doorway, drew it out, and read a text message, a smile coming over her face. She handed it to Chaska.

Don't really need tables. Take my credit card and go out to eat somewhere. See you tomorrow. XO Dad

"My dad is the best."

Chaska couldn't argue with that.

They got some Chinese takeout, making the most of their short time together by staying home. There were so many stories Naomi wanted to share with him, so many things they needed to say to each other. It seemed to her that the bond between them had somehow grown stronger since she'd left.

They made love again, Chaska settling Naomi astride him, looking up at her through dark eyes. "Ride me."

It took Naomi a few attempts to figure out the rhythm, but when she did… *Oh, yes.* It was heaven to feel him inside her, to control the angle and the depth, to see the arousal on his face as he watched her take him. He palmed her breasts, reached down to stroke her clit.

She came twice, the second time taking him over the edge with her.

Afterward, she lay on top of him, contented to her soul, their hearts beating against each other.

He traced the line of her spine. "I want you to marry me."

It took her a moment to realize what he'd said.

She raised her head, stared down at him, her breath caught in her throat. "Do you… Do you mean that?"

"I know you've got a lot going on here. I don't want to take you away from that. I'm not saying we have to get married right away or that you'd have to move to Scarlet tomorrow, but I miss you, Naomi. Being away from you—it's so much harder than I thought it would be."

Heart soaring, Naomi ran a finger down his sternum. "I would love to marry you, Chaska, but I'm a very traditional Lakota woman now."

A dark eyebrow arched. "Is that so?"

She nodded. "You'll have to gather up some horses and talk to my father."

"Your father doesn't even have a place to keep horses."

"I read about a Lakota woman whose bride price was a hundred horses," she teased, rolling off of Chaska onto her side, snuggling against him, her head resting on his shoulder.

"A *hundred*?" Chaska laughed. "Were they the plastic kind?"

"I don't think so."

"I don't have a hundred horses, but I'll see what I can pull together." He raised his head, kissed her lips. "If he accepts my bride price, you'll marry me?"

"Yes." She kissed him back. "*Tecíhila*."

Chaska drove Naomi back to Pine Ridge in the morning, then helped her father get ready for the relatives who were already rolling in. It was a hot day for early September, and Doug had a big yard, so Chaska took on the chore of mowing the lawn.

"Is this your way of saying I'm an old man?" Doug joked.

Chaska laughed. "Just trying to get on your good side."

Afterward, he helped Doug and Naomi's Uncle Tim set up a sweatlodge for the *inipi* Old Man was holding to prepare Naomi for her naming ceremony.

She came outside to watch them as they constructed the willow frame.

Chaska walked over to where she stood in the shade. "What do you think?"

"I'm starting to feel nervous."

"About the *inipi* or the naming ceremony?"

"Both, but mostly the *inipi.* I've heard stories about people freaking out and trying to get out. I don't want to be that person."

"Don't listen to the stories." Some of them were true, but hearing this wouldn't help her. "Old Man goes easy on first-timers. It won't be like the sweats we do for Sun Dance. Doug will be there. Star will be there. Win and I will be there, too. You can sit between us if you like."

She nodded. "That would make me feel a lot better."

He kissed her. "It's going to be fine."

"Hey, Naomi, I'd like you to come meet my sisters," Star called.

Naomi kissed Chaska and walked back to the house.

Chaska helped finish the lodge and stacked firewood. Then it was time to head to Rapid City to pick Winona up at the airport. He stopped in at the house to tell Naomi he was leaving. "I'll be back in plenty of time for the *inipi.*"

"I can't wait to see Win."

"She's excited to see you, too." He gave her hand a squeeze, then headed out the door and climbed into his truck, an idea forming in his mind.

Heated stones. Sage. Sweetgrass.

Naomi sat in the silent sweatlodge with a towel wrapped around her shoulders, her pulse beating a little too fast. Winona sat on her left and Star just beyond her, while Chaska sat, shirtless with a towel around his waist like the other men, on her right.

Darkness. Water hitting stone. Hot steam.

She fought back her panic, her senses stunned by the pitch black, by the suffocating heat. She held onto Chaska and Winona's hands, felt their reassuring presence beside her.

A drumbeat. Her heartbeat. The otherworldly trill of an eagle bone whistle.

She sang the songs, songs she had practiced every night with Doug, songs she knew by heart, Chaska's strong voice and Winona's joining with hers, with Grandpa Belcourt's, with Doug's, with Star's.

Tears. Prayers. Purification.

She didn't know why she was crying, but couldn't stop, old sorrows and fears rising inside her only to wash away in the steam. She prayed for everyone in the lodge, for all of her relatives, for the Lakota people, for all Native peoples, for the kind people of Scarlet, for the woman who'd abandoned her, for Peter and Ruth and their congregation.

Tunkasila, Creator, take pity on me. I am praying with my people.

Songs. Voices raised in unions. Drumbeat strong as a heartbeat.

"*Mitakuye Oyasin*!" they said together. *All my relations.*

The door went up, steam shooting into the night, cool night air rushing in.

When the *inipi* was over, Naomi felt new and clean and free.

Naomi stood in her bedroom, Winona, Star, and other women from her family, helping her put on a hundred-year-old tanned doeskin dress with quillwork that her great-grandmother had once worn. She couldn't believe they were letting her wear it. The quillwork—blue with black designs—was among the best she'd ever seen.

"You look beautiful," Star said.

When Naomi looked in the mirror, the woman who stared back at her was someone she'd never seen before, a strong Lakota woman with braids hanging over her shoulders and no makeup on her face.

It had been an amazing weekend. She'd met so many wonderful people, each one of them related to her by blood. Everyone had brought gifts for her, some simple like braids of sweetgrass, others sacred, like eagle feathers. Everyone wanted to hear her story, to know more about her, to talk with her.

It was like standing in the center of a benevolent tornado.

They walked outside together for the naming ceremony, relatives sitting in the shade or standing in groups.

Grandpa Belcourt stood next to the big tree, wearing his best blue jeans and a ribbon shirt, an eagle feather in his hair. Chaska was there, too, feather in his hair. His gaze was warm when he saw her, appreciation in his dark eyes. Winona stood beside him, looking like she wanted to run over and hug Naomi.

Naomi went to stand beside Grandpa Belcourt, who waited for quiet and then began to speak, reminding everyone that Naomi hadn't had a naming ceremony when she was little. He told them how important a Lakota name was, its spiritual power conferring protection on Lakota children.

After that, he blessed her with his ancient eagle father, painted her face with *wase*, singing ancient and sacred songs, the host drum beating out the rhythm.

Then it was time for him to speak her name, the name that the Spirit world would know her by, her true Lakota name. She knew what her name would be, of course. Everyone already called her Tanagila—Hummingbird.

Grandpa said it in Lakota first, and then in English, speaking clearly so that everyone could hear. "She Catches the Light."

Stunned, she stood there, accepting the congratulations of her family, her mind flashing to that July day when she and Grandpa had sat on the front porch.

It's all about the settings on the camera. They need to be fast enough to catch the light for just that split second when the wings are open.

And for the first time in her life, Naomi knew exactly who she was.

Chaska couldn't believe he was doing this. "The pants are too short."

Not surprising, given that they belonged to Old Man, part of an old powwow costume he still had on hand.

"You won't be able to tell when you have the moccasins on." Winona fussed with his braids, then stepped back, biting back a smile. "I think you look great. A little Hollywood maybe, but, good."

His cousin, Frankie, watched from the sofa, chuckling. He'd let them borrow his trailer as their staging area and had even helped Chaska pick out the horses he needed for Naomi's bride price. "You going to wear a shirt or just go bare-chested? Women like that bare-chested stuff, especially when the chest looks like yours."

"Thanks, Frank. I feel completely un-self-conscious now." Chaska couldn't wear the shirt that went with the pants because it was too narrow in the shoulders for him.

Frankie shook his head. "I don't know about this. Her father is either going to be impressed—or he's going to call the police on you, man."

Winona put the leather cord for the pendant Naomi had given him over his neck and fussed with it, too. "Doug is going to love this—especially the horses."

"Enough." Chaska batted Winona's hand away. "Let's get back before all the food is gone."

A thanksgiving feast always followed a naming ceremony, and Chaska was hungry. Or maybe he was nauseated from nerves.

They walked out to Frankie's driveway, where the horses waited in the bed of Chaska's pickup. The plan was that Frankie would follow him, bringing a loading ramp to make it easier for Chaska to get the horses down. Then he would ride them into the feast and offer them to Doug.

Naomi wanted a traditional Lakota betrothal? Well, she was going to get it.

"*Hoka hey*!" shouted Frankie, climbing into his truck. "Let's roll."

They drove the short distance back to the Otter Tail residence, trucks parked alongside the road for a half mile in either direction and found a parking spot. Frankie brought the loading ramp, attached it to the back of Chaska's truck, then stepped aside.

Chaska climbed into the bed of the truck, mounted the horses, and started their engine, then drove them down the ramp and up the street.

People smiled as he passed, some laughing. He didn't care. What he was doing would be the stuff of legend by tomorrow—if the bride agreed to have him and Doug didn't have him arrested.

He drove the horses into Doug's backyard, stopped the engine, and dismounted, standing there, waiting for Doug to see him.

Old Man saw him first. He gave him an approving nod, a big grin on his face.

Then Naomi noticed him. "Chaska? What in the—"

"I think he's here for your father." Star seemed to understand what was going on. A bright smile on her face, she drew Naomi aside. "Doug!"

Doug stepped out from behind the barbecue grill, walked over to Chaska, a look of confusion on his face. "What are you—"

"It's a bride price," Star whisper-shouted in Lakota.

Doug nodded, met Chaska's gaze. "You want to marry my daughter?"

"I bring twenty-two horses for her." Chaska stepped away from the yard tractor, giving Doug a chance to examine it.

It was a 22-horsepower machine that would make mowing Doug's big yard much faster and easier.

"Are they good horses?" Doug kicked a tire.

People laughed.

"They get a five-star review on the hardware store's website."

Doug nodded, fighting laughter now. "This is a good bride price."

"*Aho*!"

Laughter.

Naomi stood behind her father now, a hand over her mouth in excitement.

Doug turned to Naomi and spoke in Lakota using both of their Lakota names. "She Catches the Light, this warrior, Gray Owl, wishes to take you as his wife. Is this agreeable to you?"

He'd obviously gotten into the spirit of this.

"Yes!" Naomi answered in English, running to Chaska, throwing her arms around him, and kissing him. "Yes! Yes! Yes!"

Applause. Whoops. Drums. Or was that his heart?

"Then I accept your bride price." Doug walked over to the yard tractor, sat in the seat, and chuckled. "Twenty-two horsepower. It says right here. I guess that means it's time to get ready for a wedding."

Cheers.

But Chaska wasn't paying attention to Doug or anyone else, the woman in his arms now his entire world.

She looked up at him, her eyes bright. "I can't believe you did this."

"Are you kidding? You're worth at least five yard tractors."

She laughed, the sweet sound putting a hitch in his chest. Then her expression grew serious. "The luckiest day of my life was the day you found me."

"I was led to you, Naomi." No one would ever be able to tell him otherwise. "I love you with everything I am, and I always will."

He leaned down, kissed her.

"You look good in my old powwow pants." Old Man's voice brought their kiss to an end. "It's a special day. Let's see some fancy dancing."

The air around them filled with whoops and cheers.

Epilogue

Two months later

Naomi unlocked the front door, opening her boutique to the public for the first time. It was a cold November Saturday with a sky that threatened snow. "Do you think anyone will come?"

Chaska rested his hands on her shoulders. "It will take time to build your clientele, but I have no doubt that your shop is going to become a reason that people drive to Scarlet from Boulder and Denver."

"I hope so."

This had been Chaska's wedding present to her.

He'd handed her the lease to the shop on their wedding night and then worked beside her for two months, painting the walls, refinishing the wood floors, installing display cases and lighting, restoring the beautiful Victorian exterior. Winona had helped, too, as had her father and Star. They had made the trip down a couple of times, bringing the kids, who got to see their first moose—not to mention their first wolf. It was her father who had come up with the name for the store—Tanagila's.

Now all Naomi needed were customers.

She glanced around, wanting to make sure everything was perfect. Paintings and photographs hung on the walls, including some of her own work. Pottery and blown glass pieces in a rainbow of colors sat on glass shelves together with small sculptures of bronze and stone, bigger sculptures sitting on the floor. Glass display cases held jewelry—rings, earrings, bracelets, pendants, necklaces, tie clips, belt buckles, and more—with Naomi's signature pieces given special prominence in the center case.

Everything here had been made by Native artisans, many of them from Pine Ridge. The idea had come to Naomi the week after her naming ceremony when she'd met with some of her new artist friends and had listened to them talk about how hard it was to reach potential customers. If the shop were successful, it would give them all another source of income and funnel revenue into Native communities that desperately needed it.

A white van stopped in the street outside the shop. A man climbed out and walked to the back, then pulled out a large bouquet of flowers. Naomi didn't realize they were for her till the man ran up her front steps and pushed through the door. "Naomi Belcourt?"

Naomi stared up at Chaska, who shrugged. "They're not from me. I *wish* I'd thought of that."

She took the flowers and set them down near the cash register, then retrieved the card and opened it, her throat growing tight.

> Congratulations on your big day. We're sending all our love and prayers.
>
> *Mitakuye Oyasin.*
>
> Dad, Star, and the kids

She handed the card to Chaska, who read it and gave it back to her. "Your old man sure knows how to come through for you."

Yes, he did. He'd been true to his word, doing his best for her in everything, getting his name on her birth certificate, paying for her wedding dress and hosting the ceremony in his yard. He was still fighting to get her adoption annulled. There hadn't been a moment since getting the results of the paternity test when he'd let her down.

The back door opened, and Winona appeared, a white pastry box in her arms. "Sorry that took so long. I got a dozen scones and a dozen blueberry muffins, plus some cookies just in case. Where should I put them?"

"On the counter there next to the coffee." Naomi had wanted to have refreshments on hand, part of making the store's opening special for her customers. Except that there were no customers. "If no one comes, I guess we'll have to eat these ourselves."

Win had already picked out a scone. "I'm okay with that."

Footsteps on the wooden walkway.

Rose appeared, bundled against the cold and waving at them through the window. She walked inside. "I just had to be your first customer."

"Welcome." Naomi accepted a patchouli-scented hug. If Rose liked the shop, it would be better for business than taking out a full-page ad. "I've got coffee, scones, and muffins over there."

But Rose's gaze was on a blown glass vase. "Oh, this is lovely."

The door opened again, and Rain and Lark stepped in, followed by a woman Naomi didn't know, someone who wasn't from Scarlet.

Lark glanced around, a bright smile coming over her face. "Wow!"

Chaska leaned down, spoke for Naomi alone. "See? Things will be fine."

By noon, they'd gone through the scones, the muffins, and four pots of coffee and were down to the cookies. Winona and Chaska had gone out to get more and to grab lunch for the three of them.

Naomi answered people's questions. She'd counted sixty-five customers so far, a mix of locals, people she recognized, and people from Boulder who told her they'd read the newspaper article about the store. She'd already sold several higher-priced pieces—a painting by a Hopi artist, a Navajo squash-blossom necklace, one of her signature bracelets—along with dozens of smaller items.

If every day were like this one…

The door opened again, and a middle-aged woman stepped inside. She wasn't a local, her blue pantsuit and the diamond rings on her fingers telling Naomi that she was well off. A business traveler perhaps?

"We've got coffee and cookies over here if you'd like something. Feel free to browse. Let me know if you have any questions."

"Are you the owner?"

Naomi nodded, held out her hand. "Yes. I'm Naomi Belcourt."

"I'm Kristi," the woman said. "Tell me about this place."

Naomi explained that she was a jewelry-maker and that the boutique carried the work of Native artists from around the country.

"Show me some of your work."

Naomi pointed out her photographs, then showed Kristi her jewelry in the display cases, finishing with her signature pieces in the center case.

"These are exquisite. Can I see that one?"

It was one of Naomi's latest pieces, a bracelet with a hummingbird of inlaid abalone, mother of pearl, onyx, and green turquoise flashing its shimmering wings against a flower of inlaid rose quartz. "I made this when I got back from my honeymoon."

Okay, so it had been a week-long stay at a bed and breakfast in Estes Park, but that had been perfect, giving them time to explore each other and the mountains.

"How long have you been married?" Kristi asked.

"Just since the end of September."

"Congratulations. Oh, look at this filigree work. Beautiful." Kristi turned the bracelet in her hand, examining it. "Did you have a big ceremony?"

"We got married at my father's place on Pine Ridge. My husband's grandfather is a spiritual leader. He led the ceremony. We invited family and a few close friends from Scarlet. It was small, but for us, that was just right."

"It sounds wonderful." The woman held out the bracelet. "I'll take this."

Naomi wrapped it for her and ran her credit card. "Thanks for coming in today. Would you like my card?"

"Yes, thank you. I would." Kristi took the card, tucked it in her handbag. "How did you become interested in jewelry-making?"

Naomi didn't want to share the whole story, so she gave her the shorter, more cheerful version. She drew her medicine wheel out of her blouse, held it by its cord where Kristi could see it. "I was given this medicine wheel, made by my great-grandmother when I was very little. I was fascinated with it and wanted to learn how to make things like it."

Kristi stared at the medicine wheel, a look of recognition on her face as if she'd seen one before and knew what a medicine wheel was.

"Lunch has arrived!" Winona came up behind Naomi, holding a paper bag from *Tacos Sabrosos.*

"Oh, thank goodness! I'm starving."

Chaska appeared carrying more scones and muffins, which he set down near the almost-empty cookie plate. "Who was that?"

Naomi turned, saw Kristi disappearing down the street. "She said her name was Kristi."

Chaska shook his head. "It looked like she was in tears."

"Really?" She'd seemed perfectly cheerful to Naomi.

Winona held up a white envelope. "I think she left you something."

Naomi opened the envelope and found a letter inside. At the first words, her eyes filled with tears. She threw the letter down and ran for the door, looking up and down the street for any sign of Kristi. She was gone.

For a moment, Naomi stood on the store's front porch, fighting to get her emotions under control, cold wind biting into her skin.

Kristi was her mother.

A bell jingled, and Chaska stepped outside.

He wrapped his arms around her. "I read it. It's a powerful letter."

"I don't have time for it now. I just can't … not now, not with customers in the store, not till I'm home. Can you keep it safe for me?"

"Of course."

She walked back inside, smiled to Win, who looked worried. "I'm so hungry. Where are those tacos?"

Chaska sat on the sofa beside Naomi while she read through the letter that her biological mother had left for her today, unable to imagine how this must feel. The woman had abandoned her, had nearly killed her, and hadn't reached out—until now.

And yet Chaska couldn't help but feel for Kristi. She'd been a child in a terrible situation with no support, no one to help her. She hadn't been able to see any way out, so she'd made the problem go away by abandoning Naomi.

He couldn't excuse what she'd done, but now he could understand it.

Naomi finished the letter, tears streaming down her face.

Chaska drew her into his arms, held her while she sobbed, wishing he knew what to say to her. Hell, he didn't even know what she was feeling.

Win sat down on the other side of her, rested her hand on Naomi's back, offering silent support, a helpless expression on her face. She loved Naomi, too, and she was probably just as uncertain about what to say or do as Chaska.

Naomi drew back, picked up the letter again, tears on her cheeks. "I've spent so much of my life hating her, raging at her. Why did she leave me? Why did she dump me? Why did she think I was garbage?"

"Now you know." Chaska handed Naomi a tissue. "She never thought you were garbage."

"It's not what I expected. That's for sure."

"What does the letter say?" Win asked. "Can I read it?"

Naomi picked it up again and read it aloud, her voice breaking, new tears streaming down her cheeks. "Dear, dear Naomi: Every day since your birth, I have thought about you. Every day, I have regretted what I did. There is no excuse, so I won't offer one, but I do owe you an explanation.

"I was sixteen when I met your father at summer camp. He was the sweetest, most handsome boy I'd ever known. I didn't think about the consequences. I thought I was in love, and I just wanted to be with him.

"When I got home, my parents were furious to learn that I had a Lakota boyfriend. They refused to let me call him or even write him a letter. My mother took his phone number and threw it away. When he called, she told him to stay away from me. She even tried to take away the medicine wheel he'd given me. I hid it in my room.

"I think some part of me understood I was pregnant, but I just couldn't face it. I did my best to hide my belly from everyone, especially my parents, who had once threatened to kick me out if I ever got pregnant.

"The night you were born was the longest and toughest and most terrifying night of my life. I was in so much pain and so afraid. I had no idea what to do, no knowledge about childbirth. I had you in the basement bathroom by myself, biting a towel so that I wouldn't scream. There was so much blood.

"When you were out, I held you. You looked up at me and didn't even cry. You were the most precious, most perfect thing I'd ever seen. But you looked like your father, and I knew my parents would punish me if they saw I'd been together with an Indian boy. I knew I had no choice but to give you up.

"So I wrapped you in a blanket I'd used for one of my dolls when I was little, tucked the medicine wheel inside it along with the afterbirth (I thought it would keep you warm), and snuck out of the house.

"I had no idea what to do with you. Back then there were no laws that enabled a mother to leave her newborn at a church or fire station without answering questions. I was sure that if I went to the fire station, my parents would find out. So, I put you near the back door of a grocery store because I thought a lot of people must go in and out and that they would find you quickly. Then I went home, cleaned the mess in the bathroom, and tried to hide my bleeding.

"When I heard on the news that a baby had been found, I knew it was you. The news reports said you'd been close to dying. I have never gotten over the guilt I feel for abandoning you rather than facing my parents, for putting you in danger, for making the first hours of your life so terrible. When I think of you, lying in that alley, crying, with no one around, I am crushed and hate myself.

"I worked hard to finish high school after that and went to college. I married a man and later divorced him. I've had no other children. My life has been focused on higher education. But there hasn't been a day when I haven't thought of you and hoped you were safe and happy.

"When I saw the news stories about the young Lakota woman who'd been reunited with her father and then heard the father's name, I knew you'd found your way home, found your way to your people. I celebrated with you both in my heart, so happy that you were together.

"You should know that your father reached out to me after he found you. He located me, demanded answers, and then apologized for what I'd gone through by myself. He left it up to me how and when to reach out to you. He said he thought it would help you to know how you ended up in that alley. I hope this brings you some peace.

"I don't deserve your forgiveness, but I am sorry to the depth of my soul for what I did. Love, Kristi Larson."

When Naomi finished reading, Winona was in tears, too.

Chaska rolled onto his back, taking Naomi with him, his heart still pounding from an orgasm that had almost blown off his balls.

She snuggled against him. "You like it more this way, don't you?"

"Yeah." *Hell, yeah.*

They had agreed to wait to start trying for children till after their first year together. Chaska would have finished his fourth Sun Dance by then—he had invited his father to the wedding, and they were on speaking terms again—and Naomi would know whether the boutique was a hit or a flop. Not wanting him to be stuck with condoms, Naomi had gone to the women's clinic last week and gotten an IUD.

For Chaska, it was like discovering sex again. Without latex to separate them, he could feel her heat, her wetness. And if he didn't last quite as long?

He did his best to make up for that, and Naomi didn't seem to be holding it against him.

Chaska shifted his weight, drew her closer. "How are you?"

She'd had a big day—a successful grand opening and a letter from her biological mother.

"Relaxed. Satisfied." She gave a giggle, stretching languidly in his arms. "I'm okay. Really, I am."

"What did your father have to say?"

She'd talked with Doug for almost an hour and had scanned and emailed him a copy of the letter.

"He was really happy about how well it went at the store today—and he was glad that Kristi had finally gotten in touch with me. He knew everything that was in the letter, of course, and he was happy that she'd been as open with me as she'd been with him."

"Did he explain why he hadn't told you that he was searching for her?"

"He said he had no idea what he might find. She might have been in prison or an addict on the street or dead by suicide for all he knew. He didn't want me to have to process that. Once he'd found her and met with her, he wanted to give her the chance to do the right thing. So, he didn't tell me. A year ago, that probably would have made me angry, but …"

Chaska waited for her to finish, orgasm cooling into sleepiness.

"He has my back, and I trust him. I know that everything he does comes out of his love for me. He's done so much on my behalf. I trust you, too, and Win and Rain and Joe and everyone on the Team. I didn't realize how amazing it is to be able to trust people, to be able to rely on them, to know that they care about you and would never deliberately do anything to hurt you. You taught me that, Chaska, you and Win and my family and the people of Scarlet."

Chaska thought back to the traumatized woman who'd been reluctant to accept anything from anyone. "We all need each other. That's why we talk about communities being a circle, a hoop. Each one of us touches so many others. Connected, we're stronger."

"You're starting to sound like Grandpa—a wise man."

He kissed her hair. "Not wise—not yet."

But as Old Man had said last time they'd spoken, even a genius could learn.

Chaska turned toward his wife, held her in his arms, and the two of them fell fast asleep.

Read on for a note about this story from the author.

Author's Note

One of the most amazing experiences in my life was attending a four-day Sun Dance ceremony on sacred land. It was transformational for me, something I'll remember for the rest of my life. But I'm getting ahead of myself.

As a journalist, I made a conscious choice to give the voice I had to others, to use my ink to raise awareness about issues that otherwise weren't getting coverage. I chose to focus on women in prison and Native peoples. I devoted fifteen years of my 20-year career to learning about the challenges these two groups faced and trying to share their struggles with my readership.

From the start, I had two rules for myself when it came to covering Native American issues. The first was not to go to any reservation without being *asked* to come. The second was never to go to any ceremony without being invited. I did not want to impose myself on anyone or come across as the stereotypical journalist on the reservation who asks the wrong questions about the wrong things of the wrong people at the wrong time—and then gets the answers all wrong in print. As a result, I covered Native issues from my desk in Boulder, Colo., for the first few years of this effort.

That all changed one afternoon when I got a call from a woman in Denver who'd heard from her husband, a Sun Dancer, that the elders wanted me to come to report on the harassment of Sun Dancers by federal agents.

I dropped everything, hopped in my car, and made the twelve-hour drive over rutted, unpaved roads to the Sun Dance site, going off road to get around a federal surveillance van that was blocking the way, attempting to keep people out of this ceremony. (The reason why they were blocking the road and threatening to arrest people who were attending is very long and difficult to explain. It's also not relevant to what I'm trying to convey here, so we'll skip it.)

I covered the story to the best of my ability and, in the process, ended up participating in a Sun Dance that was being run by a hereditary Lakota Sun Dance chief. I was one of few non-Natives there. I ate mutton stew, did my reporting, and volunteered in the first-aid tent, giving elders foot massages. At night, I slept in a tent under a piñon pine, waking every morning at sunrise to the sound of the drums. I joined in the ceremony, standing under the arbor, smoking the *chanupa* for the first time, learning songs and words. Time became irrelevant. The feeling of welcome I experienced was profound.

I did my best to cover the story accurately. As a result, word got around. I was asked by other Native people to cover many other stories. This took me as far north as the Cheyenne River Reservation, where I reported on the Si Tanka riders in the coldest weather I've ever experienced (-60F with wind chill) and as far south as Navajoland in Arizona where it was 114F. I met Hopis, Cherokee, Diné, Canadian Cree, Quechua, Inuit, and Lakota/Dakota people. I listened to the stories of Native leaders of all kinds—tribal presidents, spiritual leaders, and community activists. In 2005, I even found myself in an *inipi* ceremony with Native spiritual leaders and NASA scientists. Who was pouring water at that *inipi*? The Sun Dance chief from that first Sun Dance I attended. He became a friend, though we have since lost touch.

Through the years, I participated in other ceremonies and was eventually asked by three different spiritual leaders from three different Indian Nations to act as a bridge between the white world and the Native world. This book is one attempt to continue being that bridge despite the fact that I no longer work in journalism.

I have tried to share what I know in a way that is respectful and mindful of Lakota traditions. I have attempted to bring to life a contemporary Native couple—plus relatives—who might live down the street in Anytown, USA. Any mistakes I've made with regard to Lakota customs and language are my own. I offer this story with respect and gratitude and in the hope that this broken wheel can be mended, bringing all of us together as one.

Mitakuye Oyasin.

Pamela Clare

June 26, 2017

Also by Pamela Clare

Romantic Suspense

I-Team Series

Extreme Exposure (Book 1)

Heaven Can't Wait (Book 1.5)

Hard Evidence (Book 2)

Unlawful Contact (Book 3)

Naked Edge (Book 4)

Breaking Point (Book 5)

Skin Deep: An I-Team After Hours Novella (Book 5.5)

First Strike: The Prequel to Striking Distance (Book 5.9)

Striking Distance (Book 6)

Soul Deep: An I-Team After Hours Novella (Book 6.5)

Seduction Game (Book 7)

Dead by Midnight: An I-Team Christmas (Book 7.5)

Contemporary Romance

Colorado High Country Series

Barely Breathing (Book 1)

Slow Burn (Book 2)

Falling Hard (Book 3)

Tempting Fate (Book 4)

Historical Romance

Kenleigh-Blakewell Family Saga

Sweet Release (Book 1)

Carnal Gift (Book 2)

Ride the Fire (Book 3)

MacKinnon's Rangers series

Surrender (Book I)

Untamed (Book 2)

Defiant (Book 3)

Upon A Winter's Night: A MacKinnon's Rangers Christmas (Book 3.5)

About the Author

USA Today best-selling author Pamela Clare began her writing career as a columnist and investigative reporter and eventually became the first woman editor-in-chief of two different newspapers. Along the way, she and her team won numerous state and national honors, including the National Journalism Award for Public Service. In 2011, Clare was awarded the Keeper of the Flame Lifetime Achievement Award. A single mother with two sons, she writes historical romance and contemporary romantic suspense at the foot of the beautiful Rocky Mountains. To learn more about her or her books, visit her website at www.pamelaclare.com. You can keep up with her on Goodreads, on Facebook, or search for @Pamela_Clare on Twitter to follow her there.

CPSIA information can be obtained
at www.ICGtesting.com
Printed in the USA
FSHW011041180119
55112FS